Alone

by

Norman Douglas

T0243159

The Echo Library 2007

Published by

The Echo Library

Echo Library
131 High St.
Teddington
Middlesex TW11 8HH

www.echo-library.com

Please report serious faults in the text to complaints@echo-library.com

ISBN 978-1-40682-581-7

CONTENTS

INTRODUCTION
MENTONE
LEVANTO
SIENA
PISA
VIAREGGIO (February)
VIAREGGIO (May)
ROME
OLEVANO
VALMONTONE
SANT' AGATA, SORRENTO
ROME
SORIANO
ALATRI

Introduction

What ages ago it seems, that "Great War"!

And what enthusiasts we were! What visionaries, to imagine that in such an hour of emergency a man might discover himself to be fitted for some work of national utility without that preliminary wire-pulling which was essential in humdrum times of peace! How we lingered in long queues, and stamped up and down, and sat about crowded, stuffy halls, waiting, only waiting, to be asked to do something for our country by any little guttersnipe who happened to have been jockeyed into the requisite position of authority! What innocents....

I have memories of several afternoons spent at a pleasant place near St. James's Park station, whither I went in search of patriotic employment. It was called, I think, Board of Trade Labour Emergency Bureau (or something equally lucid and concise), and professed to find work for everybody. Here, in a fixed number of rooms, sat an uncertain number of chubby young gentlemen, all of whom seemed to be of military age, or possibly below it; the Emergency Bureau was then plainly—for it may have changed later on—a hastily improvised shelter for privileged sucklings, a kind of nursery on advanced Montessori methods. Well, that was not my concern. One must trust the Government to know its own business.

During my second or third visit to this hygienic and well-lighted establishment I was introduced, most fortunately, into the sanctuary of Mr. R——, whose name was familiar to me. Was he not his brother's brother? He was. A real stroke of luck!

Mr. R——, a pink little thing, laid down the pen he had snatched up as I entered the room, and began gazing at me quizzically through enormous tortoise-shell-rimmed goggles, after the fashion of a precocious infant who tries to look like daddy. What might he do for me?

I explained.

We had a short talk, during which various forms were conscientiously filled up as to my qualifications, such as they were. Of course, there was nothing doing just then; but one never knows, does one? Would I mind calling again?

Would I mind? I should think not. I should like nothing better. It did one good to be in contact with this youthful optimist and listen to his blithe and pleasing prattle; he was so hopeful, so philosophic, so cheery; his whole nature seemed to exhale the golden words: "Never say die." And no wonder. He ought to have been at the front, but some guardian angel in the haute finance had dumped him into this soft and safe job: it was enough to make anybody cheerful. One should be cautious, none the less, how one criticises the action of the authorities. May be they kept him at the Emergency Bureau for the express purpose of infusing confidence, by his bright manner, into the minds of despondent patriots like myself, and of keeping the flag flying in a general way—a task for which he, a German Jew, was pre-eminently fitted.

Be that as it may, his consolatory tactics certainly succeeded in my case, and I went home quite infected with his rosy cheeks and words. Yet, on the occasion of my next visit a week or two later, there was still nothing doing—not just then, though one never knows, does one?

"Tried the War Office?" he added airily.

I had.

Who hadn't?

The War Office was a nightmare in those early days. It resembled Liverpool Street station on the evening of a rainless Bank Holiday. The only clear memory I carried away—and even this may have been due to some hallucination—was that of a voice shouting at me through the rabble: "Can you fly?" Such was my confusion that I believe I answered in the negative, thereby losing, probably, a lucrative billet as Chaplain to the Forces or veterinary surgeon in the Church Lads' Brigade. Things might have been different had my distinguished cousin still been on the spot; I, too, might have been accommodated with a big desk and small work after the manner of the genial Mr. R——. He died in harness, unfortunately, soon after the outbreak of war.

I said to my young friend:

"Everybody tells one to try the War Office—I don't know why. Of course I tried it. I wish I had a shilling for every hour I wasted in that lunatic asylum."

"Ah!" he replied. "I feel sure a good many men would like to be paid at that rate. Anyhow, trust me. We'll fix you up, sooner or later. (He kept his word.) Why not have a whack at the F.O., meanwhile?" "Because I have already had a whack at it."

I then possessed, indeed, in reply to an application on my part, a holograph of twelve pages in the elegant calligraphy of H.M. Under-Secretary of State for Foreign Affairs, the same gentleman who was viciously attacked by the Pankhurst section for his supposed pro-Germanism. It conveyed no grain of hope. Other Government Departments, he opined, might well be depleted at this moment; the Foreign Office was in exactly the reverse position. It overflowed with diplomatic and consular officials returned, perforce, from belligerent countries, and now in search of occupation. Was it not natural, was it not right, to give the preference to them? One was really at a loss to know what to do with all those people. He had tried, hitherto in vain, to find some kind of job for his own brother.

A straightforward, convincing statement. Acting on the hint, I visited the Education Office, notoriously overstaffed since Tudor days; it might now be emptier; clerical work might be obtained there in substitution of some youngster who had been induced to join the colours. I poked my nose into countless recesses, and finally unearthed my man.

They were full up, said Mr. F——.

Full up?

Full up.

Then, after some further conversation as to my capacities, he thought he might find me employment as teacher of science in the country, to replace somebody or other.

The notion was distasteful to me. I am not averse to learning from the young; I only once tried to teach them—at a ragged school, long since pulled down, near Ladbroke Grove, where I soon discovered that my little pupils knew a great deal more than I did, more, indeed, than was good for body or soul. Still, this was a tangible, definite offer of unremunerative but at the same time semi-pseudo-patriotic work, not to be sneezed at. An idea occurred to me.

"Supposing I stick it out and give satisfaction, shall I be able to interchange later into this department? I am more fitted for office duties. In fact, I have had a certain experience of them."

"No chance of that," he replied. "It is the German system. Their schoolmasters are sometimes taken to do administrative work at head-quarters, and vice versâ. Our English rule is: Once a teacher, always a teacher."

Here was a deadlock. For in such matters as teaching, a man may put a strain on himself for a certain length of time; he may even be a success, up to a point. But if he lacks the temperamental gift of holding classes, the results in the long run will not be fair to the children, to say nothing of himself. With reluctance I rose to depart, Mr. F——adding, by way of letting me down gently:

"Tried the War Office?"

I had.

If the War Office was too lively, this place was too slumberous by half. A cobwebby, Rip-van-Winkle-ish atmosphere brooded about those passages and chambers. One could not help thinking that a little "German system" might work wonders here. And this is merely one of several similar sites I explored, and endeavoured to exploit, for patriotic purposes; I am here only jotting down a few of the more important of those that occur to me.

And, oh! for the brush of a Hogarth to depict the gallery of faces with which I came in contact as I went along. They were all different, yet all alike; different in their degrees of beefiness, stolidity, and self-sufficiency, but plainly of the same parentage—British to the backbone; British of the wrong kind, with a sprinkling of Welshmen, Irishmen, and Jews. Not a Scotsman discoverable in that whole mob of complacent office-jacks. My countrymen were conspicuous by their absence; they were otherwise engaged, in the field, the colonies, the engine-room. I can only remember one single exception to this rule, this type; it was the head of the Censorship Department.

For of course I offered my services there, climbing up that decent red-carpeted stairway, and glad to find myself among respectable surroundings after all the unseemly holes I had lately wallowed in. I sent up a card which, to my surprise, caused me to be ushered forthwith into the presence of the Chief, who may have heard of my existence from some mutual friend. Here, at all events, was a man with a face worth looking at, a man who had done notable things in his day. What a relief, moreover, to be able to talk to a gentleman for a change! I wished I could have had him to myself for five minutes; there were one or two things one would have liked to learn from him. Unfortunately he was surrounded, as such people are, by half a dozen of the characteristic masks. For the rest, His ex-Excellency seemed to be ineffably bored with his new functions.

"What on earth brings you here?" he began in a fascinatingly absent-minded style, as if he had known me all my life, and with an inimitable nasal drawl. "This is a rotten job, my dear sir. Rotten! I cannot recommend it. Not your style at all, I should say." "But, my dear Sir F——, I am not applying for your job. Something subordinate, I mean. Anything, anything."

"What? Down there, cutting up newspapers at twenty-two shillings a week? No, no. Let's have your address, and we will communicate with you when we find something worth your while. By the way, have you tried the War Office?"

I had.

And it stands to reason that I tried the Munitions more than once. It was my rare good fortune—luck pursued me on these patriotic expeditions—to come face to face, at the Munitions, with the fons et origo; the deputy fountain-head, that is to say; a very peculiar private-secretary-in-chief for that department. He was a perpendicular, iron-grey personality, if I remember rightly, who smelt of some indifferent hair-wash and lost no time in giving you to understand that he was preternaturally busy.

Did I know anything about machinery?

Nothing to speak of, I replied. As co-manager and proprietor of some cotton mills employing several hundred hands for spinning and weaving, I naturally learnt how to handle a fair number of machines—sufficiently well, at all events, to start and stop them and tell the girls how to avoid being scalped or having their arms torn out whenever I happened to be passing that way. This life also gave me some experience, useful perhaps at the Munitions, in dealing with factory-hands——

That was not the kind of machinery he meant. Did I know anything about banking?

Nothing at all.

"You are like everybody else," he replied with a weary sigh, as much as to say: How am I going to run the British Empire with a collection of imbeciles like this? "We have several thousands of applicants like yourself," he went on. "But I will put your name down. Come again."

"You are very kind."

"Do call again," he added, in his best private-secretary manner.

I called again a couple of weeks later. It struck me, namely, that they might have acquired a sufficient stock of bankers and mechanics by this time, and be able possibly to discover a vacancy for a public-school man with a fairish knowledge of the world and some other things—one who, moreover, had himself served in a cranky and fussy Government Department and, though working in another sphere, had been thanked officially for certain labours— once by the Admiralty, twice by the Board of Trade; and anyway, hang it! one was not so infernally venerable as all that, was one?

"I called about a fortnight ago. You have my name down."

"Oh, yes, yes, yes, yes, yes. We have such thousands of applicants. I remember you! A mechanic, aren't you?"

"No. And you asked me if I understood banking, and I said I didn't."

"What a pity. Now if you knew about banking——"

Nothing, evidently, had been done about my application, nor, for that matter, about those thousands of others. We were being played with. I began to feel grumpy. It was a lovely afternoon, and I remembered, with regret, that I had thrown over an engagement to go for a walk with a friend at Wimbledon. About this hour, I calculated, we should be strolling along Beverley Brook or through the glades of Coombe Woods with sunshine filtering through the birches overhead; it would have been more pleasant, and far more instructive, than wasting my time with a hatchet-faced automaton like this. That comes, I thought, of being patriotic. I observed:

"Your department seems to require only bankers and mechanics. Would it not be well to advertise the fact and save trouble and time to those thousands of applicants who, you say, are in the same predicament as myself? I came here to do national work of some general kind."

"So I gather. And if you understood banking——"

"If I did, I should be a banker at my time of life—don't you see?—and lending money to you people, and giving you good advice, instead of asking you for employment. Isn't that fairly obvious? As a matter of fact, my acquaintance with banking is limited to a knowledge of how to draw cheques, and even that useful accomplishment is fast fading from my memory, under the stress of the times."

Being a Welshman—so I presume, from his name—he condescended to smile faintly, but not for long; his salary was too high. As for myself, I refrained from saying a few harsher things I was minded to say; indeed,

I made myself so vastly agreeable, after my own private recipe, that he was quite touched. He remarked:

"I think I had better put your name down, although we have thousands of applicants, you know. Call again, won't you?"

For which I humbly thanked him, instead of saying, as I ought to have done:

"You go to blazes. The public is a pack of idiots to run after people who merely keep them loitering about while they feather their own nests. We are out to lick the Germans, and yours is not the way to do it."

Did I understand banking? The full ineptitude of this conundrum only dawned upon me by degrees. Manifestly, if I understood banking, I might do some specialised kind of work for the Government. But in that case I would not apply to the Munitions. Granted they wanted bankers. Well, there was my friend M——, renowned in the City as a genius for banking; he could have saved them untold thousands of pounds. They would have none of him. They sent him into the trenches, where he was duly shot.

How easy it is for a disappointed place-seeker to jibe and rail against the powers that be, especially when he is not in full possession of the data! For all I know, they may have discovered my friend M——to be a dangerous character, and have been only too glad to remove him out of society without unnecessary fuss, in an outwardly honourable fashion, with a view to saving his poor but respectable parents the humiliating experience of a criminal trial and possible execution in the family.

If I understood banking…why did they want bankers at this institution? Ah, it was not my business to probe into such mysteries of administration. To my limited intelligence it would seem that the mere fact of a man applying at the Munitions was primâ facie evidence that banking was not one of his accomplishments. It seemed to me, furthermore, that there was no end to such "ifs"—patriotic or otherwise. If I were a woman, for instance, I would promptly aid the cause by jumping into a nurse's outfit, telling improper stories to the Tommies, and getting myself photographed for the Press every morning. But I am only a man. If I were a high-class trumpeter, I could qualify for a job in one of the Allied Armies or, failing that, on Judgment Day. But I can only strum the piano. And if the moon were made of green cheese, we might all try to get hold of a slice of it, mightn't we?…

Such was my pigheadedness, my boyish zeal, my belief in human nature or perverse sense of duty, that I actually broke my vow and returned to that ridiculous establishment. Yes, I "called again," flattering myself with the conjecture that, even if they had not yet obtained a requisite amount of bankers and mechanics, and even if persons of my particular aptitudes were still a drug in the market, there might nevertheless be room, amid the ramifications and interstices of so great a department, for a man or two who could help to count up or pack munitions, or, if that proposal were hopelessly wide of the mark, for the services of something even more recondite and exotic—an intelligent corpse-washer, for instance, or half a dozen astrologers. I felt I could distinguish myself, at a national crisis like this, in either capacity. Anyhow, it was only one more afternoon wasted—one out of how many!

This time I saw Mr. W——. Though I had never met him in the flesh, I once enjoyed the privilege of perusing a manuscript from his pen—a story about a girl in Kew Gardens. A nice-looking young Hebrew was Mr. W——. He had made himself indispensable, somehow or other, to the Minister, and would doubtless by this time have been pitchforked into some permanent and prominent job, but for that unfortunate name of his, with its strong Teutonic flavour.

This, by the way, was about the eighth official of his tribe, and of his age, I had come across in the course of my recent peregrinations. How did   they get there? Tell me, who can. Far be it from me to disparage the race of Israel. I have gained the conviction—firm-fixed, now, as the Polar Star—that the Hebrew is as good a man as the Christian. Yet one would like to know their method, their technique, in this instance. How was the thing done? How did they manage it, these young Jews, all healthy-looking and of military age—how did they contrive to keep out of the Army? Was there some secret society which protected them? Or were they all so preposterously clever that the Old Country would straightway evaporate into thin air unless they sat in some comfortable office, while our own youngsters were being blown to pieces out yonder?

Mr. W———, I regret to say, was not a good Oriental. He lacked the Semite's pliability. He was graceful, but not gracious. A consequence, doubtless, of having inhaled for some time past the rarefied atmosphere of the Chief, and swallowed a few pokers during the process, his manner towards me was freezingly non-committal—worthy of the best Anglo-Saxon traditions.

Had I come a little earlier, he avowed, he might perhaps have been able to squeeze me into one of his departments—thus spake this infant: "One of my departments." As it was, he feared there was nothing doing; nothing whatsoever; not just then. Tried the War Office?

I had.

I even visited, though only twice, an offshoot of that establishment in Victoria Street near the Army and Navy Stores, where candidates for the position of translator—quasi-confidential work and passable pay, five pounds a week—were interviewed. On the second occasion, after waiting in an ante-room full of bearded and be-spectacled monsters such as haunt the British Museum Library, I was summoned before a board of reverend elders, who put me through a catechism, drowsy but prolonged, as to my qualifications and antecedents. It was a systematic affair. Could I decipher German manuscripts? Let them show me their toughest one, I said. No! It was merely a pro forma question; they had enough German translators on the staff. So the interrogation went on. They were going to make sure of their man, in whom, I must say, they took little interest save when they learnt that he had passed a Civil Service examination in Russian and another in International Law. At that moment— though I may be mistaken—they seemed to prick up their ears. Not long afterwards I was allowed to depart, with the assurance that I might hear further.

Their inquiries into my attainments and references must have given satisfaction, for in the fulness of time a missive arrived to the effect that, assuming me to be a competent Turkish scholar, they would be glad to see me again with a view to a certain vacancy.

Turkish—a language I had not mentioned to them, a language of which I never possessed more than fifty words, every one of them forgotten long years ago.

"How very War Office," I thought.

These good people were mixing up Turkish and Russian—a natural error, when one comes to think of it, for, though the respective tongues might not be absolutely identical, yet the countries themselves were sufficiently close together to account for a little slip like this.

Was it a slip? Who knows? It is so easy to criticise when one is not fully informed about things. They may have suggested my acting as Turkish translator for reasons of their own—reasons which I cannot fathom, but which need not therefore be bad ones. Chagrined office-hunters like myself are prone to be bitter. In an emergency of this magnitude a citizen should hesitate before he finds fault with the wisdom of those whom the nation has chosen to steer it through troubled waters. No carping! You only hamper the Government. The general public should learn to keep a civil tongue in its head. Theirs but to do and die.

None the less, it was about this time that I began to experience certain moments of despondency, and occasionally let a whole day slip by without endeavouring to be of use to The Cause—moments when, instead of asking myself, "What have I done for my country?" I asked, "What has my country done for me?"—moments when I envied the hotel night-porters, taxi-drivers, and red-nosed old women selling flowers in Piccadilly Circus who had something more sensible to do than to bother their heads about trying to be patriotic, and getting snubbed for their pains. Yet, with characteristic infatuation for hopeless ventures, I persevered. Another "whack" at the F.O. leading to another holograph, two more whacks at the Censorship, interpreter jobs, hospital jobs, God knows what—I persevered, and might for the next three years have been kicking my heels, like any other patriot, in the corridor of some dingy Government office at the mercy of a pack of tuppenny counter-jumpers, but for a God-sent little accident, the result of sheer boredom, which counselled a trip to the sunny Mediterranean.

Fortune was nearer to me, at that supreme moment, than she had ever yet been. For on the day prior to my departure I received a communication from the Board of Trade Labour, etc., etc., whose methods of work, it was now apparent, were as expeditious as its own name was brief. That hopeful Mr. R——, that bubbling young optimist who had so conscientiously written down a number of my qualifications, such as they were—he was keeping his promise after months, and months, and months. Never say die. The dear little fellow! What job had he captured for me?

An offer to work in a factory at Gretna Green, wages to commence at 17s. 6d. per week.

H'm.

The remuneration was not on a princely scale, but I like to think that it included the free use of the lavatory, if there happened to be one on the premises.

So luck pursued me to the end, though it never quite caught me up. For bags were packed, and tickets taken. And therefore:

"What did you do in the Great War, grandpapa?"

"I loafed, my boy."

"That was naughty, grandpapa."

"Naughty, but nice…."

Mentone

Italiam petimus....

Discovered, in a local library—a genuine old maid's library: full of the trashiest novels—those two volumes of sketches by J. A. Symonds, and forthwith set to comparing the Mentone of his day with that of ours. What a transformation! The efforts of Dr. James Henry Bennet and friends, aided and abetted by the railway, have converted the idyllic fishing village into—something different. So vanishes another fair spot from earth. And I knew it. Yet some demon has deposited me on these shores, where life is spent in a round of trivialities.

One fact suffices. Symonds, driving over from Nice, at last found himself at the door of "the inn." The inn.... Are there any inns left at Mentone?

À propos of inns, here is a suggestive state of affairs. At the present moment, twenty-two of the principal hotels and pensions of Mentone are closed, because owned or controlled or managed by Germans. Does not this speak rather loudly in favour of Teuton enterprise? Where, in a German town of 18,000 inhabitants, will you find twenty-two such establishments in the hands of Frenchmen?

The statistical mood is upon me. I wander either among the tombs of that cemetery overhead, studying sepulchral inscriptions and drawing deductions, from what is therein stated regarding the age, nationality and other circumstances of the deceased, as to the relative number of consumptives here interred. Sixty per cent, shall we say? Or else, in the streets of the town, I catch myself endeavouring—hitherto without success—to count up the number of grocers' shops. They are far in excess of what is needful. Now, why? Well, your tailor or hatter or hosier—he makes a certain fixed profit on each article he sells, and he does not sell them at every moment of the day. The other, quite apart from small advantages to be gained owing to the ever-shifting prices of his wares, is ceaselessly engaged in dispensing trifles, on each of which he makes a small gain. The grocery business commends itself warmly to the French genius for garnering halfpennies. Nowhere on earth, I fancy, will you see butter more meticulously weighed than here. Buy a ton of it, and they will replace on their counter a fragment of the weight and size of a postage stamp, rather than let the balance descend on your side.

And so the days, the weeks, have passed. Will one ever again escape from Mentone? It may well be colder in Italy, but anything is preferable to this inane Riviera existence....

I am not prone to recommend restaurants, or to discommend them, for the simple reason that, if they have proved bad, I smile to think of other men being poisoned and robbed as well as myself; as to the good ones—why, only a fool would reveal their whereabouts. Since, however, I hope so to order my remaining days of life as never to be obliged to return to these gimcrack regions, there is no inducement for withholding the name of the Merle Blanc at Monte

Carlo, a quite unpretentious place of entertainment that well deserves its name—white blackbirds being rather scarcer here than elsewhere. The food is excellent—it has a cachet of its own; the wine more than merely good. And this is surprising, for the local mixtures (either Italian stuff which is dumped down in shiploads at Nice, Marseille, Cette, etc., or else the poor though sometimes aromatic product of the Var) are not gratifying to the palate. One imbibes them, none the less, in preference to anything else, as it is a peculiarity of what goes under the name of wine hereabouts that the more you pay for it, the worse it tastes. If you adventure into the Olympic spheres of Chateau Lafite and so forth, you may put your trust in God, or in a blue pill. Chateau Cassis would be a good name for these finer vintages, seeing that the harmless black currant enters largely into their composition, though not in sufficient quantity to render them wholly innocuous. Which suggests a little problem for the oenophilist. What difference of soil or exposure or climate or treatment can explain the fact that Mentone is utterly deficient in anything drinkable of native origin, whereas Ventimiglia, a stone's throw eastwards, can boast of its San Biagio, Rossese, Latte, Dolceacqua and other noble growths, the like of which are not to be found along the whole length of the French Riviera?

Having pastured the inner man, to his complete satisfaction, at the hospitable Merle Blanc, our traveller will do well to pasture his eyes on the plants in the Casino gardens. Whoever wants to see flowers and trees on their best behaviour, must come to Monte Carlo, where the spick-and-span Riviera note is at its highest development. Not a leaf is out of place; they have evidently been groomed and tubbed and manicured from the hour of their birth. And yet—is it possible? Lurking among all this modern splendour of vegetation, as though ashamed to show their faces, may be discerned a few lowly olive trees. Well may they skulk! For these are the Todas and Veddahs, the aboriginals of Monte Carlo, who peopled its sunny slopes in long-forgotten days of rustic life—once lords of the soil, now pariahs. What are they doing here? And how comes it that the eyesore has not yet been detected and uprooted by those keen-sighted authorities that perform such wonders in making the visitor feel at home, and hush up with miraculous dexterity everything in the nature of a public scandal?

In exemplification whereof, let me tell a trivial Riviera tale. There was an Englishwoman here, one of those indestructible modern ladies who breakfast off an ether cocktail and half a dozen aspirins and feel all the better for it, and who, one day, found herself losing rather heavily at the tables. "Another aspirin is going to turn my luck," she thought, and therewith swallowed surreptitiously her last tabloid of the panacea. Not unobserved, however; for straightway two elegant gentlemen—they might have been Russian princes—pounced upon her and led her to that underground operating-room where a kindly physician is in perennial attendance. He brushed aside her explanations.

"It would be a thousand pities for so charming a lady to poison herself. But since you wish to take that step, why choose the Casino which has a reputation to keep up? Are there not hotels——"

"I tell you it was only aspirin."

"Alas, we are sufficiently familiar with that tale! Now, Madam, let us not lose a moment! It is a question of life and death."

"Aspirin, I tell you——"

"Kindly submit, or the three of us will be obliged to employ force."

The stomach-pump was produced.

It is the drawback of all sea-side places that half the landscape is unavailable for purposes of human locomotion, being covered by useless water. Mentone is more unfortunate than most of them, for its Hinterland is so cloven and contorted that unless you keep on the main roads, or content yourself with short but pleasant strolls, you will soon find all progress barred by some natural obstruction. And one really cannot walk along the esplanade all day long, though it is worth while, once in a lifetime, continuing that promenade as far as Cap Martin, if only in memory of the inspiration which Symonds drew therefrom. Who, he asks—who can resist the influence of Greek ideas at the Cape St. Martin? Anybody can, nowadays. The place is encrusted with smug villas of parvenus (wherein we include the Empress Eugénie), to say nothing of that preposterous hotel at the very point, which disfigures the country for leagues around.

On other occasions you may find your way towards evening up to Gorbio and stay for supper, provided you do not mind being cheated. Or wander further afield, over Sospel to Breil by the old path—note the lavender: they make a passable perfume of it—or else to Moulinet (famous for bad food and a mastodontic breed of mosquitoes) and thence along the stream—note the bushes of wild box—and over a wooded ridge to the breezy heights of Peira Cava, there to dream away the daylight under the pines. These are summer rambles. At present the snow lies deep.

One of my favourite excursions has been up the so-called Berceau, the cradle-shaped hill which dominates Mentone on the east. I was there to-day for a solitary luncheon, resting awhile in the timbered saddle between the peaks. The summit is only about five minutes' walk from this delectable grove, but its view inland is partially intercepted by a higher ridge. From here, if you are in the mood, you may descend eastward over the Italian frontier, crossing the stream which is spanned lower down by the bridge of St. Louis, and find yourself at Mortola Superiore (try the wine) and then at Mortola proper (try the wine). Somewhere in this gulley was killed the last wolf of these regions; so a grey-haired local Nimrod told me. He had wrought much mischief in his time. That is to say, he was not killed, but accidentally drowned—drowned in one of those artificial reservoirs which are periodically filled and drawn off for irrigating the gardens lower down; an ignoble death, for a wolf! A goat lay drowned beside him. The event, he reckoned, must have taken place half a century ago. Since then, the wolf has never been seen.

This afternoon, however, I preferred to repose in that shady dell, while a flock of goldcrests were investigating the branches overhead and two buzzards cruised, in dreamy spirals, about the sunny sky of midday; to repose; to indulge my genius and review the situation; to profit, in short, by that sense of aloofness peculiar to such aerial spots, which tempts the mind to set its house in order. What are we doing, in these empty regions? Why not wander hence? That cursed traveller's gift of sitting still; of remaining stationary, no matter where, until one is actually pushed away! And yet, how enjoyable this land might be, were it inhabited by any race save one whose thousand little meannesses, public and private, are calculated to drain away a man's last ounce of self-respect! Not many are the glad memories I shall carry from Mentone. I can think of no more than two.

There is my landlady, to begin with, who spies out every detail of my daily life; of decent birth and richer than Croesus, but inflamed with a peevish penuriousness which no amount of plain speaking on my part will correct. Never a day passes that she does not permit herself some jocular observation anent my spendthrift habits. The following is an example of our matutinal converse:

"I fear, Monsieur, you omitted to put out the light in a certain place last night. It was burning when I returned home."

"Certainly not, Madame. I have been nicely brought up. I never visit places at night. You ought to be familiar with my habits after all this time."

"True. Then it must have been some one else. Ah, these electricians' bills!"

Or this:

"Monsieur, Monsieur! The English Consul called yesterday with his little dog at about five o'clock. He waited in your room, but you never came back."

"Five o'clock? I was at the baths."

"I have heard of that establishment. What do they charge for a hot bath?"

"Three francs——"

"Bon Dieu!"

"—if you take an abonnement. Otherwise, it may well be more."

"And so you go there. Why then—why must you also wash in the morning and splash water on my floor? It may have to be polished after your departure. Would you mind asking the Consul, by the way, not to sit on the bed? It weakens the springs."

Or this:

"Might I beg you, Monsieur, to tread more lightly on the carpet in your room? I bought it only nine years ago, and it already shows signs of wear."

"Nine years—that old rag? It must have survived by a miracle."

"I do not ask you to avoid using it. I only beg you will tread as lightly as possible."

"Carpets are meant to be worn out."

"You would express yourself less forcibly, if you had to pay for them."

"Let us say then: carpets are meant to be trodden on."

"Lightly."

"I am not a fairy, Madame."

"I wish you were, Monsieur."

Thrice already, in a burst of confidence, has she told me the story of an egg—an egg which rankles in the memory. Some years ago, it seems, she went to a certain shop (naming it)—a shop she has avoided ever since—to buy an egg; and paid the full price—yes, the full price—of a fresh egg. That particular egg was not fresh. So far from fresh was it, that she experienced considerable difficulty in swallowing it.

A memorable episode occurred about a fortnight ago. I was greeted towards 8 a.m. with moanings in the passage, where Madame tottered around, her entire head swathed in a bundle of nondescript woollen wraps, out of which there peered one steely, vulturesque eye. She looked more than ever like an animated fungus.

Her teeth—her teeth! The pain was past enduring. The whole jaw, rather; all the teeth at one and the same time; they were unaccountably loose and felt, moreover, three inches longer than they ought to feel. Never had she suffered such agony—never in all her life. What could it be?

It was easy to diagnose periostitis, and prescribe tincture of iodine.

"That will cost about a franc," she observed.

"Very likely."

"I think I'll wait."

Next day the pain was worse instead of better. She would give anything to obtain relief—anything!

"Anything?" I inquired. "Then you had better have a morphia injection. I have had numbers of them, for the same trouble. The pain will vanish like magic. There is my friend Dr. Théophile Fornari——"

"I know all about him. He demands five francs a visit, even from poor people like myself."

"You really cannot expect a busy practitioner to come here and climb your seventy-two stairs for much less than five francs."

"I think I'll wait. Anyhow, I am not wasting money on food just now, and that is a consolation."

Now periostitis can hardly be called an amusing complaint, and I would have purchased a franc's worth of iodine for almost anybody on earth. Not then. On the contrary, I grew positively low-spirited when, after three more days, the lamentations began to diminish in volume. They were sweet music to my ears, at the time. They are sweeter by far, in retrospect. If only one could extract the same amount of innocent and durable pleasure out of all other landladies!...

My second joyful memory centres round another thing of beauty—a spiky agave (miscalled aloe) of monstrous dimensions which may be seen in the garden of a certain hill-side hotel. Many are the growths of this kind which I have admired in various lands; none can vaunt as proud and harmonious a development as this one. You would say it had been cast in some dull blue metal. The glaucous wonder stands by itself, a prodigy of good style, more pleasing to the eye than all that painfully generated tropicality of Mr. Hanbury's Mortola paradise. It is flawless. Vainly have I teased my fancy, endeavouring to discover the slightest defect in shape or hue. Firm-seated on the turf, in exultant pose, with a pallid virginal bloom upon those mighty writhing leaves, this plant has drawn me like a magnet, day after day, to drink deep draughts of contentment from its exquisite lines.

For the rest, the whole agave family thrives at Mentone; the ferox is particularly well represented; one misses, among others, that delightful medio-picta variety, of which I have noticed only a few indifferent specimens.[1] It is the same with the yuccas; they flourish here, though one kind, again, is conspicuous by its absence—the Atkinsi (some such name, for it is long since I planted my last yucca) with drooping leaves of golden-purple. You will be surprised at the number of agaves in flower here. The reason is, that they are liable to be moved about for ornamental purposes when they want to be at rest; the plant, more sensitive and fastidious than it looks, is outraged by this forceful perambulation and, in an access of premature senility, or suicidal mania, or sheer despair, gives birth to its only flower—herald of death. The fatal climax could be delayed if gardeners, in transplanting, would at least take the trouble to set them in their old accustomed exposure so far as the cardinal points are concerned. But your professional gardener knows everything; it is useless for an amateur to offer him advice; worse than useless, of course, to ask him for it. Indeed, the flowers, even the wild ones, might almost reconcile one to a life on the Riviera. Almost.... I recall a comely plant, for instance, seven feet high at the end of June, though now slumbering underground, in the Chemin de Saint Jacques—there, where the steps begin——

Almost....

And here my afternoon musings, up yonder, took on a more acrid complexion. I remembered a recent talk with one of the teachers at the local college who lamented that his pupils displayed a singular dullness in their essays; never, in his long career at different schools, had he met with boys more destitute of originality. What could be expected, we both agreed? Mentone was of recent growth—the old settlement, Mentone of Symonds, proclaims its existence only by a ceaseless and infernal clanging of bells, rivalling Malta—no history, no character, no tradition—a mushroom town inhabited by shopkeepers and hôteliers who are there for the sole purpose of plucking foreigners: how should a youngster's imagination be nurtured in this atmosphere of savourless modernism? Then I asked myself: who comes to these regions, now that invalids have learnt the drawbacks of their climate? Decayed Muscovites, Englishmen such as you will vainly seek in England, and their painted women-folk with stony, Medusa-like gambling eyes, a Turk or two, Jews and cosmopolitan sharks and sharpers, flamboyant Americans, Brazilian, Peruvian, Chilian, Bolivian rastaqueros with names that read like a nightmare (see "List of Arrivals" in New York Herald)—the whole exotic riff-raff enlivened and perfumed by a copious sprinkling of horizontales.

And I let my glance wander along that ancient Roman road which led from Italy to Arles and can still be traced, here and there; I took in the section from Genoa to Marseille, an enormous stretch of country, and wondered: what has this coast ever produced in the way of thought or action, of great men or great women? There is Doria at Genoa, and Gaby Deslys at Marseille; that may well exhaust the list. Ah, and half-way through, a couple of generals, born at Nice. It is really an instructive phenomenon, and one that should appeal to students of Buckle—this relative dearth of every form of human genius in one of the most favoured regions of the globe. Here, for unexplained reasons, the Italian loses his better qualities; so does the Frenchman. Are the natives descended from those mysterious Ligurians? Their reputation was none of the best; they were more prompt, says Crinagoras, in devising evil than good. That Mentone man, to be sure, whose remains you may study at Monaco and elsewhere, was a fine fellow, without a doubt. He lived rather long ago. Even he, by the way, was a tourist on these shores. And were the air of Mentone not unpropitious to the composition of anything save a kind of literary omelette soufflée, one might like to expatiate on Sergi's remarkable book, and devise thereto an incongruous footnote dealing with the African origin of sundry Greek gods, and another one referring to the extinction of these splendid races of men; how they came to perish so utterly, and what might be said in favour of that novel theory of the influence of an ice-age on the germplasm producing mutations—new races which breed true...enough! Let us remain at the Riviera level.

In the little museum under those cliffs by the sea, where the Grimaldi caves are, I found myself lately together with a young French couple, newly married. The little bride was vastly interested in the attendant's explanations of the habits of those remote folk, but, as I could plainly see, growing more and more distrustful of his statements as to what happened all those hundreds of thousands of years ago.

"And this, Messieurs, is the jaw-bone of a cave-bear—the competitor, one might say, in the matter of lodging-houses, with the gentleman whose anatomy we have just inspected. Here are bones of hippopotamus, and rhinoceros, which he hunted with the weapons you saw. And the object on which your arm is reposing, Madame, is the tooth of an elephant. Our ancestor must have been pretty costaud to kill an elephant with a stone."

"Elephants?" she queried. "Did elephants scramble about these precipices and ravines? I should like to have seen that."

"Pardon me, Madame. He probably killed them down there," and his arm swept over the blue Mediterranean, lying at our feet. "Do you mean to say that elephants paddled across from Algiers in order to be assassinated by your old skeleton? I should like to have seen that."

"Pardon me, Madame. The Mediterranean did not exist in those days."

The suggestion that this boundless sea should ever have been dry land, and in the time of her own ancestors, was too much for the young lady. She smiled politely, and soon I heard her whispering to her husband:

"I had him there, eh? Quel farceur!"

"Yes. You caught him nicely, I must say. But one must not be too hard on these poor devils. They have got to earn their bread somehow."

This will never do. Italiam petimus....

Levanto

I have loafed into Levanto, on the recommendation of an Irish friend who, it would seem, had reasons of his own for sending me there.

"Try Levanto," he said. "A little place below Genoa. Nice, kindly people. And sunshine all the time. Hotel Nazionale. Yes, yes! The food is all right. Quite all right. Now please do not let us start that subject——"

We started it none the less, and at the end of the discussion he added:

"You must go and see Mitchell there. I often stayed with him. Such a good fellow! And very popular in the place. He built an aqueduct for the peasants—that kind of man. Mind you look him up. He will be bitterly disappointed if you don't call. So make a note of it, won't you? By the way, he's dead. Died last year. I quite forgot."

"Dead, is he? What a pity."

"Yes; and what a nuisance. I promised to send him down some things by the next man I came across. You would have been that man. I know you do not carry much luggage, but you could have taken one or two trifles at least. He wanted a respectable English telescope, I remember, to see the stars with—a bit of an astronomer, you know. Chutney, too—devilish fond of chutney, the old boy was; quite a gastro-maniac. What a nuisance! Now he will be thinking I forgot all about it. And he needed a clothes-press; I was on no account to forget that clothes-press. Rather fussy about his trousers, he was. And a type-writer; just an ordinary one. But I doubt whether you could have managed a type-writer."

"Easily. And a bee-hive or two. You know how I like carrying little parcels about for other people's friends. What a nuisance! Now I shall have to travel with my bags half empty."

"Don't blame me, my dear fellow. I did not tell him to die, did I?"....

It must have been about midnight as the train steamed into Levanto station. Snow was falling; you could hear the moan of the sea hard by; an icy wind blew down from the mountains.

Sunshine all the time!

Everybody scurried off the platform. A venerable porter, after looking in dubious fashion at my two handbags, declared he would return in a few moments to transport them to the hotel, and therewith vanished round the corner. The train moved on. Lamps were extinguished. Time passed. I strode up and down in the semi-darkness, trying to keep warm and determined, whatever happened, not to carry those wretched bags myself, when suddenly a figure rose out of the gloom—a military figure of youthful aspect and diminutive size, armed to the teeth.

"A cold night," I ventured.

"Do you know, Sir, that you are in the war-zone—the zona di difesa?"

He began to fumble at his rifle in ominous fashion.

Nice, kindly people!

I said:

"It is hard to die so young. And I particularly dislike the looks of that bayonet, which is half a yard longer than it need be. But if you want to shoot me, go ahead. Do it now. It is too cold to argue."

"Your papers! Ha, a foreigner. Hotel Nazionale? Very good. To-morrow morning you will report yourself to the captain of the carbineers. After that, to the municipality. Thereupon you will take the afternoon train to Spezia. When you have been examined by the police inspector at the station you will be accompanied, if he sees fit, to head-quarters in order that your passport may be investigated. From there you will proceed to the Prefecture for certain other formalities which will be explained to you. Perhaps—who knows?—they will allow you to return to Levanto."

"How can you expect me to remember all that?" Then I added: "You are a Sicilian, I take it. And from Catania."

He was rather surprised. Sicilians, because they learn good Italian at their schools, think themselves indistinguishable from other men.

Yes; he explained. He was from a certain place in the Catania part of the country, on the slopes of Etna.

I happened to know a good deal of that place from an old she-cook of mine who was born there and never wearied of telling me about it. To his still greater surprise, therefore, I proceeded to discourse learnedly about that region, extolling its natural beauties and healthy climate, reminding him that it was the birthplace of a man celebrated in antiquity (was it Diodorus Siculus?) and hinting, none too vaguely, that he would doubtless live up to the traditions of so celebrated a spot.

Straightway his manner changed. There is nothing these folks love more than to hear from foreign lips some praise of their native town or village. He waxed communicative and even friendly; his eyes began to sparkle with animation, and there we might have stood conversing till sunrise had I not felt that glacial wind searching my garments, chilling my humanity and arresting all generous impulses. Rather abruptly I bade farewell to the cheery little reptile and snatched up my bags to go to the hotel, which he said was only five minutes' walk from there.

Things turned out exactly as he had predicted. Arrived at Spezia, however, I found an unpleasant surprise awaiting me. The officer in command, who was as civil as the majority of such be-medalled jackasses, suggested that one single day would be quite sufficient for me to see the sights of Levanto; I could then proceed to Pisa or anywhere else outside his priceless "zone of defence." I pleaded vigorously for more time. After all, we were allies, were we not? Finally, a sojourn of seven days was granted for reasons of health. Only seven days: how tiresome! From the paper which gave me this authorisation and contained a full account of my personal appearance I learnt, among other less flattering details, that my complexion was held to be "natural." It was a drop of sweetness in the bitter cup.

No butter for breakfast.

The landlord, on being summoned, avowed that to serve crude butter on his premises involved a flagrant breach of war-time regulations. The condiment could not be used save for kitchen purposes, and then only on certain days of the week; he was liable to heavy penalties if it became known that one of his guests…. However, since he assumed me to be a prudent person, he would undertake to supply a due allowance to-morrow and thenceforward, though never in the public dining-room; never, never in the dining-room!

That is the charm of Italy, I said to myself. These folks are reasonable and gifted with imagination. They make laws to shadow forth an ideal state of things and to display their good intentions towards the community at large; laws which have no sting for the exceptional type of man who can evade them—the sage, the millionaire, and the "friend of the family." Never in the dining-room. Why, of course not. Catch me breakfasting in any dining-room.

Was it possible? There, at luncheon in the dining-room, while devouring those miserable macaroni made with war-time flour, I beheld an over-tall young Florentine lieutenant shamelessly engulfing huge slices of what looked uncommonly like genuine butter, a miniature mountain of which stood on a platter before him, and overtopped all the other viands. I could hardly believe my eyes. How about those regulations? Pointing to this golden hillock, I inquired softly:

"From the cow?"

"From the cow."

"Whom does one bribe?"

He enjoyed a special dispensation, he declared—he need not bribe. Returned from Albania with shattered health, he had been sent hither to recuperate. He required not only butter, but meat on meatless days, as well as a great deal of rest; he was badly run down…. And eggs, raw eggs, drinking eggs; ten a day, he vows, is his minimum. Enviable convalescent!

The afternoon being clear and balmy, he took me for a walk, smoking cigarettes innumerable. We wandered up to that old convent picturesquely perched against the slope of the hill and down again, across the rivulet, to the inevitable castle-ruin overhanging the sea. Like all places along this shore, Levanto lies in a kind of amphitheatre, at a spot where one or more streams, descending from the mountains, discharge themselves into the sea. Many of these watercourses may in former times have been larger and even navigable up to a point. Their flow is now obstructed, their volume diminished. I daresay they have driven the sea further out, with silt swept down from the uplands. The same thing has struck me in England—at Lyme Regis, for instance, whose river was also once navigable to small craft and at Seaton, about a mile up whose stream stands that village—I forget its name—which was evidently the old port of the district in pre-Seaton days. Local antiquarians will have attacked these problems long ago. The sea may have receded.

A glance from this castle-height at the panorama bathed in that mellow sunshine made me regret more than ever the enforced brevity of my stay at

Levanto. Seven days, for reasons of health: only seven days! Those mysterious glades opening into the hill-sides, the green patches of culture interspersed with cypresses and pines, dainty villas nestling in gardens, snow-covered mountains and blue sea—above all, the presence of running water, dear to those who have lived in waterless lands—why, one could spend a life-time in a place like this!

The lieutenant spoke of Florence, his native city. He would be there again before long, in order to present himself to the medical authorities and be weighed and pounded for the hundredth time. He hoped they would then let him stay there. He was tired to death of Levanto and its solitude. How pleasant to bid farewell to this "melancholy" sea which was supposed to be good for his complaints. He asked:

"Do you know why Florentines, coming home from abroad, always rejoice to see that wonderful dome of theirs rising up from the plain?"

"Why?"

"Can't you guess?"

"Let me see. It is sure to be something not quite proper. H'm.... The tower of Giotto, for example, has certain asperities, angularities, anfractuosities——"

"You are no Englishman whatever!" he laughed. "Now try that joke on the next Florentine you meet.... There was a German here," he went on, "who loved Levanto. The hotel people have told me all about him. He began writing a book to prove that there was a different walk to be taken in this neighbourhood for every single day of the year."

"How German. And then?"

"The war came. He cleared out. The natives were sorry. This whole coast seems to be saturated with Teutons—of a respectable class, apparently. They made themselves popular, they bought houses, drank wine, and joked with the countrymen."

"What do you make of them?" I inquired.

"I am a Tuscan," he began (meaning: I am above race-prejudices; I can view these things with olympic detachment). "I think the German says to himself: we want a world-empire, like those damned English. How did they get it? By piracy. Two can play at that game, though it may be a little more difficult now than formerly. Of course," he added, "we have a certain sprinkling of humanitarians even here, the kind of man, I mean, who stands aside in fervent prayer while his daughter is being ravished by the Bulgars, and then comes forward with some amateurish attempt at First Aid, and probably makes a mess of it. But Italians as a whole—well, we are lovers of violent and disreputable methods; it is our heritage from mediaeval times. The only thing that annoys the ordinary native of the country is, if his own son happens to get killed."

"I know. That makes him very angry."

"It makes him angry not with the Germans who are responsible for the war, but with his own government which is responsible for conscripting the boys. Ah, what a stupid subject of conversation! And how God would laugh, if he had any sense of humour! Suppose we go down to the beach and lie on the sand. I need rest: I am very dilapidated."

"You look thin, I must say."

"Typhoid, and malaria, and pleurisy—it is a respectable combination. Thin? I am the merest framework, and so transparent that you can see clean through my stomach. Perhaps you would rather not try? Count my ribs, then."

"Count your ribs? That, my dear Lieutenant, is an occupation for a rainy afternoon. Judging by your length, there must be a good many of them...."

"We should be kind to our young soldiers," said the Major to whom I was relating, after dinner, the story of our afternoon promenade. A burly personage is the Major, with hooked nose and black moustache and twinkling eyes—retired, now, from a service in the course of which he has seen many parts of the world; a fluent raconteur, moreover, who keeps us in fits of laughter with naughty stories and imitations of local dialects. "We must be nice with them, and always offer them cigarettes. What say you, Mr. Lieutenant?"

"Yes, sir. Offer them cigarettes and everything else you possess. The dear fellows! They seldom have the heart to refuse."

"Seldom," echoes the judge.

That is our party; the judge, major, lieutenant and myself. We dine together and afterwards sit in that side room while the fat little host bustles about, doing nearly all the work of the war-diminished establishment himself. Presently the first two rise and indulge in a lively game of cards, amid vigorous thumpings of the table and cursings at the ways of Providence which always contrives to ruin the best hands. I order another litre of wine. The lieutenant, to keep me company, engulfs half a dozen eggs. He tells me about Albanian women. I tell him about Indian women. We thrash the matter out, pursuing this or that aspect into its remotest ramifications, and finally come to the conclusion that I, at the earliest opportunity, must emigrate to Albania, and he to India.

As for the judge, he was born under the pale rays of Saturn. He has attached himself to my heart. Never did I think to care so much about a magistrate, and he a Genoese.

There are some men, a few men, very few, about whom one craves to be precise. Viewed through the mist of months, I behold a corpulent and almost grotesque figure of thirty-five or thereabouts; blue-eyed, fair-haired but nearly bald, clean-shaven, bespectacled. So purblind has he grown with poring over contracts and precedents that his movements are pathologically awkward—embryonic, one might say; his unwieldy gestures and contortions remind one of a seal on shore. The eyes being of small use, he must touch with his hands. Those hands are the most distinctive feature of his person; they are full of expression; tenderly groping hands, that hesitate and fumble in wistful fashion like the feelers of some sensitive creature of night. There is trouble, too, in that obese and sluggish body; trouble to which the unhealthy complexion testifies. He may drink only milk, because wine, which he dearly loves—"and such good wine, here at Levanto"—it always deranges the action of some vital organ inside.

The face is not unlike that of Thackeray.

A man of keen understanding who can argue the legs off a cow when duly roused, he seems far too good for a small place like this, where, by the way, he is a newcomer. Maybe his infinite myopia condemns him to relative seclusion and obscurity. He has a European grip of things; of politics and literature and finance. Needless to say, I have discovered his cloven hoof; I make it my business to discover such things; one may (or may not) respect people for their virtues, one loves them only for their faults. It is a singular tinge of mysticism and credulity which runs through his nature. Can it be the commercial Genoese, the gambling instinct? For he is an authority on stocks and shares, and a passionate card-player into the bargain. Gambling and religion go hand-in-hand—they are but two forms of the same speculative spirit. Think of the Poles, an entire nation of pious roulette-lovers! I have yet to meet a full-blown agnostic who relished these hazards. The unbeliever is not adventurous on such lines; he knows the odds against backing a winner in heaven or earth.

Often, listening to this lawyer's acute talk and watching his uncouth but sympathetic face, I ask myself a question, a very obvious question hereabouts: How could you cause him to swerve from the path of duty? How predispose him in your favour? Sacks of gold would be unavailing: that is certain. He would wave them aside, not in righteous Anglo-Saxon indignation, but with a smile of tolerance at human weakness. To simulate clerical leanings? He is too sharp; he would probably be vexed, not at your attempt to deceive, but at the implication that you took him for a fool. A good tip on the stock exchange? It might go a little way, if artfully tendered. Perhaps an apt and unexpected quotation from the pages of some obsolete jurist—the intellectual method of approach; for there is a kinship, a kind of freemasonry, between all persons of intelligence, however antagonistic their moral outlook. In any case, it would be a desperate venture to override the conscience of such a man. May I never have to try!

His stern principles must often cause him suffering, needless suffering. He is for ever at the mercy of some categorical imperative. This may be the reason why I feel drawn to him. Such persons exercise a strange attraction upon those who, convinced of the eternal fluidity of all mundane affairs, and how that our most sacred institutions are merely conventionalities of time and place, conform to only one rule of life—to be guided by no principles whatever. They miss so much, those others. They miss it so pathetically. One sees them staggering gravewards under a load of self-imposed burdens. A lamentable spectacle, when one thinks of it. Why bear a cross? Is it pleasant? Is it pretty?

He also has taken me for walks, but they are too slow and too short for my taste. Every twenty yards or so he must stand still to "admire the view"—that is, to puff and pant.

"What it is," he then exclaims, "to be an old man in youth, through no fault of one's own. How many are healthy, and yet vicious to the core!"

I inquire:

"Are you suggesting that there may be a connection between sound health and what society, in its latest fit of peevish self-maceration, is pleased to call viciousness?"

"That is a captious question," he replies. "A man of my constitution, unfit for pleasures of the body, is prone to judge severely. Let me try to be fair. I will go so far as to say that to certain natures self-indulgence appears to be necessary as—as sunshine to flowers."

Self-indulgence, I thought. Heavily-fraught is that word; weighted with meaning. The history of two thousand years of spiritual dyspepsia lies embedded in its four syllables. Self-indulgence—it is what the ancients blithely called "indulging one's genius." Self-indulgence! How debased an expression, nowadays. What a text for a sermon on the mishaps of good words and good things. How all the glad warmth and innocence have faded out of the phrase. What a change has crept over us....

Glancing through a glass window not far from the hotel, I was fortunate enough to espy a young girl seated in a sewing shop. She is decidedly pretty and not altogether unaware of the fact, though still a child. We have entered upon an elaborate, classical flirtation. With all the artfulness of her years she is using me to practise on, as a dummy, for future occasions when she shall have grown a little bigger and more admired; she has already picked up one or two good notions. I pretend to be unaware of this fact. I treat her as if she were grown up, and profess to feel that she has really cast a charm—a state of affairs which, if true, would greatly amuse her. And so she has, up to a point. Impossible not to sense the joy which radiates from her smile and person. That is all, so far. It is an orthodox entertainment, merely a joke. God knows what might happen, under given circumstances. Some of a man's most terrible experiences—volcanic cataclysms that ravaged the landscape and left a trail of bitter ashes in their rear—were begun as a joke. You can say so many things in a joking way, you can do so many things in a joking way—especially in Northern countries, where it is easy to joke unseen.

Meanwhile, with Ninetta, I discourse sweet nothings in my choicest idiom which has grown rather rusty in England.

Italian is a flowery language whose rhetorical turns and phrases require constant exercise to keep them in smooth working order. No; that is not correct. It is not the vocabulary which deteriorates. Words are ever at command. What one learns to forget in England is the simplicity to use them; to utter, with an air of deep conviction, a string of what we should call the merest platitudes. It sometimes takes your breath away—the things you have to say because these folks are so enamoured of rhetoric and will not be happy without it.

An English girl of her social standing—I lay stress upon the standing, for it prescribes the conduct—an English girl would never listen to such outpourings with this obvious air of approbation; maybe she would ask where you had been drinking; in every case, your chances would be seriously diminished. She prefers an impromptu frontal attack, a system which is fatal to success in this country. The affair, here, must be a siege. It must move onward by those gradual and inevitable steps ordained of old in the unwritten code of love; no lingering by the wayside, no premature haste. It must march to its end with the measured stateliness of a quadrille. Passion, well-restrained passion, should be written on every line of your countenance. Otherwise you are liable to be dubbed a savage. I know what it is to be called a "Scotch bear," and only because I trembled too much, or too little—I forget which—on a certain occasion.

I have heard those skilled in amatory matters say that the novice will do well to confine his attentions to young girls, avoiding married women or widows. They, the older ones, are a bad school—too prone to pardon infractions of the code, too indulgent towards foreigners and males in general. The girls are not so easily pleased; in fact (entre nous) they are often the devil to propitiate. There is something remorseless about them. They put you on your mettle. They keep you dangling. Quick-witted and accustomed to all the niceties of love-badinage, they listen to every word you have to say, pondering its possibly veiled signification. Thus far and no further, they seem to imply. Yet each hour brings you nearer the goal, if—if you obey the code. Weigh well your conduct during the preliminary stage; remember you are dealing with a professional in the finer shades of meaning. Presumption, awkwardness, imprudence; these are the three cardinal sins, and the greatest of these is imprudence. Be humble; be prepared.

Her best time for conversation, Ninetta tells me, is after luncheon, when she is generally alone for a little while. At that hour therefore I appear with a shirt or something that requires a button—would she mind? The hotel people are so dreadfully understaffed just now—this war!—and one really cannot live without shirts, can one? Would she mind very much? Or perhaps in the evening…is she more free in the evening?

Alas, no; never in the evenings; never for a single moment; never save on religious festivals, one of which, she suddenly remembers, will take place in a week or so.

This is innocent coquetry and perhaps said to test my self-restraint, which is equal to the occasion. An impatient admirer might exclaim——

"Ah, let us meet, then!"

—language which would be permissible after four meetings, and appropriate after six; not after two. With submissive delicacy I reply hoping that the may shine brightly, that she may have all the joy she deserves and give her friends all the pleasure they desire. One of them, assuredly, would be pained in his heart not to see her on that evening. Could she guess who it is? Let her try to discover him tonight, when she is just closing her eyes to sleep, all alone, and thinking about things——

There I leave it, for the present. Unless a miracle occurs, I fear I will have quitted Levanto before that festival comes round. True, they have played the fool with me—how often! Yet, such is my interest in religious ceremonies, that I am frankly annoyed at the prospect of missing that evening.

One would like to be able to stroll about the beach with her, or up to the old castle, instead of sitting in that formal little shop. Such enterprises are impossible. To be seen together for five minutes in any public place might injure her reputation. It is the drawback of her sex, in this country. I am sorry. For though she hides it as best she can, striving to impress me with the immensity of her worldly experiences, there is an unsophisticated freshness in her outlook. The surface has not been scored over.

So it is, with the young. From them you may learn what their elders, having forgotten it, can nevermore teach you. New horizons unroll themselves; you are treading untrodden ground. Talk to a simple creature, farmer or fisherman—well, there is always that touch of common humanity, that sense of eternal needs, to fashion a link of conversation. From a professional—lawyer, doctor, engineer—you may pick up some pungent trifle which yields food for thought; it is never amiss to hearken to a specialist. But the ordinary man of the street, the ordinary man or woman of society, of the world—what can they tell you about art or music or life or religion, about tailors and golf and exhaust-pipes and furniture—what on earth can they tell you that you have not heard already? A mere grinding-out of commonplaces! How often one has covered the same field! They cannot even put their knowledge, such as it is, into an attractive shape or play variations on the theme; it is patter; they have said the same thing, in the same language, for years and years; you have listened to the same thing from other lips, in the same language, for years and years. How one knows it all beforehand—every note in that barrel-organ of echoes! One leaves them feeling like an old, old man, vowing one will never again submit to such a process of demoralization, and understanding, better than ever, the justification of monarchies and tyrannies: these creatures are born to act and think and believe as others tell them. You may be drawn to one or the other, detecting an unusual kindliness of nature or some endearing trick; for the most part, one studies them with a kind of medical interest. How comes it that this man, respectably equipped by birth, has grown so warped and atrophied, an animated bundle of deficiencies?

Life is the cause—life, the onward march of years. It has a cramping effect; it closes the pores, intensifying one line of activity at the expense of all the others; often enough it encrusts the individual with a kind of shell, a veneer of something akin to hypocrisy. Your ordinary adult is an egoist in matters of the affections; a specialist in his own insignificant pursuit; a dull dog. Dimly aware of these defects, he confines himself to generalities or, grown confidential, tells you of his little fads, his little love-affairs—such ordinary ones! Like those millions of his fellows, he has been transformed into a screw, a bolt, a nut, in the machine. He is standardised.

A man who has tried to remain a mere citizen of the world and refused to squeeze himself into the narrow methods and aspirations of any epoch or country, will discover that children correspond unconsciously to his multifarious interests. They are not standardised. They are more generous in their appreciations, more sensitive to pure ideas, more impersonal. Their curiosity is disinterested. The stock may be rudimentary, but the outlook is spacious; it is the passionless outlook of the sage. A child is ready to embrace the universe. And, unlike adults, he is never afraid to face his own limitations. How refreshing to converse with folks who have no bile to vent, no axe to grind, no prejudices to air; who are pagans to the core; who, uninitiated into the false value of externals, never fail to size you up from a more spiritual point of view than do their elders; who are not oozing politics and sexuality, nor afflicted with some stupid ailment or other which prevents them doing this and that. To be in contact with physical health—it would alone suffice to render their society a dear delight, quite apart from the fact that if you are wise and humble you may tiptoe yourself, by inches, into fairyland.

That scarlet sash of hers set me thinking—thinking of the comparative rarity of the colour red as an ingredient of the Italian panorama. The natives seem to avoid it in their clothing, save among certain costumes of the centre and south. You see little red in the internal decorations of the houses—in their wallpapers, the coloured tiles underfoot, the tapestries, table-services and carpets, though a certain fondness for pink is manifest, and not only in Levanto. There is a gulf between pink and red.

It is essentially a land of blue and its derivatives—cool, intellectual tints. The azure sea follows you far inland with its gleams. Look landwards from the water—purple Apennines are ever in sight. And up yonder, among the hills, you will rarely escape from celestial hues.

Speaking of these mountains in a general way, they are bare masses whose coloration trembles between misty blue and mauve according to distance, light, and hour of day. As building-stone, the rock imparts a grey-blue tint to the walls. The very flowers are blue; it is a peculiarity of limestone formation, hitherto unexplained, to foster blooms of this colour. Those olive-coloured slopes are of a glaucous tone.

Or wander through the streets of any town and examine the pottery whether ancient or modern—sure index of national taste. Greens galore, and blues and bilious yellows; seldom will you see warmer shades. And if you do, it is probably Oriental or Siculo-Arabic work, or their imitations.

One does not ask for wash-hand basins of sang-de-boeuf. One wonders, merely, whether this avoidance of sanguine tints in the works of man be an instinctive paraphrase of surrounding nature, or due to some cause lying deep down in the roots of Italian temperament. I am aware that the materials for producing crimson are not common in the peninsula. If they liked the colour, the materials would be forthcoming.

The Spaniards, a different race, sombre and sensuous, are not averse to red. Nor are the Greeks. Russians have a veritable cult of it; their word for "beautiful" means red. It is therefore not a matter of climate.

In Italy, those rare splashes of scarlet—the flaming horse-cloths of Florence, a ruddy sail that flecks the sea, some procession of ruby-tinted priests—they come as a shock, a shock of delight. Cross the Mediterranean, and you will find emotional hues predominating; the land is aglow with red, the very shadows suffused with it. Or go further east....

Meanwhile, Attilio hovers discreetly near the hotel-entrance, ready to convey me to Jericho. He is a small mason-boy to whom I contrived to be useful in the matter of an armful of obstreperous bricks which refused to remain balanced on his shoulder. Forthwith, learning that I was a stranger unfamiliar with Levanto, he conceived the project of abandoning his regular work and becoming my guide, philosopher and friend.

"Drop your job for the sake of a few days?" I inquired. "You'll get the sack, my boy."

Not so, he thought. He was far too serviceable to those people. They would welcome him with open arms whenever—if ever—he cared to return to them. Was not the mason-in-chief a cousin of his? Everything could be arranged, without a doubt.

And so it was.

He knows the country; every nook of the hills and sea-shore. A pleasanter companion could not be found; observant and tranquil, tinged with a gravity beyond his years—a gravity due to certain family troubles—and with uncommon sweetness of disposition. He has evidently been brought up with sisters.

We went one day up the valley to a village, I forget its name, that sits on a hill-top above the spot where two streams unite; the last part of the way is a steep climb under olives. Here we suddenly took leave of spring and encountered a bank of wintry snow. It forced us to take refuge in the shop of a tobacconist who provided some liquid and other refreshment. Would I might meet him again, that genial person: I never shall! We conversed in English, a language he had acquired in the course of many peregrinations about the globe (he used to be a seaman), and great was Attilio's astonishment on hearing a man whom he knew from infancy now talking to me in words absolutely incomprehensible. He asked:

"You two—do you really understand each other?"

On our homeward march he pointed to some spot, barely discernible among the hills on our left. That was where he lived. His mother would be honoured to see me. We might walk on to Monterosso afterwards. Couldn't I manage it?

To be sure I could. And the very next day. But the place seemed a long way off and the country absolutely wild. I said:

"You will have to carry a basket of food."

"Better than bricks which grow heavier every minute. Your basket, I daresay, will be pretty light towards evening."

The name of his natal village, a mere hamlet, has slipped my memory. I only know that we moved at daybreak up the valley behind Levanto and presently turned to our right past a small mill of some kind; olives, then chestnuts, accompanied the path which grew steeper every moment, and was soon ankle-deep in slush from the melted snow. This was his daily walk, he explained. An hour and a half down, in the chill twilight of dawn; two hours' trudge home, always up hill, dead tired, through mud and mire, in pitch darkness, often with snow and rain.

"Do you wonder," he added, "at my preferring to be with you?"

"I wonder at my fortune, which gave me such a charming friend. I am not always so lucky."

"Luck—it is the devil. We have had no news from my father in America for two years. No remittances ever come from him. He may be dead, for all we know. Our land lies half untilled; we cannot pay for the hire of day labourers. We live from hand to mouth; my mother is not strong; I earn what I can; one of my sisters is obliged to work at Levanto. Think what that means, for us! Perhaps that is why you call me thoughtful. I am the oldest male in the family; I must conduct myself accordingly. Everything depends on me. It is enough to make anyone thoughtful. My mother will tell you about it."

She doubtless did, though I gleaned not so much as the drift of her speech. The mortal has yet to be born who can master all the dialects of Italy; this one seemed to bear the same relation to the Tuscan tongue which that of the Basses-Pyrenées bears to French—it was practically another language. Listening to her, I caught glimpses, now and then, of familiar Mediterranean sounds; like lamps shining through a fog, they were quickly swallowed up in the murk. Unlike her offspring, she had never been to school. That accounted for it. A gentle woman, frail in health and manifestly wise; the look of the house, of the children, bore witness to her sagacity. Understanding me as little as I understood her, our conversation finally lapsed into a series of smiles, which Attilio interpreted as best he could. She insisted upon producing some apples and a bottle of wine, and I was interested to notice that she poured out to her various male offspring, down to the tiniest tot, but drank not a drop herself, nor gave any to her big daughters.

"She is sorry they will not let you stay at Levanto."

"Carrara lies just beyond the war-zone. I want to visit the marble-mines when the weather grows a little warmer, and perhaps write something about them. Ask her whether you can join me there for a week or so, if I send the money. Make her say yes."

She said yes.

With a companion like this, to reflect my moods and act as buffer between myself and the world, I felt I could do anything. Already I saw myself exploring those regions, interviewing directors as to methods of work and output, poking my nose into municipal archives and libraries to learn the history of those various quarries of marble, plain and coloured; tracking the footsteps of Michael Angelo at Seravezza and Pietrasanta and re-discovering that old road of his and the inscription he left on the rock; speculating why the Romans, who ransacked the furthermost corners of the earth for tinted stones, knew so little of the treasures here buried; why the Florentines were long content to use that grey bigio, when the lordly black portovenere,[2] with its golden streaks, was lying at their very doors....

The gods willed otherwise.

Then, leaving that hospitable dame, we strolled forth along a winding road—a good road, once more—ever upwards, under the bare chestnuts. At last the watershed was reached and we began a zigzag descent towards the harbour of Monterosso, meeting not a soul by the way. Snow lay on these uplands; it began to fall softly. As the luncheon hour had arrived we took refuge in a small hut of stone and there opened the heavy basket which gave forth all that heart could desire—among other things, a large fiasco of strong white wine which we drank to the dregs. It made us both delightfully tipsy. So passed an hour of glad confidences in that abandoned shelter with the snowflakes drifting in upon us— one of those hours that sweeten life and compensate for months of dreary harassment.

A long descent, past some church or convent famous as a place of pilgrimage, led to the strand of Monterosso where the waves were sparkling in tepid sunshine. Then up again, by a steep incline, to a signal station perched high above the sea. Attilio wished to salute a soldier-relative working here. I remained discreetly in the background; it would never do for a foreigner to be seen prying into Marconi establishments in this confounded "zone of defense." Another hour by meandering woodland paths brought us to where, from the summit of a hill, we looked down upon Levanto, smiling merrily in its conch-shaped basin....

All this cloudless afternoon we conversed in a flowery dell under the pine trees, with the blue sea at our feet. It was a different climate from yesterday; so warm, so balmy. Impossible to conceive of snow! I thought I had definitely bidden farewell to winter.

Trains, an endless succession of trains, were rumbling through the bowels of the mountain underneath, many of them filled with French soldiers bound for Salonika. They have been going southward ever since my arrival at Levanto.

Attilio was more pensive than usual; the prospect of returning to his bricks was plainly irksome. Why not join for a change, I suggested, one of yonder timber-felling parties? He knew all about it. The pay is too poor. They are cutting the pines all along this coast and dragging them to the water, where they are sawn into planks and despatched to the battle-front. It seemed a pity to Attilio; at this rate, he thought, there would soon be none left, and how then would we be able to linger in the shade and take our pleasure on some future day?

"Have no fear of that," I said. "And yet—would you believe it? Many years ago these hills, as far as you can see to right and left and behind, were bare like the inside of your hand. Then somebody looked at the landscape and said: 'What a shame to make so little use of these hundreds of miles of waste soil. Let us try an experiment with a new kind of pine tree which I think will prosper among the rocks. One of these days people may be glad of them.'"

"Well?"

"You see what has happened. Right up to Genoa, and down below Levanto—nothing but pines. You Italians ought to be grateful to that man. The value of the timber which is now being felled along this stretch of coast cannot be less than a thousand francs an hour. That is what you would have to pay, if you wanted to buy it. Twelve thousand francs a day; perhaps twice as much."

"Twelve thousand francs a day!"

"And do you know who planted the trees? It was a Scotsman."

"A Scozzese. What kind of animal is that?"

"A person who thinks ahead."

"Then my mother is a Scotsman."

I glanced from the sea into his face; there was something of the same calm depth in both, the same sunny composure. What is it, this limpid state of the mind? What do we call this alloy of profundity and frankness? We call it intelligence. I would like to meet that man or woman who can make Attilio say something foolish. He does not know what it is to feel shy. Serenely objective, he discards those subterfuges which are the usual safeguard of youth or inexperience—the evasions, reservations and prevarications that defend the shallow, the weak, the self-conscious. His candour rises above them. He feels instinctively that these things are pitfalls.

"Have you no sweetheart, Attilio?"

"Certainly I have. But it is not a man's affair. We are only children, you understand—siamo ancora piccoli."

"Did you ever give her a kiss?"

"Never. Not a single one."

I relight my pipe, and then inquire:

"Why not give her a kiss?"

"People would call me a disrespectful boy."

"Nobody, surely, need be any the wiser?"

"She is not like you and me."

A pause....

"Not like us? How so?"

"She would tell her sister."

"What of it?"

"The sister would tell her mother, who would say unpleasant things to mine. And perhaps to other folks. Then the fat would be in the fire. And that is why."

Another pause....

"What would your mother say to you?"

"She would say: 'You are the oldest male; you should conduct yourself accordingly. What is this lack of judgment I hear about?'"

"I begin to understand."

Siena

Driven from the Paradise of Levanto, I landed not on earth but—with one jump—in Hell. The Turks figure forth a Hell of ice and snow; this is my present abode; its name is Siena. Every one knows that this town lies on a hill, on three hills; the inference that it would be cold in January was fairly obvious; how cold, nobody could have guessed. The sun is invisible. Streets are deep in snow. Icicles hang from the windows. Worst of all, the hotels are unheated. Those English, you know,—they refuse to supply us with coal....

Could this be the city where I was once nearly roasted to death? It is an effort to recall that glistening month of the Palio festival, a month I spent at a genuine pension for a set purpose, namely, to write a study on the habits of "The Pension-cats of Europe"—those legions of elderly English spinsters who lead crepuscular lives in continental boarding-houses. I tore it up, I remember; it was unfair. These ladies have a perfect right to do as they please and, for that matter, are not nearly as ridiculous as many married couples that live outside boarding-houses. But when Siena grew intolerable—a stark, ill-provisioned place; you will look in vain for a respectable grocer or butcher; the wine leaves much to be desired; indeed, it has all the drawbacks of Florence and none of its advantages—why, then we fled into Mr. Edward Hutton's Unknown Tuscany. There, at Abbadia San Salvatore (though the summit of Mount Amiata did not come up to expectation) we at last felt cool again, wandering amid venerable chestnuts and wondrously tinted volcanic blocks, mountain-fragments, full of miniature glens and moisture and fernery—a green twilight, a landscape made for fairies....

Was this the same Siena from which we once escaped to get cool? Muffled up to the ears, with three waistcoats on, I move in and out of doors, endeavouring to discover whether there be any appreciable difference in temperature between the external air and that of my bedroom. There cannot be much to choose between them. They say I am the only foreigner now in Siena. That, at least, is a distinction, a record. Furthermore, no matches, not even of the sulphur variety, were procurable in any of the shops for the space of three days; that also, I imagine, cannot yet have occurred within the memory of living man.

While stamping round the great Square yesterday to keep my feet warm, a Florentine addressed me; a commercial gentleman, it would seem. He disapproved of this square—it was not regular in shape, it was not even level. What a piazza! Such was his patriotism that he actually went on to say unfriendly things about the tower. Who ever thought of building a tower at the bottom of a hill? It was good enough, he dared say, for Siena. Oh, yes; doubtless it satisfied their artistic notions, such as they were.

This tower being one of my favourites, I felt called upon to undertake its defence. Recollecting all I had ever heard or read to its credit, citing authorities neither of us had ever dreamt of—improvising lustily, in short, as I warmed to my work—I concluded by proving it to be one of the seven wonders of the world. He said:

"Now really! One would think you had been born in this miserable hole. You know what we Florentines say:

Siena
Di tre cose è piena:
Torri, campane,
E figli di putane."

"I admit that Siena is deficient in certain points," I replied. "That wonderful dome of yours, for example—there is nothing like it here."

"No, indeed. Ah, that cupola! Ah, Brunelleschi—che genio!"

"I perceive you are a true Florentine. Could you perhaps tell me why Florentines, coming home from abroad, always rejoice to see it rising out of the plain?"

"Some enemy has been talking to you...."

A little red-haired boy from Lucca, carrying for sale a trayful of those detestable plaster-casts, then accosted me.

Who bought such abominations, I inquired?

Nobody. Business was bad.

Bad? I could well believe it. Having for the first time in my life nothing better to do, I did my duty. I purchased the entire collection of these horrors, on the understanding that he should forthwith convey them in my presence to the desolate public garden, where they were set up, one after the other, on the edge of a bench and shattered to fragments with our snow-balls. Thus perished, not without laughter and in a good cause, three archangels, two Dantés, a nondescript lady with brocade garments and a delectable amorino whose counterpart, the sole survivor, was reserved for a better fate—being carried home and presented as a gift to my chambermaid.

She was polite enough to call it a beautiful work of art.

I was polite enough not to contradict her.

Both of us know better....

This young girl has no illusions (few Tuscans have) and yet a great charm. Her lover is at the front. There is little for her to do, the hotel being practically empty. There is nothing whatever for me to do, in these Arctic latitudes. Bored to death, both of us, we confabulate together huddled in shawls and greatcoats, each holding a charcoal pan to keep the fingers from being frostbitten. I say to myself: "You will never find a maidservant of this type in Rome, so sprightly of tongue, distinguished in manner and spotless in person—never!"

The same with her words. The phrases trip out of her mouth, immaculate, each in full dress. Seldom does she make an original remark, but she says ordinary things in a tone of intense conviction and invests them with an appetizing savour. Wherein lies that peculiar salt of Tuscan speech? In its emphasis, its air of finality. They are emphatic, rather than profound. Their deepest utterances, if you look below the surface, are generally found to be variants of one of those ancestral saws or proverbs wherewith the country is saturated. Theirs is a crusted charm. A hard and glittering sanity, a kind of ageless enamel, is what confronts us in their temperament. There are not many deviations from this Tuscan standard. Close by, in Umbria, you will find a softer type.

One can be passably warm in bed. Here I lie for long, long hours, endeavouring to generate the spark of energy which will propel me from this inhospitable mountain. Here I lie and study an old travel-book. I mean to press it to the last drop.

One seldom presses books out, nowadays. The mania for scraps of one kind or another, the general cheapening of printed matter, seem to have dulled that faculty and given us a scattered state of mind. We browse dispersedly, in goatish fashion, instead of nibbling down to the root like that more conscientious quadruped whose name, if I mentioned it, would degrade the metaphor. Devouring so much, so hastily, so irreverentially, how shall a man establish close contact with the mind of him who writes, and impregnate himself with his peculiar outlook to such an extent as to be able to take on, if only momentarily, a colouring different from his own? It is a task requiring submissiveness and leisure.

And yet, what could be more interesting than really to observe things and men from the angle of another individual, to install oneself within his mentality and make it one's habitation? To sit in his bones—what glimpses of unexplored regions! Were a man to know what his fellow truly thinks; could he feel in his own body those impulses which drive the other to his idiomatic acts and words—what an insight he would gain! Morally, it might well amount to "tout comprendre, c'est ne rien pardonner"; but who troubles about pardoning or condemning? Intellectually, it would be a feast. Thus immersed into an alien personality, a man would feel as though he lived two lives, and possessed two characters at the same time. One's own life, prolonged to an age, could never afford such unexpected revelations.

The thing can be done, up to a point, with patient humility; for everybody writes himself down more or less, though not everybody is worth the trouble of deciphering.

I purpose to apply this method; to squeeze the juice, the life-blood, out of what some would call a rather dry Scotch traveller. I read his book in England for the first time two years ago, and have brought it here with a view to further dissection. Would I had known of its existence five years earlier! Strange to say, despite my deplorable bookishness (vide Press) this was not the case; I could never ascertain either the author's name or the title of his volume, though I had heard about him, rather vaguely, long before that time. It was Dr. Dohrn of the Naples Aquarium who said to me in those days:

"Going to the South? Whatever you do, don't forget to read that book by an old Scotch clergyman. He ran all over the country with a top-hat and an umbrella, copying inscriptions. He was just your style: perfectly crazy."

Flattered at the notion of being likened to a Scottish divine, I made all kinds of inquiries—in vain. I abandoned hope of unearthing the top-hatted antiquarian and had indeed concluded him to be a myth, when a friend supplied me with what may be absurdly familiar to less bookish people: "The Nooks and By-ways of Italy." By Craufurd Tait Ramage, LL.D. Liverpool, 1868.

A glance sufficed to prove that this Ramage belonged to the brotherhood of David Urquhart, Mure of Caldwell, and the rest of them. Where are they gone, those candid inquirers, so full of gentlemanly curiosity, so informative and yet shrewdly human; so practical—think of Urquhart's Turkish Baths—though stuffed with whimsicality and abstractions? Where is the spirit that gave them birth?

One grows attached to these "Nooks and By-ways." An honest book, richly thoughtful, and abounding in kindly twinkles.

Now, regarding the top-hat. I find no mention of it in these letters. For letters they are; letters extracted from a diary which was written on his return from Italy in 1828 from "very full notes made from day to day during my journey." 1828: that date is important. It was in 1828, therefore, when the events occurred which he relates, and he allowed an interval of forty years to elapse ere making them public.

The umbrella on the other hand is always cropping up. It pervades the volume like a Leitmotif. It is "a most invaluable article" for protecting the head against the sun's rays; so constantly is it used that after a single month's wear we find it already in "a sad state of dilapidation." Still, he clings to it. As a defence against brigands it might prove useful, and on one occasion, indeed, he seizes it in his hand "prepared to show fight." This happened, be it remembered, in 1828. Vainly one conjectures what the mountain folk of South Italy thought of such a phenomenon. Even now, if they saw you carrying an umbrella about in the sunshine, they would cross themselves and perhaps pray for your recovery—perhaps not. Yet Ramage was not mad at all. He was only more individualistic and centrifugal than many people. Having formed by bitter experience a sensible theory—to wit, that sunstroke is unpleasant and can be avoided by the use of an umbrella—he is not above putting it into practice. Let others think and do as they please!

For the rest, his general appearance was quite in keeping. How delightful he must have looked! Why have we no such types nowadays? Wearing a "white merino frock-coat, nankeen trowsers, a large-brimmed straw hat, and white shoes," he must have been a fairly conspicuous object in the landscape. That hat alone will have alarmed the peasantry who to this day and hour wear nothing but felt on their heads. And note the predominance of the colour white in his attire; it was popular, at that period, with English travellers. Such men, however, were unknown in most of the regions which Ramage explored. The colour must have inspired feelings akin to awe in the minds of the natives, for white is their bête noire. They have a rooted aversion to it and never employ it in their clothing, because it suggests to their fancy the idea of bloodlessness—of anaemia and death. If you want to make one of them ill over his dinner, wear a white waistcoat.

Accordingly, it is not surprising that he sometimes finds himself "an object of curiosity." An English Vice-Consul, at one place, was "quite alarmed at my appearance." Elsewhere he meets a band of peasant-women who "took fright at my appearance and scampered off in the utmost confusion." And what happened at Taranto? By the time of his arrival in that town his clothes were already in such a state that "they would scarcely fit an Irish beggar." Umbrella in hand—he is careful to apprise us of this detail—and soaked moreover from head to foot after an immersion in the river Tara, he entered the public square, which was full of inhabitants, and soon found himself the centre of a large crowd. Looking, he says, like a drowned rat, his appearance caused "great amazement."

"What is the matter? Who is he?" they asked.

The muleteer explained that he was an Englishman, and "that immediately seemed to satisfy them."

Of course it did. People in those times were prepared for anything on the part of an Englishman, who was a far more self-assertive and self-confident creature than nowadays.

Thus arrayed in snowy hue, like the lilies of the field, he perambulates during the hot season the wildest parts of South Italy, strangely unprejudiced, heedless of bugs and brigands—a real danger in 1828: did he not find the large place Rossano actually blocked by them?—sleeping in stables and execrable inns, viewing sites of antiquity and natural beauty, interrogating everybody about everything and, in general, "satisfying his curiosity." That curiosity took a great deal to satisfy. It is a positive relief to come upon a sentence in this book, a sentence unique, which betrays a relaxing or waning of this terrible curiosity. "It requires a strong mania for antiquities to persevere examining such remains as Alife furnishes, and I was soon satisfied with what I had seen." Nor did he climb to the summit of Mount Vulture, as he would have done if the view had not been obscured by a haze.

His chief concern could not be better summed up than in the sub-title he has chosen for this volume: Wanderings in search of ancient remains and modern superstitions. To any one who knows the country it appears astonishing how much he contrived to see, and in how brief a space of time. He accomplished wonders. For it was no mean task he had proposed to himself, namely, "to visit every spot in Italy which classic writers had rendered famous."

To visit every spot—what a Gargantuan undertaking! None but a quite young man could have conceived such a project, and even Ramage, with all his good health and zest, might have spent half a lifetime over the business but for his habit of breathless hustle, which leaves the reader panting behind. He is always on the move. He reminds one of Mr. Phineas Fogg in that old tale. The moment he has "satisfied his curiosity" there is no holding him; off he goes; the smiles of the girls whom he adores, the entreaties of some gentle scholar who fain would keep him as guest for the night—they are vain; he is tired to death, but "time is precious" and he "tears himself away from his intelligent host" and scampers into the wilderness once more, as if the Furies were at his heels. He thinks nothing of rushing from Catanzaro to Cotrone, from Manduria to Brindisi, in a single day—at a time when there was hardly a respectable road in the country. Up to the final paragraph of the book he is "hurrying" because time is "fast running out."

This sense of fateful hustle—this, and the umbrella—they impart quite a peculiar flavour to his pages.

One would like to learn more about so lovable a type—for such he was, unquestionably; one would like to know, above all things, why his descriptions of other parts of Italy have never been printed. Was the enterprise interrupted by his death? He tells us that the diaries of his tours through the central and northern regions were written; that he visited "every celebrated spot in Umbria and Etruria" and wandered "as far as the valley of the Po." Where are these notes? Those on Etruria, especially, would make good reading at this distance of time, when even Dennis has acquired an old-world aroma. The Dictionary of National Biography might tell us something about him, but that handy little volume is not here; moreover, it has a knack of telling you everything about people save what you ought to know.

So, for example, I had occasion not long ago to look up the account of Charles Waterton the naturalist.[3] He did good work in his line, but nothing is more peculiar to the man than his waywardness. It was impossible for him to do anything after the manner of other folks. In all his words and actions he was a freak, a curiosity, the prince of eccentrics. Yet this, the essence of the man, the fundamental trait of his character which shines out of every page of his writing and every detail of his daily life—this, the feature by which he was known to his fellows and ought to be known to posterity—it is intelligible from that account only if you read between the lines. Is that the way to write "biography"?

Fortunately he has written himself down; so has Ramage; and it is instructive to compare the wayside reflections of these two contemporaries as they rove about the ruins of Italy; the first, ardent Catholic, his horizon close-bounded by what the good fathers of Stonyhurst had seen fit to teach him; the other, less complacent, all alive indeed with Calvinistic disputatiousness and ready to embark upon bold speculations anent the origin of heathen gods and their modern representatives in the Church of Rome; amiable scholars and gentlemen, both of them; yet neither venturing to draw those plain conclusions which the "classic remains of paganism" would have forced upon anybody else—upon anybody, that is, who lacked their initial warp, whose mind had not been twisted in youth or divided, rather, into watertight compartments.

A long sentence....

Pisa

After a glacial journey—those English! They will not even give us coal for steam-heating—I arrived here. It is warmer, appreciably warmer. Yet I leave tomorrow or next day. The streets of the town, the distant beach of San Rossore and its pine trees—they are fraught with sad memories; memories of an autumn month in the early nineties. A city of ghosts....

The old hotel had put on a new face; freshly decorated, it wears none the less a poverty-stricken air. My dinner was bad and insufficient. One grows sick of those vile maccheroni made with war-time flour. The place is full of rigid officers taking themselves seriously. Odd, how a uniform can fill a simpleton with self-importance. What does Bacon say? I forget. Something apposite—something about the connection between military costumes and vanity. For the worst of this career is that it is liable to transform even a sensible man into a fool. I never see these sinister-clanking marionettes without feelings of distrust. They are the outward symbol of an atavistic striving: the modern infâme. We have been dying for sometime past from over-legislation. Now we are caught in the noose. A bureaucracy is bad enough. A bureaucracy can at least be bribed. Militarism dries up even that little fount of the imagination.

Another twenty years of this, and we may be living in caves again; they came near it, at the end of the Thirty Years' War. Such a cataclysm as ours may account for the extinction of the great Cro-Magnon civilization—as fine a race, physically, as has yet appeared on earth; they too may have been afflicted with the plague of nationalism, unless, as is quite likely, that horrid work was accomplished by a microbe of some kind....

In the hour of evening, under a wintry sky amid whose darkly massed vapours a young moon is peering down upon this maddened world, I wander alone through deserted roadways towards that old solitary brick-tower. Here I stand, and watch the Arno rolling its sullen waves. In Pisa, at such an hour, the Arno is the emblem of Despair. Swollen with melted snow from the mountains, it has gnawed its miserable clay banks and now creeps along, leaden and inert, half solid, like a torrent of liquid mud—irresolute whether to be earth or water; whether to stagnate here for ever at my feet, or crawl onward yet another sluggish league into the sea. So may Lethe look, or Styx: the nightmare of a flood.

There is dreary monotony in all Italian rivers, once they have reached the plain. They are livelier in their upper reaches. At Florence—where those citron-tinted houses are mirrored in the stream—you may study the Arno in all its ever-changing moods. Seldom is its colour quite the same. The hue of café-au-lait in full spate, it shifts at other times between apple-green and jade, between celadon and chrysolite and eau-de-Nil. In the weariness of summer the tints are prone to fade altogether out of the waves. They grow bleached, devitalized; they are spent, withering away like grass that has lain in the sun.[1] Yet with every thunder-storm on yonder hills the colour-sprite leaps back into the waters.

Your Florentine of the humbler sort loves to dawdle along the bank on a bright afternoon, watching the play of the river and drawing a kind of philosophic contentment out of its cool aquatic humours. Presently he reaches that bridge—the jewellers' bridge. He thinks he must buy a ring. Be sure the stone will reflect his Arno in one of its moods. I will wager he selects a translucent chrysoprase set in silver, a cheap and stubborn gem whose frigidly uncompromising hue appeals in mysterious fashion to his own temperament.

Whoever suffers from insomnia will find himself puzzling at night over questions which have no particular concern for him at other times. And one seems to be more wide awake, during those moments, than by day. Yet the promptings of the brain, which then appear so lucid, so novel and convincing, will seldom bear examination in the light of the sun. To test the truth of this, one has only to jot down one's thoughts at the time, and peruse them after breakfast. How trite they read, those brilliant imaginings!

For reasons which I cannot fathom, I pondered last night upon the subject of heredity; a subject that had a certain fascination for me in my biological days. The lacunae of science! We weigh the distant stars and count up their ingredients. Yet here is a phenomenon which lies under our very hand and to which is devoted the most passionate study: what have we learnt of its laws? Be that as it may, there occurred to me last night a new idea. It consisted in putting together two facts which have struck me separately on many occasions, but never conjointly. Taken together, I said to myself, and granted that both are correct, they may help to elucidate a dark problem of national psychology.

The first one I state rather tentatively, having hardly sufficient material to go upon. It is this. You will find it more common in Italy than in England for the male offspring of a family to resemble the father and the female the mother. I cannot suggest a reason for this. I have observed the fact—that is all.

Let me say, in parenthesis, that it is well to confine oneself to adults in such researches. Childhood and youth is a period of changing lights and half-tones and temperamental interplay. Characteristics of body and mind are held, as it were, in solution. We think a child takes after its mother because of this or that feature. If we wait for twenty-five years, we see the true state of affairs; the hair has grown dark like the father's, the nose, the most telling item of the face, has also approximated to his type, likewise the character—in fact the offspring is clearly built on paternal lines. And vice-versa. To study children for these purposes would be waste of time.

The second observation I regard as axiomatic. It is this. You will nowhere find an adult offspring which reproduces in any marked degree the physical features of one parent displaying in any marked degree the mental features of the other. That man whose external build and complexion is entirely modelled upon that of his hard materialistic father and who yet possesses all the artistic idealism of his maternal parent—such creatures do not exist in nature, though you may encounter them as often as you please in the pages of novelists.

Let me insert another parenthesis to observe that I am speaking of the broad mass, the average, in a general way. For it stands to reason that the offspring may be vaguely intermediate between two parents, may resemble one or both in certain particulars and not in others, may hark back to ancestral types or bear no appreciable likeness to any one discoverable. It is a theme admitting of endless combinations and permutations. Or again, in reference to the first proposition, it would be easy for any traveller in this country to point out, for example, a woman who portrays the qualities of her father in the clearest manner. I know a dozen such cases. Hundreds of them would not make them otherwise than what I think they are—rarer here than in England.

Granting that both these propositions are correct, what should we expect to find? That in Italy the male type of character and temperament is more constant, more intimately associated with the male type of feature; and the same with the female. In other words, that the categories into which their men and women fall are fewer and more clearly defined, by reason of the fact that their mental and moral sex-characteristics are more closely correlated with their physical sex-characteristics. That the Englishman, on the other hand, male or female, does not fall so easily into categories; he is complex and difficult to "place," the psychological sex-boundaries being more hazily demarcated. There is iridescence and ambiguity here, whereas Italians of either sex, once the rainbow period of youth is over, are relatively unambiguous; easily "placed."

Is this what we find? I think so.

Speculations….

I never pass through Pisa without calling to mind certain rat-hunts in company with J. O. M., who was carried out of the train at this very station, dead, because he refused to follow my advice. He was my neighbour at one time; he lived near the river Mole in relative seclusion; coursing rats with Dandie Dinmonts was the only form of exercise which entailed no strain on his weakened constitution. How he loved it!

This O——was a man of mystery and violence, who threw himself into every kind of human activity with superhuman, Satanic, zest; traveller, sportsman, financier, mining expert, lover of wine and women, of books and prints; one of the founders, I believe, of the Rhodesia Company; faultlessly dressed, infernally rich and, when he chose—which was fairly often—preposterously brutal. Neither manner nor face were winning. He was swarthy almost to blackness, quite un-English in looks, with rather long hair, a most menacing moustache and the fiercest eyes imaginable; a king of the gipsies, so far as features went. Something sinister hung about his personality. A predatory type, unquestionably; never so happy as when pitting his wits or strength against others, tracking down this or that—by choice, living creatures. He had taken life by the throat, and excesses of various kinds having shattered his frame, there was an end, for the time being, of deer-stalking and tigers; it was a tame period of rat-hunts with those terriers whose murderous energies were a pis aller, yielding a sort of vicarious pleasure. The neighbourhood was depopulated of such beasts, purchased at fancy prices; when a sufficient quantity (say, half a hundred) had been collected together, I used to receive a telegram containing the single word "rats." Then the pony was saddled, and I rode down for the grand field day.

We once gave the hugest of these destroyed rodents, I remember, to an amiable old sow, a friend of the family. What was she going to do? She ate it, as you would eat a pear. She engulfed the corpse methodically, beginning at the head, working her way through breast and entrails while her chops dripped with gore, and ending with the tail, which gave some little trouble to masticate, on account of its length and tenuity. Altogether, decidedly good sport....

Then O——disappeared from my ken. Years went by. Improving health, in the course of time, tempted him back into his former habits; he built himself a shooting lodge in the Alps. We were neighbours again, having no ridge worth mentioning save the Schadona pass between us. I joined him once or twice— chamois, instead of rats. This place was constructed on a pretentious scale, and he must have paid fantastic sums for the transport of material to that remote region (you could watch the chamois from the very windows) and for the rights over all the country round about.[5] O——told me that the superstitious Catholic peasants raised every kind of difficulty and objection to his life there; it was a regular conspiracy. I suggested a more friendly demeanour, especially towards their priests. That was not his way. He merely said: "I'll be even with them. Mark my words."....

There followed another long interval, during which he vanished completely. Then, one April afternoon on the Posilipo, a sailor climbed up with a note from him. The Consul-General said I lived here. If so, would I come to Bertolini's hotel at once? He was seriously ill.

Neighbours once more!

I left then and there, and was appalled at the change in him. His skin was drawn tight as parchment over a face the colour of earth, there was no flesh on his hands, the voice was gone, though fire still gleamed viciously in the hollows of his eyes. That raven-black hair was streaked with grey and longer than ever, which gave him an incongruously devout appearance. He had taken pitiful pains to look fresh and appetizing.

So we sat down to dinner on Bertolini's terrace, in the light of a full moon. O——ate nothing whatever.

He arrived from Egypt some time ago, on his way to England. The doctor had forbidden further travelling or any other exertion on account of various internal complications; among other things, his heart, he told me, was as large as a child's head.

"I hope you can stand this food," he whispered, or rather croaked. "For God's sake, order anything you fancy. As for me, I can't even eat like you people. Asses' milk is what I get, and slops. Done for, this time. I'm a dying man; anybody can see that. A dying man——"

"Something," I said, "is happening to that moon."

It was in eclipse. Half the bright surface had been ominously obscured since we took our seats. O——scowled at the satellite, and went on:

"But I won't be carried out of this dirty hole (Bertolini's)—not feet first. Would you mind my gasping another day or two at your place? Rolfe has told me about it."

We moved him, with infinite trouble. The journey woke his dormant capacities for invective. He cursed at the way they jolted him about; he cursed himself into a collapse that day, and we thought it was all over. Then he rallied, and became more abusive than before. Nothing was right. Stairs being forbidden, the whole lower floor of the house was placed at his disposal; the establishment was dislocated, convulsed; and still he swore. He swore at me for the better part of a week; at the servants, and even at the good doctor Malbranc, who came every morning in a specially hired steam-launch to make that examination which always ended in his saying to me: "You must humour him. Heart-patients are apt to be irritable." Irritable was a mild term for this particular patient. His appetite, meanwhile, began to improve.

It was soon evident that my cook had not the common sense to prepare his invalid dishes; a second one was engaged. Then, my gardener and sailor-boy being manifest idiots, it became necessary to procure an extra porter to fetch the numberless odd things he needed from town every day, and every hour of the day. I wrote to the messenger people to send the most capable lad on their books; we would engage him by the week, at twice his ordinary pay. He arrived; a limp and lean nonentity, with a face like a boiled codfish.

This miserable youth promptly became the object of O——'s bitterest execration. I soon learnt to dread those conferences, those terrific scenes which I was forced to witness in my capacity of interpreter. O——revelled in them with exceeding gusto. He used to gird his loins for the effort of vituperation; I think he regarded the performance as a legitimate kind of exercise—his last remaining one. As soon as the boy returned from town and presented himself with his purchases, O——would glare at him for two or three minutes with such virulence, such concentration of hatred and loathing, such a blaze of malignity in his black eyes, that one fully expected to see the victim wither away; all this in dead silence. Then he would address me in his usual whisper, quite calmly, as though referring to the weather:

"Would you mind telling that double-distilled abortion that if he goes on making such a face I shall have to shoot him. Tell him, will you; there's a good fellow."

And I had to "humour" him.

"The gentleman"—I would say—"begs you will try to assume another expression of countenance," or words to that effect; whereto he would tearfully reply something about the will of God and the workmanship of his father and mother, honest folks, both of them. I was then obliged to add gravely:

"You had better try, all the same, or he may shoot you. He has a revolver in his pocket, and a shooting licence from your government."

This generally led to the production of a most ghastly smile, calculated to convey an ingratiating impression.

"Look at him," O——would continue. "He is almost too good to be shot. And now let's see. What does he call these things? Ask him, will you?"

"Asparagus."

"Tell him that when I order asparagus I mean asparagus and not walking-sticks. Tell him that if he brings me such objects again, I'll ram the whole bundle up—down his throat. What does he expect me to do with them, eh? You might ask him, will you? And, God! what's this? Tell him (accellerando) that when I send a prescription to be made up at the Royal Pharmacy——"

"He explained about that. He went to the other place because he wanted to hurry up."

"To hurry up? Tell him to hurry up and get to blazes. Oh, tell him——"

"You'll curse yourself into another collapse, at this rate."

To the doctor's intense surprise, he lingered on; he actually grew stronger. Although never seeming to gain an ounce in weight, he could eat a formidable breakfast and used to insist, to my horror and shame, in importing his own wine, which he accused my German maid Bertha of drinking on the sly. Callers cheered him up—Rolfe the Consul, Dr. Dohrn of the Aquarium, and old Marquis Valiante, that perfect botanist—all of them dead now! After a month and a half of painful experiences, we at last learnt to handle him. The household machinery worked smoothly.

A final and excruciating interview ended in the dismissal of the errand-boy, and I personally selected another one—a pretty little rascal to whom he took a great fancy, over-tipping him scandalously. He needed absolute rest; he got it; and I think was fairly happy or at least tranquil (when not writhing in agony) at the end of that period. I can still see him in the sunny garden, his clothes hanging about an emaciated body—a skeleton in a deck-chair, a death's head among the roses. Humiliated in this inactivity, he used to lie dumb for long hours, watching the butterflies or gazing wistfully towards those distant southern mountains which I proposed to visit later in the season. Once a spark of that old throttling instinct flared up. It was when a kestrel dashed overhead, bearing in its talons a captured lizard whose tail fluttered in the air: the poor beast never made a faster journey in its life. "Ha!" said O——. "That's sport."

At other times he related, always in that hoarse whisper, anecdotes of his life, a life of reckless adventure, of fortunes made and fortunes lost; or spoke of his old passion for art and books. He seemed to have known, at one time or another, every artist and connoisseur on either side of the Atlantic; he told me it had cost about £10,000 to acquire his unique knowledge and taste in the matter of mezzotints, and that he was concerned about the fate of his "Daphnis and Chloe" collection which contained, he said, a copy of every edition in every language—all except the unique Elizabethan version in the Huth library (now British Museum). I happened to have one of the few modern reprints of that stupid and ungainly book: would he accept it? Not likely! He was after originals.

One day he suddenly announced:

"I am leaving you my small library of erotic literature, five or six hundred pieces, worth a couple of thousand, I should say. Some wonderful old French stuff, and as many Rops as you like, and Persian and Chinese things—I can see you gloating over them! Don't thank me. And now I'm off to England."

"To England?"

The doctor peremptorily forbade the journey; if he must go, let him wait another couple of weeks and gain some more strength. But O——was obdurate; buoyed up, I imagine, with the prospect of movement and of causing some little trouble at home. As the weather had grown unusually hot, I booked at his own suggestion a luxurious cabin on a home-bound liner and engaged a valet for the journey. On my handing him the tickets, he said he had just changed his mind; he would travel overland; there were some copper mines in Etruria of which he was director; he meant to have a look at them en route and "give those people Hell" for something or other. I tried to dissuade him, and all in vain. Finally I said:

"You'll die, if you travel by land in this heat."

So he did. They carried him out of the train in the early days of June, here at Pisa, feet first....

I never learnt the fate of that library of erotic literature. But his will contained one singular provision: the body was to be cremated and its ashes scattered among the hills of his Alpine property. This was his idea of "being even" with the superstitious peasantry, who would thenceforward never have ventured out of doors after dark, for fear of encountering his ghost. He would harass them eternally! It was no bad notion of revenge. A sandy-haired gentleman came from Austria to Italy to convey this handful of potential horrors to the mountains, but the customs officials at Ala refused to allow it to enter the country and it ultimately came to rest in England.

Another queer thing happened. Since his arrival from Egypt, O——had never been able to make up his mind to pay any of his innumerable bills; the creditors, aware of the man's wealth and position, not pressing for a settlement. I rather think that this procrastination, this reluctance to disburse ready money, is a symptom of his particular state of ill-health; I have observed it with several heart-patients (and others as well); however that may be, it became a source of real vexation to me, for hardly was the news of his death made public before I began to be deluged with outstanding accounts from every quarter— tradespeople, hotel keepers, professional men, etc. I finally sent the documents with a pressing note to his representatives who, after some demur, paid up, English-fashion, in full. Then a noteworthy change came over the faces of men. Everybody beamed upon me in the streets, and there arrived multitudinous little gifts at my house—choice wines, tie-pins, game, cigars, ebony walking-sticks, confectionery, baskets of red mullets, old prints, Capodimonte ware, candied fruits, amber mouthpieces, maraschino—all from donors who plainly desired to remain anonymous. Such things were dropped from the clouds, so to speak, on my doorstep: an enigmatic but not unpleasant state of affairs. Gradually it dawned upon me, it was forced upon me, that I had worked a miracle. These good people, thinking that their demands upon O——'s executors would be cut down, Italian-fashion, by at least fifty per cent, had anticipated that eventuality by demanding twice or thrice as much as was really due to them. And they got it! No wonder men smiled, when the benefactor of the human race walked abroad.

Viareggio (February)

Viareggio, dead at this season, is a rowdy place in summer; not rowdy, however, after the fashion of Margate. There is a suggestive difference between the two. The upper classes in both towns are of course irreproachable in externals—it is their uniformity of behaviour throughout the world which makes them so uninteresting from a spectacular point of view. A place does not receive its tone from them (save possibly Bournemouth) but from their inferiors; and here, in this matter of public decorum, the comparison is to the credit of Italy. It is beside the point to say that the one lies relatively remote, while the other is convenient for cheap trips from a capital. Set Viareggio down at the very gate of Rome and fill it with the scum of Trastevere: the difference would still be there. It might be more noisy than Margate. It would certainly be less blatant.

As for myself, I hate Viareggio at all seasons, and nothing would have brought me here but the prospect of visiting the neighbouring Carrara mines with Attilio to whom I have written, enclosing a postcard for reply.

For this is a modern town built on a plain of mud and sand, a town of heartrending monotony, the least picturesque of all cities in the peninsula, the least Italian. It has not even a central piazza! You may conjure up visions of Holland and detect something of an old-world aroma, if you stroll about the canal and harbour where sails are now flapping furiously in the north wind; you may look up to the snow-covered peaks and imagine yourself in Switzerland, and then thank God you are not there; of Italy I perceive little or nothing. The people are birds of prey; a shallow and rapacious brood who fleece visitors during those summer weeks and live on the proceeds for the rest of the year. There is no commerce to liven them up and make them smilingly polite; no historical tradition to give them self-respect; no agriculture worth mentioning (the soil is too poor)—in other words, no peasantry to replenish the gaps in city life and infuse an element of decency and depth. An inordinate amount of singing and whistling goes on all day long. Is it not a sign of empty-headedness? I would like the opinion of schoolmasters on this point, whether, among the children committed to their charge, the habitual whistlers be not the dullest of wit.

And so five days have passed. A pension proving uninhabitable, and most of the better-class hotels being closed for the winter, I threw myself upon the mercy of an octroi official who stood guarding a forlorn gate somewhere in the wilderness. He has sent me to a villa bearing the name of a certain lady and situated in a street called after a certain politician. He has done well.

A kindlier dame than my hostess could nowhere be found. She hails from the province of the Marche and has no high opinion of this town, where she only lives on account of her husband, a retired something-or-other who owns the house. Although convulsed with grief, both of them, at the moment of my arrival—a favourite kitten had just been run over—they at once set about making me comfortable in a room with exposure due south. The flooring is of cement: the usual Viareggio custom. Bricks are cold, stone is cold, tiles are cold;

but cement! It freezes your marrow through double carpets. For meals I go to the "Assassino" or the Vittoria hotel; the fare is better at the first, the company at the other....

The large dining-room at the "Vittoria" is not in use just now. We take our meals in two smaller rooms adjoining each other, one of which leads into the kitchen where privileged guests may talk secrets with the cook and poke their noses into saucepans. At a table by herself sits the little signorina who controls the establishment, wide awake, pale of complexion, slightly hump-backed, close-fisted as the devil though sufficiently vulnerable to a bluff masculine protest. Our waiter is noteworthy in his line. He is that exceptional being, an Italian snob; he can talk of nothing but dukes and princes, Bourbons by choice, because he once served at a banquet given by some tuppenny Parma royalties round the corner.

The food would be endurable, save for those vile war-time maccheroni. The wine is of doubtful origin. Doubtful, at least, to the uninitiated who smacks his lips and wonders vaguely where he has tasted the stuff before. The concoction has so many flavours—a veritable Proteus! I know it well, though its father and mother would be hard to identify. It was born on the banks of the Tiber and goes by the name of ripa: ask any Roman. Certain cheap and heady products of the south—Sicily, Sardinia, Naples, Apulia, Ischia—have contributed their share to its composition; Tiber-water is the one and constant ingredient. This ripa is exported by the ton to wine-less centres like Genoa and there drunk under any name you please. A few butts have doubtless been dropped overboard at Viareggio for the poisoning of its ten thousand summer visitors.

Quite a jolly crowd of folk assembles here every evening. There is, of course, the ubiquitous retired major; also some amusing gentlemen who run up and down between this place and Lucca on mysterious errands connected, I fancy, with oil; as well as a dissipated young marquis sent hither from Rimini by the ridiculously old-fashioned father to expiate his sins—his gambling debts, his multifarious and costly love-adventures, and the manslaughter of a carpenter whom he ran over in his car.[6] My favourite is a fat creature with a glorious fleshy face, the face of some Neronian parvenu—a memorable face, full of the brutal prosperity of Trimalchio's Banquet. He told me, yesterday, a long story about a local saint in one of their villages—a saint of yesterday who, curing diseases and performing various other miracles, began to think himself, as their manner is, God Almighty, or something to that effect. The police shot him as a revolutionary, because he had gathered a few adherents.

"Rather an extreme measure," I suggested.

"It is. Not that I love the saints. But I love the police still less."

"Like every good Italian."

"Like every good Italian...."

News from Attilio. He cannot come. Both mother and sister are ill. He delayed writing in the hopes of their getting better; he wanted to join me, but they are always "auguale"—the same; in short, he must stay at home, as appears from the following plaintive and rather puzzling postcard, the address of which I had providentially written myself:

Caro G. N. Dorcola ho ricevuto la sua cara lettera e son cozi contento da sentire le sue notizzie io non posso venire perche mia madre e amalata e mia sorella Enrica era tardato ascirvere perche mi credevo che tesano mellio ma invece sono sempre auguale perche volevo venire ci mando dici mille baci e una setta dimano addio al Signior D. Dor.

But for the fact that, counting on a fortnight's trip to Carrara, I have asked for certain printed matter to be forwarded here from England, I would jump into the next train for anywhere.

Running along the sea on either side of Viareggio is a noble forest of stone pines where the wind is scarce felt, though you may hear it sighing overhead among the crowns. This is the place for a promenade at all hours of the day. Children climb the trunks to fetch down a few remaining cones or break off dried branches as fuel. A sportsman told me that several of them lose their lives every year at this adventure. What was he doing here, with a gun? Waiting for a hare, he said. They always wait for hares. There are none!

Then a poor thin woman, dressed in black and gathering the prickly stalks of gorse for firewood, began to converse with me, reasonably enough at first. All of a sudden her language changed into a burning torrent of insanity, with wild gesticulations. She was the Queen of the country, she avowed, the rightful Queen, and they had robbed her of all her children, every one of them, and all her jewels. I agreed—what else could one do? Being in the combustible stage, she went over the argument again and again, her eyes fiercely flashing. Nothing could stop the flow of her words. I was right glad when another woman came to my rescue and pushed her along, as you would a calf, saying:

"You go home now, it's getting dark, run along!—yes, yes! you're the Queen right enough—she was in the asylum, Sir, for three months and then they let her out, the fools—of course you are, everybody knows that! But you really mustn't annoy this gentleman any more—her husband and son were both killed in the war, that's what started it—we'll fetch them tomorrow at the palace, all those things, and the children, only don't talk so much—they thought she was cured, but just hark at her!—va bene, it's all yours, only get along—she'll be back there in a day or two, won't she?—really, you are chattering much too much, for a Queen; va bene, va bene, va bene—"

A sad little incident, under the pines....

A fortnight has elapsed.

I refuse to budge from Viareggio, having discovered the village of Corsanico on the heights yonder and, in that village, a family altogether to my liking. How one stumbles upon delightful folks! Set me down in furthest Cathay and I will undertake to find, soon afterwards, some person with whom I am quite prepared to spend the remaining years of life.

The driving-road to Corsanico is a never-ending affair. Deep in mire, it meanders perversely about the plain; meanders more than ever, but of necessity, once the foot of the hills is reached. I soon gave it up in favour of the steam-tram to Cammaiore which deposits you at a station whose name I forget, whence you may ascend to Corsanico through a village called, I think, Momio. That route, also, was promptly abandoned when the path along the canal was revealed to me. This waterway runs in an almost straight line from Viareggio to the base of that particular hill on whose summit lies my village. It is a monotonous walk at this season; the rich marsh vegetation slumbers in the ooze underground, waiting for a breath of summer. At last you cross that big road and strike the limestone rock.

Here is no intermediate region, no undulating ground, between the upland and the plain. They converge abruptly upon each other, as might have been expected, seeing that these hills used to be the old sea-board and this green level, in olden days, the Mediterranean. Three different tracks, leading steeply upward through olives and pines and chestnuts from where the canal ends, will bring you to Corsanico. I know them all. I could find my way in darkest midnight.

Days have passed; days of delight. I climb up in the morning and descend at nightfall, my mind well stored with recollections of pleasant talk and smiling faces. A large place, this Corsanico, straggling about the hill-top with scattered farms and gardens; to reach the tobacconist—near whose house, by the way, you obtain an unexpected glimpse into the valley of Cammaiore—is something of an excursion. As a rule we repose, after luncheon, on a certain wooded knoll. We are high up; seven or eight hundred feet above the canal. The blue Tyrrhenian is dotted with steamers and sailing boats, and yonder lies Viareggio in its belt of forest; far away, to the left, you discern the tower of Pisa. A placid lake between the two, wood-engirdled, is now famous as being the spot selected by the great Maestro Puccini to spend a summer month in much-advertised seclusion. I am learning the name of every locality in the plain, of every peak among the mountains at our back.

"And that little ridge of stone," says my companion, "—do you see it, jutting into the fields down there? It has a queer name. We call it La Sirena."

La Sirena….

It is good to live in a land where such memories cling to old rocks.

By what a chance has the name survived to haunt this inland crag, defying geological changes, outlasting the generations of men, their creeds and tongues and races! How it takes one back—back into hoary antiquity, into another landscape altogether! One thinks of those Greek mariners coasting past this promontory, and pouring libations to the Siren into an ocean on whose untrampled floor the countryman now sows his rice and turnips.

Paganisme immortel, es-tu mort? On le dit.
Mais Pan, tout bas, s'en moque, et la Sirène en rit.

They are still here, both sea and Siren; they have only agreed to separate for a while. The ocean shines out yonder in all its luminous splendour of old. And the Siren, too, can be found by those to whom the gods are kind. My Siren dwells at Corsanico.

Viareggio (May)

Those Sirens! They have called me back, after nearly three months in Florence, to that village on the hill-top. Nothing but smiles up there.

And never was Corsanico more charming, all drenched in sunlight and pranked out with fresh green. On this fourteenth of May, I said to myself, I am wont to attend a certain yearly festival far away, and there enjoy myself prodigiously. Yet—can it be possible?—I am even happier here. Seldom does the event surpass one's hopes.

Later than usual, long after sunset, under olives already heavy-laden, through patches of high-standing corn and beans, across the little brook, past that familiar and solitary farmhouse, I descended to the canal, in full content. Another golden moment of life! Strong exhalations rose up from the swampy soil, that teemed and steamed under the hot breath of spring; the pond-like water, once so bare, was smothered under a riot of monstrous marsh-plants and loud with the music of love-sick frogs. Stars were reflected on its surface.

Star-gazing, my Star? Would I were Heaven, to gaze on thee with many eyes.

Such was my mood, a Hellenic mood, a mood summed up in that one word [Greek: tetelestai]—not to be taken, however, in the sense of "all's over." Quite the reverse! Did Shelley ever walk in like humour along this canal? I doubt it. He lacked the master-key. An evangelist of a kind, he was streaked, for all his paganism, with the craze of world-improvement. One day he escaped from his chains into those mountains and there beheld a certain Witch—only to be called back to mortality by a domestic and critic-bitten lady. He tried to translate the Symposium. He never tried to live it....

I have now interposed a day of rest.

My welcome in the villa situated in the street called after a certain politician was that of the Prodigal Son. There was a look bordering on affection in the landlady's eyes. She knew I would come back, once the weather was warmer. She would now give me a cool room, instead of that old one facing south. Those much-abused cement floors—they were not so inconvenient, were they, at this season? The honey for breakfast? Assuredly; the very same. And there was a tailor she had discovered in the interval, cheaper and better than that other one, if anything required attention.

And thus, having lived long at the mercy of London landladies and London charwomen—having suffered the torments of Hell, for more years than I care to remember, at the hands of these pickpockets and hags and harpies and drunken sluts—I am now rewarded by the services of something at the other end of the human scale. Impossible to say too much of this good dame's solicitude for me. Her main object in life seems to be to save my money and make me comfortable. "Don't get your shoes soled there!" she told me two days ago. "That man is from Viareggio. I know a better place. Let me see to it. I will say they are my husband's, and you will pay less and get better work." With a kind of motherly instinct she forestalls my every wish, and at the end of a few days had already known my habits better than one of those London sharks and furies would have known them at the end of a century....

My thoughts go back to her of Florence, whom I have just left. Equally efficient, she represented quite a different type. She was not of the familiar kind, but rather grave and formal, with spectacles, dyed hair and an upright carriage. She never mothered me; she conversed, and gave me the impression of being in the presence of a grande dame. Such, I used to say to myself, while listening to her well-turned periods enlivened with steely glints of humour—such were the feelings of those who conversed with Madame de Maintenon; such and not otherwise. It would be difficult to conceive her saying anything equivocal or vulgar. Yet she must have been a naughty little girl not long ago. She never dreams that I know what I do know: that she is mistress of a high police functionary and greatly in favour with his set—a most useful landlady, in short, for a virtuous young bachelor like myself.

On learning this fact, I made it my business to study her weaknesses and soon discovered that she was fond of a particular brand of Chianti. A flask of this vintage was promptly secured; then, dissatisfied with its materialistic aspect, I caused it to be garlanded with a wreath of violets and despatched it to her private apartment by the prettiest child I could pick up in the street. That is the way to touch their hearts. The offering was repeated at convenient intervals.

A little item in the newspaper led to some talk, one morning, about the war. I found she shared the view common to many others, that this is an "interested" war. Society has organized itself on new lines, lines which work against peace. There are so many persons "interested" in keeping up the present state of affairs, people who now make more money than they ever made before. Everybody has a finger in the pie. The soldier in the field, the chief person concerned, is voiceless and of no account when compared with this army of civilians, every one of whom would lose, if the war came to an end. They will fight like demons, to keep the fun going. What else should they do? Their income is at stake. A man's heart is in his purse.

I asked:

"Supposing, Madame, you desired to end the war, how would you set about it?"

Whereupon a delightfully Tuscan idea occurred to her.

"I think I would abolish this Red-Cross nonsense. It makes things too pleasant. It would bring the troops to their senses and cause them to march home and say: Basta! We have had enough."

"Don't you find the Germans a little prepotenti?" "Prepotenti: yes. By all means let us break their heads. And then, caro Lei, let us learn to imitate them...."

That afternoon, I remember, being wondrously fine and myself in such mellow mood that I would have shared my last crust with some shipwrecked archduchess and almost forgiven mine enemies, though not until I had hit them back—I strolled about the Cascine. They have done something to make this place attractive; just then, at all events, the shortcomings were unobserved amid the burst of green things overhead and underfoot. Originally it must have been an unpromising stretch of land, running, as it does, in a dead level along the Arno. Yet there is earth and water; and a good deal can be done with such materials to diversify the surface. More might have been accomplished here. For in the matter of hill and dale and lake, and variety of vegetation, the Cascine are not remarkable. One calls to mind what has been attained at Kew Gardens in an identical situation, and with far less sunshine for the landscape gardener to play with. One thinks of a certain town in Germany where, on a plain as flat as a billiard table, they actually reared a mountain, now covered with houses and timber, for the disport of the citizens. To think that I used to skate over the meadows where that mountain now stands!

There was no horse-racing in the Cascine that afternoon; nothing but the usual football. The pastime is well worth a glance, if only for the sake of sympathizing with the poor referee. Several hundred opprobrious epithets are hurled at his head in the course of a single game, and play is often suspended while somebody or other hotly disputes his decision and refuses to be guided any longer by his perverse interpretation of the rules. And whoever wishes to know whence those plastic artists of old Florence drew their inspiration need only come here. Figures of consummate grace and strength, and clothed, moreover, in a costume which leaves little to the imagination. Those shorts fully deserve their name. They are shortness itself, and their brevity is only equalled by their tightness. One wonders how they can squeeze themselves into such an outfit or, that feat accomplished, play in it with any sense of comfort. Play they do, and furiously, despite the heat.

Watching the game and mindful of that morning's discourse with Madame de Maintenon, a sudden wave of Anglo-Saxon feeling swept over me. I grew strangely warlike, and began to snort with indignation. What were all these young fellows doing here? Big chaps of eighteen and twenty! Half of them ought to be in the trenches, damn it, instead of fooling about with a ball.

It would have been instructive to learn the true ideas of the rising generation in regard to the political outlook; to single out one of the younger spectators and make him talk. But these better-class lads cluster together at the approach of a stranger, and one does not want to start a public discussion with half a dozen of them. My chance came from another direction. It was half-time and a certain player limped out of the field and sat down on the grass. I was beside him before his friends had time to come up. A superb specimen, all dewy with perspiration.

"Any damage?"

Nothing much, he gasped. A man on the other side had just caught him with the full swing of his fist under the ribs. It hurt confoundedly.

"Hardly fair play," I commented.

"It was cleverly done."

"Ah, well," I said, warming to my English character, "you may get harder knocks in the trenches. I suppose you are nearly due?"

Not for a year or so, he replied. And even then...of course, he was quite eligible as to physique...it was really rather awkward...but as to serving in the army...there were other jobs going....Was anything more precious than life?...Could anything replace his life to him?...To die at his age....

"It would certainly be a pity from an artistic point of view. But if everybody thought like that, where would the Isonzo line be?"

If everybody thought as he did, there would be no Isonzo line at all. German influence in Italy—why not? They had been there before; it was no dark page in Italian history. Was his own government so admirable that one should regret its disappearance? A pack of knaves and cutthroats. Patriotism—a phrase; auto-intoxication. They say one thing and mean another. The English too. Yes, the English too. Purely mercenary motives, for all their noble talk.

It is always entertaining to see ourselves as others see us. I had the presence of mind to interject some anti-British remark, which produced the desired effect.

"Now they howl about the sufferings of Belgium, because their money-bags are threatened. They fight for poor Belgium. They did not fight for France in 1870, or for Denmark or Poland or Armenia. Trade was not threatened. There was no profit in view. Profit! And they won't even supply us with coal——"

Always that coal.

It is clear as daylight. England has failed in her duty—her duty being to supply everybody with coal, ships, money, cannons and anything else, at the purchaser's valuation.

He made a few more statements of this nature, and I think he enjoyed his little fling at that, for him, relatively speaking, since the war began, rara avis, a genuine Englishman (Teutonic construction); I certainly relished it. Then I asked:

"Where did you learn this? About Armenia, I mean, and Poland?"

"From my father. He was University Professor and Deputy in Parliament. One also picks up a little something at school. Don't you agree with me?"

"Not altogether. You seem to forget that a nation cannot indulge in those freaks of humanitarianism which may possibly befit an individual. A certain heroic dreamer told men to give all they had to the poor. You, if you like, may adopt this idealistic attitude. You may do generous actions such as your country cannot afford to do, since a nation which abandons the line of expediency is on the high road to suicide. If I have a bilious attack, by all means come and console me; if Poland has a bilious attack, there is no reason why England should step in as dry-nurse; there may be every reason, indeed, why England should stand aloof. Now in Belgium, as you say, money is involved. Money, in this national sense, means well-being; and well-being, in this national sense, is one of the few things worth fighting for. However, I am only throwing out one or two suggestions. On some other day, I would like to discuss the matter with you point by point—some other day, that is, when you are not playing football and have just a few clothes on. I am now at a disadvantage. You could never get me to impugn your statements courageously—not in that costume. It would be like haggling with Apollo Belvedere. Why do you wear those baby things?"

"We are all wearing them, this season."

"So I perceive. How do you get into them?"

"Very slowly."

"Are they elastic?"

"I wish they were."....

Four minutes' talk. It gave me an insight. He was an intellectualist. As such, he admired brute force but refused to employ it. He was civilized. Like many products of civilization, he was unaware of its blessings and unconcerned in its fate. Is it not a feature peculiar to civilization that it thinks of everything save war? That is why they are uprooted, these flowerings, each in its turn.

My father told me; often one hears that remark, even from adults. As if a father could not be a fool like anybody else! That a child should have hard-and-fast opinions—it is engaging. Children are egocentric. A fellow of this size ought to be less positive.

These refined youths are fastidious about their clothes. They would not dream of buying a ready-made suit, however well-fitting. They are content to take their opinions second-hand. Unlike ours, they are seldom alone; they lack those stretches of solitude during which they might wrestle with themselves and do a little thinking on their own account. When not with their family, they are always among companions, being far more sociable and fond of herding together than their English representatives. They talk more; they think less; they seem to do each other's thinking, which takes away all hesitation and gives them a precocious air of maturity. If this decorative lad engages in some profession like medicine or engineering there is hope for him, even as others of his age rectify their perspective by contact with crude facts—groceries and calicoes and carburettors and so forth. Otherwise, his doom is sealed. He remains a doctrinaire. This country is full of them.

And then—the sterilizing influence of pavements. Even when summer comes round, they all flock in a mass to some rowdy place like this Viareggio or Ancona where, however pleasant the bathing, spiritual life is yet shallower than at home. What says Craufurd Tait Ramage, LL.D.? "Their country life consists merely in breathing a different air, though in nothing else does it differ from the life they live in town."

He notices things, does Ramage; and might, indeed, have elaborated this argument. The average Italian townsman seems to have lost all sense for the beauty of rural existence; he is incurious about it; dislodge him from the pavement—no easy task—and he gasps like a fish out of water. Squares and cafés—they stimulate his fancy; the doings and opinions of fellow-creatures—thence alone he derives inspiration. What is the result? A considerable surface polish, but also another quality which I should call dewlessness. Often glittering like a diamond, he is every bit as dewless. His materialistic and supercilious outlook results, I think, from contempt or nescience of nature; you will notice the trait still more at Venice, whose inhabitants seldom forsake their congested mud-flat. Depth of character and ideality and humour—such things require a rustic landscape for their nurture. These citizens are arid, for lack of dew; unquestionably more so than their English representatives.

POSTSCRIPT.—The pavements of Florence, by the way, have an objectionable quality. Their stone is too soft. They wear down rapidly and an army of masons is employed in levelling them straight again all the year round. And yet they sometimes use this very sandstone, instead of marble, for mural inscriptions. How long are these expected to remain legible? They employ the same material for their buildings, and I observe that the older monuments last, on the whole, better than the new ones, which flake away rapidly—exfoliate or crack, according to the direction from which the grain of the rock has been attacked by the chisel. It may well be that Florentines of past centuries left the hewn blocks in their shady caverns for a certain length of time, as do the Parisians of to-day, in order to allow for the slow discharge and evaporation of liquid; whereas now the material, saturated with moisture, is torn from its damp and cool quarries and set in the blazing sunshine. At the Bourse, for instance,— quite a modern structure—the columns already begin to show fissures. [7]

Amply content with Viareggio, because the Siren dwells so near, I stroll forth. The town is awake. Hotels are open. Bathing is beginning. Summer has dawned upon the land.

I am not in the city mood, three months in Florence having abated my interest in humanity. Past a line of booths and pensions I wander in the direction of that pinery which year by year is creeping further into the waves, and driving the sea back from its old shore. There is peace in this green domain; all is hushed, and yet pervaded by the mysterious melody of things that stir in May-time. Here are no sombre patches, as under oak or beech; only a tremulous interlacing of light and shade. A peculiarly attractive bole not far from the sea, gleaming rosy in the sunshine, tempts me to recline at its foot.

This insomnia, this fiend of the darkness—the only way to counteract his mischief is by guile; by snatching a brief oblivion in the hours of day, when the demon is far afield, tormenting pious Aethiopians at the Antipodes. How well one rests at such moments of self-created night, merged into the warm earth! The extreme quietude of my present room, after Florentine street-noises, may have contributed to this restlessness. Also, perhaps, the excitement of Corsanico. But chiefly, the dream—that recurrent dream.

Everybody, I suppose, is subject to recurrent dreams of some kind. My present one is of a painful or at least sad nature; it returns approximately every three months and never varies by a hair's breadth. I am in a distant town where I lived many years back, and where each stone is familiar to me. I have come to look for a friend—one who, as a matter of fact, died long ago. My sleeping self refuses to admit this fact; once embarked on the dream-voyage, I hold him to be still alive. Glad at the prospect of meeting my friend again, I traverse cheerfully those well-known squares in the direction of his home…. Where is it, that house; where has it gone? I cannot find it. Ages seem to pass while I trample up and down, in ever-increasing harassment of mind, along interminable rows of buildings and canals; that door, that well-remembered door—vanished! All search is vain. I shall never meet him: him whom I came so far to see. The dismal truth, once established, fills me with an intensity of suffering such as only night-visions can inspire. There is no reason for feeling so strongly; it is the way of dreams! At this point I wake up, thoroughly exhausted, and say to myself: "Why seek his house? Is he not dead?"

This stupid nightmare leaves me unrefreshed next morning, and often bears in its rear a trail of wistfulness which may endure a week. Only within the last few years has it dared to invade my slumbers. Before that period there was a series of other recurrent dreams. What will the next be? For I mean to oust this particular incubus. The monster annoys me, and even our mulish dream-consciousness can be taught to acquiesce in a fact, after a sufficient lapse of time.

There are dreams peculiar to every age of man. That celebrated one of flying, for instance—it fades away with manhood. I once indulged in a correspondence about it with a well-known psychologist,[8] and would like to think, even now, that this dream is a reminiscence of leaping habits in our tree-haunting days; a ghost of the dim past, therefore, which revisits us at night when recent adjustments are cast aside and man takes on the credulity and savagery of his remotest forefathers; a ghost which comes in youth when these ancient etchings are easier to decypher, being not yet overscored by fresh personal experiences. What is human life but a never-ending palimpsest?

So I pondered, when my musings under that pine tree were interrupted by the arrival on the scene of a young snake. I cannot say with any degree of truthfulness which of us two was more surprised at the encounter. I picked him up, as I always do when they give me a chance, and began to make myself agreeable to him. He had those pretty juvenile markings which disappear with maturity. Snakes of this kind, when they become full-sized, are nearly always of a uniform shade, generally black. And when they are very, very old, they begin to grow ears and seek out solitary places. What is the origin of this belief? I have come across it all over the country. If you wish to go to any remote or inaccessible spot, be sure some peasant will say: "Ah! There you find the serpent with ears."

These snakes are not easy to catch with the hand, living as they do among stones and brushwood, and gliding off rapidly once their suspicions are aroused. This one, I should say, was bent on some youthful voyage of discovery or amorous exploit; he walked into the trap from inexperience. As a rule, your best chance for securing them is when they bask on the top of some bush or hedge in relative unconcern, knowing they are hard to detect in such places. They climb into these aerial situations after the lizards, which go there after the insects, which go there after the flowers, which go there after the sunshine, struggling upwards through the thick undergrowth. You must have a quick eye and ready hand to grasp them by the tail ere they have time to lash themselves round some stem where, once anchored, they will allow themselves to be pulled in pieces rather than yield to your efforts. If you fail to seize them, they trickle earthward through the tangle like a thread of running water.

He belonged to that common Italian kind which has no English name—Germans call them Zornnatter, in allusion to their choleric disposition. Most of them are quite ready to snap at the least provocation; maybe they find it pays, as it does with other folks, to assume the offensive and be first in the field, demanding your place in the sun with an air of wrathful determination. Some of the big fellows can draw blood with their teeth. Yet the jawbones are weak and one can force them asunder without much difficulty; whereas the bite of a full-grown emerald lizard, for instance, will provide quite a novel sensation. The mouth closes on you like a steel trap, tightly compressing the flesh and often refusing to relax its hold. In such cases, try a puff of tobacco. It works! Two puffs will daze them; a fragment of a cigar, laid in the mouth, stretches them out dead. And this is the beast which, they say, will gulp down prussic acid as if it were treacle.

But snakes vary in temperament as we do, and some of these Zamenis serpents are as gentle and amiable as their cousin the Aesculap snake. My friend of this afternoon could not be induced to bite. Perhaps he was naturally mild, perhaps drowsy from his winter sleep or ignorant of the ways of the world; perhaps he had not yet shed his milk teeth. I am disposed to think that he forgot about biting because I made a favourable impression on him from the first. He crawled up my arm. It was pleasantly warm, but a little too dark; soon he emerged again and glanced around, relieved to discover that the world was still in its old place. He was not clever at learning tricks. I tried to make him stand on his head, but he refused to stiffen out. Snakes have not much sense of humour.

Lizards are far more companionable. During two consecutive summers I had a close friendship with a wall-lizard who spent in my society certain of his leisure moments—which were not many, for he always had an astonishing number of other things on hand. He was a full-grown male, bejewelled with blue spots. A fierce fighter was Alfonso (such was his name), and conspicuous for a most impressive manner of stamping his front foot when impatient. Concerning his other virtues I know little, for I learnt no details of his private life save what I saw with my eyes, and they were not always worthy of imitation. He was a polygamist, or worse; obsessed, moreover, by a deplorable habit of biting off the tails of his own or other people's children. He went even further. For sometimes, without a word of warning, he would pounce upon some innocent youngster and carry him in his powerful jaws far away, over the wall, right out of my sight. What happened yonder I cannot guess. It was probably a little old-fashioned cannibalism.

Though my meals in those days were all out of doors, his attendance at dinner-time was rather uncertain; I suspect he retired early in order to spend the night, like other polygamists, in prayer and fasting. At the hours of breakfast and luncheon—he knew them as well as I did—he was generally free, and then quite monopolized my company, climbing up my leg on to the table, eating out of my hand, sipping sugar-water out of his own private bowl and, in fact, doing everything I suggested. I did not suggest impossibilities. A friendship should never be strained to breaking-point. Had I cared to risk such a calamity, I might have taught him to play skittles....

For the rest, it is not very amusing to be either a lizard or a snake in Italy. Lizards are caught in nooses and then tied by one leg and made to run on the remaining three; or secured by a cord round the neck and swung about in the air—mighty good sport, this; or deprived of their tails and given to the baby or cat to play with; or dragged along at the end of a string, like a reluctant pig that is led to market. There are quite a number of ways of making lizards feel at home.

With snakes the procedure is simple. They are killed; treated to that self-same system to which they used to treat us in our arboreal days when the glassy eye of the serpent, gleaming through the branches, will have caused our fur to stand on end with horror. No beast provokes human hatred like that old coiling serpent. Long and cruel must have been his reign for the memory to have lingered—how many years? Let us say, in order to be on the safe side, a million. Here, then, is another ghost of the past, a daylight ghost.

And look around you; the world is full of them. We live amid a legion of ancestral terrors which creep from their limbo and peer in upon our weaker moments, ready to make us their prey. A man whose wits are not firmly rooted in earth, in warm friends and warm food, might well live a life of ceaseless trepidation. Many do. They brood over their immortal soul—a ghost. Others there are, whose dreams have altogether devoured their realities. These live, for the most part, in asylums.

There flits, along this very shore, a ghost of another kind—that of Shelley. Maybe the spot where they burnt his body can still be pointed out. I have forgotten all I ever read on that subject. An Italian enthusiast, the librarian of the Laurentian Library in Florence, garnered certain information from ancient fishermen of Viareggio in regard to this occurrence and set it down in a little book, a book with white covers which I possessed during my Shelley period. They have erected a memorial to the English poet in one of the public squares here. The features of the bust do not strike me as remarkably etherial, but the inscription is a good specimen of Italian adapted to lapidary uses—it avoids those insipid verbal terminations which weaken the language and sometimes render it almost ridiculous.

Smollet lies yonder, at Livorno; and Ouida hard by, at Bagni di Lucca. She died in one of these same featureless streets of Viareggio, alone, half blind, and in poverty....

I know Suffolk, that ripe old county of hers, with its pink villages nestling among drowsy elms and cornfields; I know their "Spread Eagles" and "Angels" and "White Horses" and other taverns suggestive—sure sign of antiquity—of zoological gardens; I know their goodly ale and old brown sherries. Her birthplace, despite those venerable green mounds, is comparatively dull—I would not care to live at Bury; give me Lavenham or Melford or some place of that kind. While looking one day at the house where she was born, I was sorely tempted to crave permission to view the interior, but refrained; something of her own dislike of prying and meddlesomeness came over me. Thence down to that commemorative fountain among the drooping trees. The good animals for whose comfort it was built would have had some difficulty in slaking their thirst just then, its basin being chocked up with decayed leaves.

We corresponded for a good while and I still possess her letters somewhere; I see in memory that large and bold handwriting, often only two words to a line, on the high-class slate-coloured paper. The sums she spent on writing materials! It was one of her many ladylike traits.

I tried to induce her to stay with me in South Italy. She made three conditions: to be allowed to bring her dogs, to have a hot bath every day, and two litres of cream. Everything could be managed except the cream, which was unprocurable. Later on, while living in the Tyrolese mountains, I renewed the invitation; that third condition could now be fulfilled as easily as the other two. She was unwell, she replied, and could not move out of the house, having been poisoned by a cook. So we never met, though she wrote me much about herself and about "Helianthus," which was printed after her death. In return, I dedicated to her a book of short stories; they were published, thank God, under a pseudonym, and eight copies were sold.

She is now out of date. Why, yes. Those guardsmen who drenched their beards in scent and breakfasted off caviare and chocolate and sparkling Moselle—they certainly seem fantastic. They really were fantastic. They did drench their beards in scent. The language and habits of these martial heroes are authenticated in the records of their day; glance, for instance, into back numbers of Punch. The fact is, we were all rather ludicrous formerly. The characters of Dickens, to say nothing of Cruikshank's pictures of them: can such beings ever have walked the earth?

If her novels are somewhat faded, the same cannot be said of her letters and articles and critiques. To our rising generation of authors—the youngsters, I mean; those who have not yet sold themselves to the devil—I should say: read these things of Ouida's. Read them attentively, not for their matter, which is always of interest, nor yet for their vibrant and lucid style, which often rivals that of Huxley. Read them for their tone, their temper; for that pervasive good breeding, that shining honesty, that capacity of scorn. These are qualities which our present age lacks, and needs; they are conspicuous in Ouida. Abhorrence of meanness was her dominant trait. She was intelligent, fearless; as ready to praise without stint as to voice the warmest womanly indignation. She was courageous not only in matters of literature; courageous, and how right! Is it not satisfactory to be right, when others are wrong? How right about the Japanese, about Feminism and Conscription and German brutalitarianism! How she puts her finger on the spot when discussing Marion Crawford and D'Annunzio! Those local politicians—how she hits them off! Hers was a sure touch. Do we not all now agree with what she wrote at the time of Queen Victoria and Joseph Chamberlain? When she remarks of Tolstoy, in an age which adored him (I am quoting from memory), that "his morality and monogamy are against nature and common sense," adding that he is dangerous, because he is an "educated Christ"—out of date? When she says that the world is ruled by two enemies of all beauty, commerce and militarism—out of date? When she dismisses Oscar Wilde as a cabotin and yet thinks that the law should not have meddled with him—is not that the man and the situation in a nutshell?

No wonder straightforward sentiments like these do not appeal to our age of neutral tints and compromise, to our vegetarian world-reformers who are as incapable of enthusiasm as they are of contempt, because their blood-temperature is invariably two degrees below the normal. Ouida's critical and social opinions are infernally out of date—quite inconveniently modern, in fact. There is the milk of humanity in them, glowing conviction and sincerity; they are written from a standpoint altogether too European, too womanly, too personally-poignant for present-day needs; and in a language, moreover, whose picturesque and vigorous independence comes as a positive shock after the colourless Grub-street brand of to-day.

They come as a shock, these writings, because in the brief interval since they were published our view of life and letters has shifted. A swarm of mystics and pragmatists has replaced the lonely giants of Ouida's era. It is an epoch of closed pores, of constriction. The novel has changed. Pick up the average one and ask yourself whether this crafty and malodorous sex-problem be not a deliberately commercial speculation—a frenzied attempt to "sell" by scandalizing our unscandalizable, because hermaphroditic, middle classes? Ouida was not one of these professional hacks, but a personality of refined instincts who wrote, when she cared to write at all, to please her equals; a rationalistic anti-vulgarian; a woman of wide horizons who fought for generous issues and despised all shams; the last, almost the last, of lady-authors. What has such a genial creature in common with our anaemic and woolly generation? "The Massarenes" may have faults, but how many of our actual woman-scribes, for all their monkey-tricks of cleverness, could have written it? The haunting charm of "In Maremma": why ask our public to taste such stuff? You might as well invite a bilious nut-fooder to a Lord Mayor's banquet.

The mention of banquets reminds me that she was blamed for preferring the society of duchesses and diplomats to that of the Florentine literati, as if there were something reprehensible in Ouida's fondness for decent food and amusing talk when she could have revelled in Ceylon tea and dough-nuts and listened to babble concerning Quattro-Cento glazes in any of the fifty squabbling art-coteries of that City of Misunderstandings. It was one of her several failings, chiefest among them being this: that she had no reverence for money. She was unable to hoard—an unpardonable sin. Envied in prosperity, she was smugly pitied in her distress. Such is the fate of those who stand apart from the crowd, among a nation of canting shopkeepers. To die penniless, after being the friend of duchesses, is distinctly bad form—a slur on society. True, she might have bettered her state by accepting a lucrative proposal to write her autobiography, but she considered such literature a "degrading form of vanity" and refused the offer. She preferred to remain ladylike to the last, in this and other little trifles—in her lack of humour, her redundancies, her love of expensive clothes and genuinely humble people, of hot baths and latinisms and flowers and pet dogs and sealing-wax. All through life she made no attempt to hide her woman's nature, her preference for male over female company; she was even guilty of saying that disease serves the world better than war, because it kills more women than men. Out of date, with a vengeance!

There recurs to me a sentence in a printed letter written by a celebrated novelist of the artificial school, a sentence I wish I could forget, describing Ouida as "a little terrible and finally pathetic grotesque." Does not a phrase like this reveal, even better than his own romances, the essentially non-human fibre of the writer's mind? Whether this derivative intellectualist spiderishly spinning his own plots and phrases and calling Ouida a "grotesque"—whether this echo ever tried to grasp the bearing of her essays on Shelley or Blind Guides or Alma Veniesia or The Quality of Mercy—tried to sense her burning words of pity for those that suffer, her hatred of hypocrisy and oppression and betrayal of friendship, her so righteous pleadings, coined out of the heart's red blood, for all that makes life worthy to be lived? He may have tried. He never could succeed. He lacked the sympathy, the sex. He lacked the sex. Ah, well—Schwamm drueber, as the Norwegians say. Ouida, for all her femininity, was more than this feline and gelatinous New Englander.

Rome

The railway station at Rome has put on a new face. Blown to the winds is that old dignity and sense of leisure. Bustle everywhere; soldiers in line, officers strutting about; feverish scurryings for tickets. A young baggage employé, who allowed me to effect a change of raiment in the inner recesses of his department, alone seemed to keep up the traditions of former days. He was unruffled and polite; he told me, incidentally, that he came from———. That was odd, I said; I had often met persons born at———, and never yet encountered one who was not civil beyond the common measure. His native place must be worthy of a visit.

"It is," he replied. "There are also certain fountains...."

That restaurant, for example—one of those few for which a man in olden days of peace would desert his own tavern in the town—how changed! The fare has deteriorated beyond recognition. Where are those succulent joints and ragouts, the aromatic wine, the snow-white macaroni, the cafe-au-lait with genuine butter and genuine honey?

War-time!

Conversed awhile with an Englishman at my side, who was gleefully devouring lumps of a particular something which I would not have liked to touch with tongs.

"I don't care what I eat," he remarked.

So it seemed.

I don't care what I eat: what a confession to make! Is it not the same as saying, I don't care whether I am dirty or clean? When others tell me this, I regard it as a pose, or a poor joke. This person was manifestly sincere in his profession of faith. He did not care what he ate. He looked it. Were I afflicted with this peculiar ailment, this attenuated form of coprophagia, I should try to keep the hideous secret to myself. It is nothing to boast of. A man owes something to those traditions of our race which has helped to raise us above the level of the brute. Good taste in viands has been painfully acquired; it is a sacred trust. Beware of gross feeders. They are a menace to their fellow-creatures. Will they not act, on occasion, even as they feed? Assuredly they will. Everybody acts as he feeds.

Then lingered on the departure platform, comparing its tone with that of similar places in England. A mournful little crowd is collected here. Conscripts, untidy-looking fellows, are leaving—perhaps for ever. They climb into those tightly packed carriages, loaded down with parcels and endless recommendations. Some of the groups are cheerful over their farewells, though the English note of deliberate jocularity is absent. The older people are resigned; in the features of the middle generation, the parents, you may read a certain grimness and hostility to fate; they are the potential mourners. The weeping note predominates among the sisters and children, who give themselves away pretty freely. An infectious thing, this shedding of tears. One little girl, loth to part from that big brother, contrived by her wailing to break down the reserve of the entire family....

It rains persistently in soft, warm showers. Rome is mirthless.

There arises, before my mind's eye, the vision of a sweet old lady friend who said to me, in years gone by:

"When next you go to Rome, please let me know if it is still raining there."

It was here that she celebrated her honeymoon—an event which must have taken place in the 'sixties or thereabouts. She is dead now. So is her husband, the prince of moralizers, the man who first taught me how contemptible the human race may become. Doubtless he expired with some edifying platitude on his lips and is deblatterating them at this very moment in Heaven, where the folks may well be seasoned to that kind of talk.

Let us be charitable, now that he is gone!

To have lived so long with a person of this incurable respectability would have soured any ordinary woman's temper. Hers it refined; it made her into something akin to an angel. He was her cross; she bore him meekly and not, I like to think, without extracting a kind of sly, dry fun out of the horrible creature. A past master in the art of gentle domestic nagging, he made everybody miserable as long as he lived, and I would give something for an official assurance that he is now miserable himself. He was a worm; a good man in the worse sense of the word. It was the contrast—the contrast between his gentle clothing and ungentle heart, which moved my spleen. What a self-sufficient and inhuman brood were the Victorians of that type, hag-ridden by their nightmare of duty; a brood that has never yet been called by its proper name. Victorians? Why, not altogether. The mischief has its roots further back. Addison, for example, is a fair specimen.

Why say unkind things about a dead man? He cannot answer back.

Upon my word, I am rather glad to think he cannot. The last thing I ever wish to hear again is that voice of his. And what a face: gorgonizing in its assumption of virtue! Now the whole species is dying out, and none too soon. Graft abstract principles of conduct upon natures devoid of sympathy and you produce a monster; a sanctimonious fish; the coldest beast that ever infested the earth. This man's affinities were with Robespierre and Torquemada—both of them actuated by the purest intentions and without a grain of self-interest: pillars of integrity. What floods of tears would have been spared to mankind, had they only been a little corrupt! How corrupt a person of principles? He lacks the vulgar yet divine gift of imagination.

That is what these Victorians lacked. They would never have subscribed to this palpable truth: that justice is too good for some men, and not good enough for the rest. They cultivated the Cato or Brutus tone; they strove to be stern old Romans—Romans of the sour and imperfect Republic; for the Empire, that golden blossom, was to them a period of luxury and debauch. Nero—most reprehensible! It was not Nero, however, but our complacent British reptiles, who filled the prisons with the wailing of young children, and hanged a boy of thirteen for stealing a spoon. I wish I had it here, that book which everybody ought to read, that book by George Ives on the History of Penal Methods—it would help me to say a few more polite things. The villainies of the virtuous: who shall recount them? I can picture this vastly offensive old man acting as judge on that occasion and then, his "duties towards society" accomplished, being driven home in his brougham to thank Providence for one of those succulent luncheons, the enjoyment of which he invariably managed to ruin for every one except himself.

God rest his soul, the unspeakable phenomenon! He ought to have throttled himself at his mother's breast. Only a woman imbued with ultra-terrestrial notions of humour could have tolerated such an infliction. Anybody else would have poisoned him in the name of Christian charity and common sense, and earned the gratitude of generations yet unborn.

Well, well! R.I.P....

On returning to Rome after a considerable absence—a year or so—a few things have to be done for the sake of auld lang syne ere one may again feel at home. Rites must be performed. I am to take my fill of memories and conjure up certain bitter-sweet phantoms of the past. Meals must be taken in definite restaurants; a certain church must be entered; a sip of water taken from a fountain—from one, and one only (no easy task, this, for most of the fountains of Rome are so constructed that, however abundant their flow, a man may die of thirst ere obtaining a mouthful); I must linger awhile at the very end, the dirty end, of the horrible Via Principe Amedeo and, again, at a corner near the Portico d'Ottavia; perambulate the Protestant cemetery, Monte Mario, and a few quite uninteresting modern sites; the Acqua Acetosa, a stupid place, may on no account be forgotten, nor yet that bridge on the Via Nomentana—not the celebrated bridge but another one, miles away in the Campagna, the dreariest of little bridges, in the dreariest of landscapes. Why? It has been hallowed by the tread of certain feet.

Thus, by a kind of sacred procedure, I immerge myself into those old stones and recreate my peculiar Roman mood. It is rather ridiculous. Tradition wills it.

To-day came the turn of the Protestant cemetery. I have a view of this place, taken about the 'seventies—I wish I could reproduce it here, to show how this spot has been ruined. A woman who looks after the enclosure was in a fairly communicative mood; we had a few minutes' talk, among the tombs. What a jumble of names and nationalities, by the way! What a mixed assemblage lies here, in this foreign earth! One would like to write down all their names, shake them in a bag, pick out fifty at random and compose their biographies. It would be a curious cosmopolitan document.

They have now a dog, the woman tells me, a ferocious dog who roams among the tombs, since several brass plates have been wrenched off by marauders. At night? I inquire. At night. At night.... Slowly, warily, I introduce the subject of fiammelle. It is not a popular theme. No! She has heard of such things, but never seen them; she never comes here at night, God forbid!

What are fiammelle? Little flames, will-o'-the-wisps which hover about the graves at such hours, chiefly in the hot months or after autumn rains. It is a well-authenticated apparition; the scientist Bessel saw one; so did Casanova, here at Rome. He describes it as a pyramidal flame raised about four feet from the ground which seemed to accompany him as he walked along. He saw the same thing later, at Cesena near Bologna. There was some correspondence on the subject (started by Dr. Herbert Snow) in the Observer of December 1915 and January 1916. Many are the graveyards I visited in this country and in others with a view to "satisfying my curiosity," as old Ramage would say, on this point, and all in vain. My usual luck! The fiammelle, on that particular evening, were coy—they were never working. They are said to be frequently observed at Scanno in the Abruzzi province, and the young secretary of the municipality there, Mr. L. O., will tell you of our periodical midnight visits to the local cemetery. Or go to Licenza and ask for my intelligent friend the schoolmaster. What he does not know about fiammelle is not worth knowing. Did he not, one night, have a veritable fight with a legion of them which the wind blew from the graveyard into his face? Did he not return home trembling all over and pale as death?...

Here reposes, among many old friends, the idealist Malwida von Meysenbug; that sculptured medallion is sufficient to proclaim her whereabouts to those who still remember her. It is good to pause awhile and etheralize oneself in the neighbourhood of her dust. She lived a quiet life in an old brown house, since rebuilt, that overlooks the Coliseum, on whose comely ellipse and blood-stained history she loved to pasture eyes and imagination. Often I walked thence with her, in those sparkling mornings, up the Palatine hill, to stroll about the ilexes and roses in view of the Forum, to listen to the blackbirds, or the siskins in that pine tree. She was of the same type, the same ethical parentage, as the late Mathilde Blind, a woman of benignant and refined enthusiasm, full of charity to the poor and, in those later days, almost shadowy—remote from earth. She had saturated herself with Rome, for whose name she professed a tremulous affection untainted by worldly considerations such as mine; she loved its "persistent spiritual life"; it was her haven of rest. So, while her arm rested lightly on mine, we wandered about those gardens, the saintly lady and myself; her mind dwelling, maybe, on memories of that one classic love-adventure and the part she came nigh to playing in the history of Europe, while mine was lost in a maze of vulgar love-adventures, several of which came nigh to making me play a part in the police-courts of Rome.

What may have helped to cement our strange friendship was my acquaintance, at that time, with the German metaphysicians. She must have thought me a queer kind of Englishman to discuss with such familiarity the tenets of these cloudy dreamers. Malwida loved them in a bland and childlike fashion. She would take one of their dicta as a starting-point—establish herself, so to speak, within this or that nebular hypothesis—and argue thence in academic fashion for the sake of intellectual exercise and the joy of seeing where, after a thousand twists and turnings, you were finally deposited. A friend of ours—some American—had lately published a Socratic dialogue entitled "The Prison"; it formed a fruitful theme of conversation.[9] Nietzsche was also then to the fore, and it pleases me to recollect that even in those days I detected his blind spot; his horror of those English materialists and biologists. I did not pause to consider why he hated them so ardently; I merely noted, more in sorrow than in anger, this fact which seemed to vitiate his whole outlook—as indeed it does. Now I know the reason. Like all preacher-poets, he is anthropocentric. To his way of thinking the human mind is so highly organized, so different from that of beasts, that not all the proofs of ethnology and physiology would ever induce him to accept the ape-ancestry of man. This monkey-business is too irksome and humiliating to be true; he waives it aside, with a sneer at the disgusting arguments of those Englishmen.

That is what happens to men who think that "the spirit alone lives; the life of the spirit alone is true life." A philosopher weighs the value of evidence; he makes it his business, before discoursing of the origin of human intellect, to learn a little something of its focus, the brain; a little comparative anatomy. These men are not philosophers. Metaphysicians are poets gone wrong. Schopenhauer invents a "genius of the race"—there you have his cloven hoof, the pathetic fallacy, the poet's heritage. There are things in Schopenhauer which make one blush for philosophy. The day may dawn when this man will be read not for what he says, but for how he says it; he being one of the few of his race who can write in their own language. Impossible, of course, not to hit upon a good thing now and then, if you brood as much as he did. So I remember one passage wherein he adumbrates the theory of "Recognition Marks" propounded later by A. R. Wallace, who, when I drew his attention to it, wrote that he thought it a most interesting anticipation. [10]

He must have stumbled upon it by accident, during one of his excursions into the inane.

And what of that jovial red-bearded personage who scorned honest work and yet contrived to dress so well? Everyone liked him, despite his borrowing propensities. He was so infernally pleasant, and always on the spot. He had a lovely varnish of culture; it was more than varnish; it was a veneer, a patina, an enamel: weather-proof stuff. He could talk most plausibly—art, music, society gossip—everything you please; everything except scandal. No bitter word was known to pass his lips. He sympathized with all our little weaknesses; he was too blissfully contented to think ill of others, he took it for granted that everybody, like himself, found the world a good place to inhabit. That, I believe, was the secret of his success. He had a divine intuition for discovering the soft spots of his neighbours and utilizing the knowledge, in a frank and gentlemanly fashion, for his own advantage. It was he who invented a saying which I have since encountered more than once: "Never run after an omnibus or a woman. There will be another one round in a minute." And also this: "Never borrow from a man who really expects to be paid back. You may lose a friend."

What lady is he now living on?

"A good-looking fellow like me—why should I work? Tell me that. Especially with so many rich ladies in the world aching for somebody to relieve them of their spare cash?"

"The wealthy woman," he once told me, after I had begun to know him more intimately, "is a great danger to society. She is so corruptible! People make her spend money on all kinds of empty and even harmful projects. Think of the mischief that is done, in politics alone, by the money of these women. Think of all the religious fads that spring up and are kept going in a state of prosperity because some woman or other has not been instructed as to the proper use of her cheque-book. I foresee a positive decline ahead of us, if this state of affairs is allowed to go on. We must club together, we reasonable men, and put an end to the scandal. These women need trimmers; an army of trimmers. I have done a good deal of trimming in my day. Of course it involves some trouble and a close degree of intimacy, now and then. But a sensible man will always know where to draw the line."

"Where do you draw it?"

"At marriage."

Whether he ever dared to tap the venerable Malwida for a loan? Likely enough. He often played with her feelings in a delicate style, and his astuteness in such matters was only surpassed by his shamelessness. He was capable of borrowing a fiver from the Pope—or at least of attempting the feat; of pocketing some hungry widow's last mite and therewith purchasing a cigarette before her eyes. All these sums he took as his due, by right of conquest. Whether he ever "stung" Malwida? I should have liked to see the idealist's face when confronted in that cheery off-hand manner with the question whether she happened to have five hundred francs to spare.

"No? Whatever does it matter, my dear Madame de Meysenbug? Perhaps I shall be more fortunate another day. But pray don't put yourself out for an extravagant rascal like myself. I am always spending money—can't live without it, can one?—and sometimes, though you might not believe it, on quite worthy objects. There is a poor family I would like to take you to see one day; the father was cut to pieces in some wretched agricultural machine, the mother is dying in a hospital for consumption, and the six little children, all shivering under one blanket—well, never mind! One does what one can, in a small way. That was an interesting lecture, wasn't it, on Friday? He made a fine point in what he said about the relation of the Ego to the Cosmos. All the same, I thought he was a little hard on Fichte. But then, you know, I always felt a sort of tenderness for Fichte. And did you notice that the room was absolutely packed? I doubt whether that would have been the case in any other European capital. This must be the secret charm of Rome, don't you think so? This is what draws one to the Eternal City and keeps one here and makes one love the place in spite of a few trivial annoyances—this sense of persistent spiritual life."

The various sums derived from ladies were regarded merely as adventitious income. I found out towards the end of our acquaintance, when I really began to understand his "method," that he had a second source of revenue, far smaller but luckily "fixed." It was drawn from the other sex, from that endless procession of men passing through Rome and intent upon its antiquities. Rome, he explained, was the very place for him.

"This is what keeps me here and makes me love the place in spite of a few trivial annoyances—this persistent coming and going of tourists. Everybody on the move, all the time! A man must be daft if he cannot talk a little archaeology or something and make twenty new friends a year among such a jolly crowd of people. They are so grateful for having things explained to them. Another lot next year! And there are really good fellows among them; fellows, mind you, with brains; fellows with money. From each of those twenty he can borrow, say, ten pounds; what is that to a rich stranger who comes here for a month or so with the express purpose of getting rid of his money? Of course I am only talking about the medium rich; one need never apply to the very rich—they are always too poor. Well, that makes about two hundred a year. It's not much, but, thank God, it's safe as a house and it supplements the ladies. Women are so distressingly precarious, you know. You cannot count on a woman unless you have her actually under your thumb. Under your thumb, my boy; under your thumb. Don't ever forget it."

I have never forgotten it.

Where is he now? Is he dead? A gulf intervenes between that period and this. What has become of him? You might as well ask me about his contemporary, the Piccadilly goat. I have no idea what became of the Piccadilly goat, though I know pretty well what would become of him, were he alive at this moment.

Mutton-chops. [11]

Yet I can make a guess at what is happening to my red-haired friend. He is not dead, but sleepeth. He is being lovingly tended, in a crapulous old age, by one of the hundred ladies he victimized. He takes it as a matter of course. I can hear him chuckling dreamily, as she smooths his pillow for him. He will die in her arms unrepentant, and leave her to pay for the funeral.

"Work!" he once said. "To Hell with work. The man who talks to me about work is my enemy."

One sunny morning during this period there occurred a thunderous explosion which shattered my windows and many others in Rome. A gunpowder magazine had blown up, somewhere in the Campagna; the concussion of air was so mighty that it broke glass, they said, even at Frascati.

We drove out later to view the site. It resembled a miniature volcano.

There I left the party and wandered alone into one of those tortuous stream-beds that intersect the plain, searching for a certain kind of crystal which may be found in such places, washed out of the soil by wintry torrents. I specialized in minerals in those days—minerals and girls. Dangerous and unprofitable studies!

Even at that tender age I seem to have dimly discerned what I now know for certain: that dangerous and unprofitable objects are alone worth pursuing. The taste for minerals died out later, though I clung to it half-heartedly for a long while, Dr. Johnston-Lavis, Professor Knop and others fanning the dying embers. One day, all of a sudden, it was gone. I found myself riding somewhere in Asiatic Turkey past a precipice streaked in alternate veins of purest red and yellow jasper, with chalcedony in between: a discovery which in former days would have made me half delirious with joy. It left me cold. I did not even dismount to examine the site. "Farewell to stones" I thought....

Often we lingered by the Fontana Trevi to watch the children disporting themselves in the water and diving for pennies—a pretty scene which has now been banished from the politer regions of Rome (the town has grown painfully proper). There, at the foot of that weedy and vacuous and yet charming old Neptune—how perfectly he suits his age!—there, if you look, you will see certain gigantic leaves sculptured into the rock. I once overheard a German she-tourist saying to her companion, as she pointed to these things: "Ist doch sonderbar, wie das Wasser so die Pflanzen versteinert." She thought they were natural plants petrified by the water's action.

What happened yesterday was equally surprising. We were sitting at the Arch of Constantine and I was telling my friend about the Coliseum hard by and how, not long ago, it was a thicket of trees and flowers, looking less like a ruin than some wooded mountain. Now the Coliseum is surely one of the most famous structures in the world. Even they who have never been to the spot would recognize it from those myriad reproductions—especially, one would think, an Italian. Nevertheless, while thus discoursing, a man came up to us, a well-dressed man, who politely inquired:

"Could you tell me the name of this castello?"

I am glad to think that some account of the rich and singular flora of the Coliseum has been preserved by Deakin and Sebastiani, and possibly by others. I could round their efforts by describing the fauna of the Coliseum. The fauna of the Coliseum—especially after 11 p.m.—would make a readable book; readable but hardly printable.

These little local studies are not without charm. Somebody, one day, may be induced to tell us about the fauna of Trafalgar Square. He should begin with a description of the horse standing on three legs and gazing inanely out of those human eyes after the fashion of its classic prototype; then pass on to the lions beloved of our good Richard Jefferies which look like puppy-dogs modelled in cotton-wool (why did the sculptor not take a few lessons in lions from the sand-artist on Yarmouth beach?), and conclude by dwelling as charitably as possible on the human fauna—that droll little man, barely discernible, perched on the summit of his lead pencil....

There was a slight earthquake at sunrise. I felt nothing....

And, appropriately enough, I encountered this afternoon M. M., that most charming of persons, who, like Shelley and others, has discovered Italy to be a "paradise of exiles." His friends may guess whom I mean when I say that M. M. is connoisseur of earthquakes social and financial; his existence has been punctuated by them to such an extent that he no longer counts events from dates in the ordinary calendar, from birthdays or Christmas or Easter, but from such and such a disaster affecting himself. Each has left him seemingly more mellow than the last. Just then, however, he was in pensive mood, his face all puckered into wrinkles as he glanced upon the tawny flood rolling beneath that old bridge. There he stood, leaning over the parapet, all by himself. He turned his countenance aside on seeing me, to escape detection, but I drew nigh none the less.

"Go away," he said. "Don't disturb me just now. I am watching the little fishes. Life is so complicated! Let us pray. I have begun a new novel and a new love-affair."

"God prosper both!" I replied, and began to move off.

"Thanks. But supposing the publisher always objects to your choicest paragraphs?"

"I am not altogether surprised, if they are anything like what you once read to me out of your unexpurgated 'House of the Seven Harlots.' Why not try another firm? They might be more accommodating. Try mine."

He shook his head dubiously.

"They are all alike. It is with publishers as with wives: one always wants somebody else's. And when you have them, where's the difference? Ah, let us pray. These little fishes have none of our troubles."

I inquired about the new romance. At first he refused to disclose anything. Then he told me it was to be entitled "With Christ at Harvard," and that it promised some rather novel situations. I shall look forward to its appearance.

What good things one could relate of M. M., but for the risk of incurring his wrath! It is a thousand pities, I often tell him, that he is still alive; I am yearning to write his biography, and cannot afford to wait for his dissolution.

"When I am dead," he always says.

"By that time, my dear M., I shall be in the same fix myself."

"Try to survive. You may find it worth your while, when you come to look into my papers. You don't know half. And I may be taking that little sleeping-draught of mine any one of these days...." [12]

Mused long that night, and not without a certain envy, on the lot of M. M. and other earthquake-connoisseurs—or rather on the lot of that true philosopher, if he exists, who, far from being damaged by such convulsions, distils therefrom subtle matter of mirth, I have only known one single man—it happened to be a woman, an Austrian—who approached this ideal of splendid isolation. She lived her own life, serenely happy, refusing to acquiesce in the delusions and conventionalities of the crowd; she had ceased to trouble herself about neighbours, save as a source of quiet amusement; a state of affairs which had been brought about by a succession of benevolent earthquakes that refined and clarified her outlook.

Such disasters, obviously, have their uses. They knock down obsolete rubbish and enable a man to start building anew. The most sensitive recluse cannot help being a member of society. As such, he unavoidably gathers about him a host of mere acquaintances, good folks who waste his time dulling the edge of his wit and infecting him with their orthodoxy. Then comes the cataclysm. He loses, let us say, all his money, or makes a third appearance in the divorce courts. He can then at last (so one of them expressed it to me) "revise his visiting-list," an operation which more than counterbalances any damage from earthquakes. For these same good folks are vanished, the scandal having scattered them to the winds. He begins to breathe again, and employ his hours to better purpose. If he loses both money and reputation he must feel, I should think, as though treading on air. The last fools gone! And no sage lacks friends.

Consider well your neighbour, what an imbecile he is. Then ask yourself whether it be worth while paying any attention to what he thinks of you. Life is too short, and death the end of all things. Life must be lived, not endured. Were the day twice as long as it is, a man might find it diverting to probe down into that unsatisfactory fellow-creature and try to reach some common root of feeling other than those physiological needs which we share with every beast of earth. Diverting; hardly profitable. It would be like looking for a flea in a haystack, or a joke in the Bible. They can perhaps be found; at the expense of how much trouble!

Therefore the sage will go his way, prepared to find himself growing ever more out of sympathy with vulgar trends of opinion, for such is the inevitable development of thoughtful and self-respecting minds. He scorns to make proselytes among his fellows: they are not worth it. He has better things to do. While others nurse their griefs, he nurses his joy. He endeavours to find himself at no matter what cost, and to be true to that self when found—a worthy and ample occupation for a life-time. The happiness-of-the-greatest-number, of those who pasture on delusions: what dreamer is responsible for this eunuchry? Mill, was it? Bentham, more likely. As if the greatest number were not necessarily the least-intelligent! As if their happiness were not necessarily incompatible with that of the sage! Why foster it? He is a poor philosopher, who cuts his own throat. Away with their ghosts; de-spiritualize yourself; what you cannot find on earth is not worth seeking.

That charming M. M., I fear, will never compass this clarity of vision, this perfect de-spiritualization and contempt of illusions. He will never remain curious, to his dying day, in things terrestrial and in nothing else. From a Jewish-American father he has inherited that all too common taint of psychasthenia (miscalled neurasthenia); he confesses, moreover,—like other men of strong carnal proclivities—to certain immaterial needs and aspirations after "the beyond." Not one of these earthquake-specialists, in fact, but has his Achilles heel: a mental crotchet or physical imperfection to mar the worldly perspective. Not one of them, at close of life, will sit beside some open window in view of a fair landscape and call up memories of certain moments which no cataclysms have taken from him; not one will lay them in the balance and note how they outweigh, in their tiny grains of gold, the dross of an age of other men's lives. Not one of them! They will be preoccupied, for the most part, with unseasonable little concerns. Pleasant folk, none the less. And sufficiently abundant in Italy. Altogether, the Englishman here is as often an intenser being than the home product. Alien surroundings awaken fresh and unexpected notes in his nature. His fibres seem to lie more exposed; you have glimpses into the man's anatomy. There is something hostile in this sunlight to the hazy or spongy quality which saturates the domestic Anglo-Saxon, blurring the sharpness of his moral outline. No doubt you will also meet with dull persons; Rome is full of them, but, the type being easier to detect among a foreign environment, there is still less difficulty in evading them....

Thus I should have had no compunction, some nights ago, in making myself highly objectionable to Mr. P. G. who has turned up here on some mission connected with the war—so he says, and it may well be true; no compunction whatever, had that gentleman been in his ordinary social state. Mr. P. G., the acme of British propriety, inhabiting a house, a mansion, on the breezy heights of north London, was on that occasion decidedly drunk. "Indulging in a jag," he would probably have called it. He tottered into a place where I happened to be sitting, having lost his friends, he declared; and soon began pouring into my ear, after the confidential manner of a drunkard, a flood of low talk, which if I attempted to set it down here, would only result in my being treated to the same humiliating process as the excellent M. M. with his "choicest paragraphs." It was highly instructive—the contrast between that impeccable personality which he displays at home and his present state. I wish his wife and two little girls could have caught a few shreds of what he said—just a few shreds; they would have seen a new light on dear daddy.

In vino veritas. Ever avid of experimentum in some corpore vili and determined to reach the bed-rock of his gross mentality, I plied him vigorously with drink, and was rewarded. It was rich sport, unmasking this Philistine and thanking God, meanwhile, that I was not like unto him. We are all lost sheep; and none the worse for that. Yet whoso is liable, however drunk, to make an exhibition of himself after the peculiar fashion of Mr. P. G., should realize that there is something fundamentally wrong with his character and take drastic measures of reform—measures which would include, among others, a total abstention from alcohol. Old Aristotle, long ago, laboured to define wherein consisted the trait known as gentlemanliness; others will have puzzled since his day, for we have bedaubed ourselves with so thick a coating of manner and phrase that many a cad will pass for something better. Well, here is the test. Unvarnish your man; make him drink, and listen. That was my procedure with P. G. Esquire. I listened to his outpouring of inanity and obscenity and, listening sympathetically, like some compassionate family doctor, could not help asking myself: Is such a man to be respected, even when sober? Be that as it may, he gave me to understand why some folk are rightly afraid of exposing, under the influence of drink, the bête humaine which lurks below their skin of decency. His language would have terrified many people. Me it rejoiced. I would not have missed that entertainment for worlds. He finally wanted to have a fight, because I refused to accompany him to a certain place of delights, the address of which—I might have given him a far better one—had been scrawled on the back of a crumpled envelope by some cabman. Unable to stand on his legs, what could he hope to do there?

Olevano

I have loafed into Olevano.

A thousand feet below my window, and far away, lies the gap between the Alban and Volscian hills; veiled in mists, the Pontine marches extend beyond, and further still—discernible only to the eye of faith—the Tyrrhenian.

The profile of these Alban craters is of inimitable grace. It recalls Etna, as viewed from Taormina. How the mountain cleaves to earth, how reluctantly it quits the plain before swerving aloft in that noble line! Velletri's ramparts, twenty miles distant, are firmly planted on its lower slope. Standing out against the sky, they can be seen at all hours of the day, whereas the dusky palace of Valmontone, midmost on the green plain and rock-like in its proportions, fades out of sight after midday.

Hard by, on your right, are the craggy heights of Capranica. Tradition has it that Michael Angelo was in exile up there, after doing something rather risky. What had he done? He crucified his model, desirous, like a true artist, to observe and reproduce faithfully in marble the muscular contractions and facial agony of such a sufferer. To crucify a man: this was going almost too far, even for the Pope of that period, who seems to have been an unusually sensitive pontiff—or perhaps the victim was a particular friend of his. However that may be, he waxed wroth and banished the conscientious sculptor in disgrace to this lonely mountain village, there to expiate his sins, for a day or two....

One sleeps badly here. Those nightingales—they are worse than the tram-cars in town. They begin earlier. They make more noise. Surely there is a time for everything? Will certain birds never learn to sing at reasonable hours?

A word as to these nightingales. One of them elects to warble, in deplorably full-throated ease, immediately below my bedroom window. When this particular fowl sets up its din at about 3.45 a.m. it is a veritable explosion; an ear-rending, nerve-shattering explosion of noise. I use that word "noise" deliberately. For it is not music—not until your ears are grown accustomed to it.

I know a little something about music, having studied the art with considerable diligence for a number of years. Impossible to enumerate all the composers and executants on various instruments, the conductors and opera-singers and ballet-girls with whom I was on terms of familiarity during that incarnation. Perhaps I am the only person now alive who has shaken hands with a man (Lachner) who shook hands with Beethoven and heard his voice; all of which may appear when I come to indite my musical memoirs. I have written a sonata in four movements, opus 643, hitherto unpublished, and played the organ during divine service to a crowded congregation. Furthermore I performed, not at my own suggestion, his insipid Valse Caprice to the great Antoine Rubinstein, who was kind enough to observe: "Yes, yes. Quite good. But I rather doubt whether you could yet risk playing that in a concert." And in the matter of sheer noise I am also something of an expert, having once, as an infant prodigy, broken five notes in a single masterly rendering of Liszt's polonaise in E

Major—I think it is E Major—whereupon my teacher, himself a pupil of Liszt, genially remarked: "Now don't cry, and don't apologize. A polonaise like yours is worth a piano." I set these things down with modest diffidence, solely in order to establish my locus standi as a person who might be expected to know the difference between sound and noise. As such, I have no hesitation in saying that the first three bars of that nightingale performance are, to sleeping ears, not music. They break upon the stillness with the crash of Judgment Day.

And every night the same scare. It causes me to start up, bathed in sudden perspiration, out of my first, and best, and often only sleep, with the familiar feeling that something awful is happening. Windows seem to rattle, plaster drops from the ceiling—an earthquake? Lord, no. Nothing so trivial. Nothing so brief. It is that blasted bird clearing its throat for a five hours' entertainment. Let it not be supposed that the song of these southerners bears any resemblance to that of an English nightingale. I could stand a hatful of English nightingales in my bedroom; they would lull me to sleep with their anaemic whispers. You might as well compare the voice of an Italian costermonger, the crowing of a cock, the braying of a local donkey, with their representatives in the north—those thin trickles of sound, shadowy as the squeakings of ghosts. Something will have to be done about those nightingales unless I am to find my way into a sanatorium. For hardly is this bird started on its work before five or six others begin to shout in emulation—a little further off, I am glad to say, but still near enough to be inconvenient; still near enough to be reached by a brick from this window———A brick. Methinks I begin to see daylight....

Meanwhile one can snatch a little rest out of doors, in the afternoon. A delectable path, for example, runs up behind the cemetery, bordered by butterfly orchids and lithospermum and aristolochia and other plants worthy of better names; it winds aloft, under shady chestnuts, with views on either side. Here one can sit and smoke and converse with some rare countryman passing by; here one can dream, forgetful of nightingales—soothed, rather, by the mellifluous note of the oriole among the green branches overhead and the piping, agreeably remote, of some wryneck in the olives down yonder. The birds are having a quiet time, for the first time in their lives; sportsmen are all at the front. I kicked up a partridge along this track two days ago.

Those wrynecks, by the way, are abundant but hard to see. They sit close, relying on their protective colour. And it is the same with the tree-creepers. I have heard Englishmen say there are no tree-creepers in Italy. The olive groves are well stocked with them (there are numbers even in the Borghese Gardens in Rome), but you must remain immovable as a rock in order to see them; for they are yet shyer, more silent, more fond of interposing the tree-trunk between yourself and them, than those at home. Mouse-like in hue, in movement and voice—a strange case of analogous variation....

As to this Scalambra, this mountain whose bleak grey summit overtops everything near Olevano, I could soon bear the sight of it no longer. It seemed to shut out the world; one must up and glance over the edge, to see what is happening on the other side. I looked for a guide and porter, for somebody more solid than Giulio, who is almost an infant; none could be found. Men are growing scarce as the Dodo hereabouts, on account of the war. So Giulio came, though he had never made the ascent.

Now common sense, to say nothing of a glance at the map, would suggest the proper method of approach: by the village of Serrano, the Saint Michael hermitage, and so up. Scouting this plan, I attacked the mountain about half-way between that village and Rojate. I cannot recommend my route. It was wearisome to the last degree and absolutely shadeless save for a small piece of jungle clothing a gulley, hung with myriads of caterpillars and not worth mentioning as an incident in that long walk. No excitement—not the faintest chance, so far as I could see, of breaking one's neck, and uphill all the time over limestone. One never seems to get any nearer. This Scalambra, I soon discovered, is one of those artful mountains which defend their summits by thrusting out escarpments with valleys in between; you are kept at arm's length, as it were, by this arrangement of the rock, which is invisible at a distance. And when at last you set foot on the real ridge and climb laboriously to what seems to be the top—lo! there is another peak a little further off, obviously a few feet higher. Up you go, only to discover a third, perhaps a few inches higher still. Alpine climbers know these tricks.

We reached the goal none the less and there lay, panting and gasping; while an eagle, a solitary eagle with tattered wings, floated overhead in the cloudless sky.

The descent to Rojate under that blazing sun was bad enough. My flask had been drained to the dregs long ago, and the Scalambra, true to its limestone tradition, had not supplied even a drop of water. Arriving at the village at about two in the afternoon, we found it deserted; everybody enjoying their Sunday nap. Rojate is a dirty hole. The water was plainly not to be trusted; it might contain typhoid germs, and I was responsible for Giulio's health; wine would be safer, we agreed. There, in a little shop near the church—a dark and cool place, the first shade we had entered for many hours—we drank without ever growing less thirsty. We felt like cinders, so hot, so porous, that the liquid seemed not only to find its way into the legitimate receptacle but to be obliged to percolate, by some occult process of capillarity, the remotest regions of the body. As time went on, the inhabitants dropped in after their slumbers and kept us company. We told our adventures, drank to the health of the Allies one by one and several times over; and it was not until we had risen to our feet and passed once more into the sunshine of the square that we suddenly felt different from what we thought we felt.

The first indication was conveyed by Giulio, who called upon the populace of Rojate, there assembled, to bear solemn witness to the fact that I was his one and only friend, and that he would nevermore abandon me—a sentiment in which I stoutly concurred. (A fellow-feeling makes us wondrous blind.) Other symptoms followed. His hat, for example, which had hitherto behaved in exemplary fashion, now refused to remain steadily balanced on his head; it took some first-class gymnastics to prevent it from falling to the ground. In fact, while I confined myself to the minor part of Silenus—my native role—this youngster gave a noteworthy representation of the Drunken Faun....

Now I see no harm in appreciating wine up to a certain point, and am consoled to observe that Craufurd Tait Ramage, LL.D., was of the same way of thinking. He says so himself, and there is no reason for doubting his word. He frankly admits, for instance, that he enjoys the stuff called moscato "with great zest." He samples the Falernian vintage and pronounces it to be "particularly good, and not degenerated." Arrived at Cutro, he is not averse to reviving his spirits with "a pretty fair modicum of wine." He also lets slip—significant detail—the fact that Dr. Henderson was one of his friends, and that he travelled about with him. You may judge a man by the company he keeps. Who was this Dr. Henderson? He was the author of "The History of Ancient Wines." Old Henderson, I should say, could be trusted to know something of local vintages.

And so far good.

At Licenza, however, Ramage tells us that he "got glorious on the wine of Horace's Sabine farm." I do not know what he means by this expression, which seems to be purposely ambiguous; in any case, it does not sound very nice. At another place, again, he and his entertainer consumed some excellent liquor "in considerable quantity"—so he avows; adding that "it was long past midnight ere we closed our bacchanalian orgies, and he (the host) ended by stating that he was happy to have made my acquaintance." Note the lame and colourless close of that sentence: he ended by stating. One always ends that way after bacchanalian orgies, though one does not always gloss over the escapade with such disingenuous language.

We can guess what really took place. It was something like what happened at Rojate. Did not the curly-haired Giulio end by "stating" something to the same effect?

I cannot make up my mind whether to be pleased with this particular trait in friend Ramage's character. For let it never be forgotten that our traveller was a young man at the time. He says so himself, and there is no reason for doubting his word. Was he acting as beseemed his years?

I am not more straight-laced than many people, yet I confess it always gives me a kind of twinge to see a young man yielding to intemperance of any kind. There is something incongruous in the spectacle, if not actually repellent. Rightly or wrongly, one is apt to associate that time of life with stern resolve. A young man, it appears to me, should hold himself well in hand. Youth has so much to spare! Youth can afford to be virtuous. With such stores of joy looming ahead, it should be a period of ideals, of self-restraint and self-discipline, of earnestness of purpose. How well the Greek Anthology praises "Temperance, the nurse of Youth!" The divine Plato lays it down that youngsters should not touch wine at all, since it is not right to heap fire on fire. He adds that older men like ourselves may indulge therein as an ally against the austerity of their years—agreeing, therefore, with Theophrastus who likewise recommends it for the "natural moroseness" of age.

Observe in this connection what happened to Craufurd Tait Ramage, LL.D., at Trebisacce. Here was a poor old coastguard who had been taken prisoner by the Corsairs thirty years earlier, carried to Algiers, and afterwards ransomed. Having "nothing better to do" (says our author) "I confess I furnished him with somewhat more wine than was exactly consistent with propriety"; with so liberal a quantity, indeed, that the coastguard became quite "obstreperous in his mirth"; whereupon Ramage hops on his mule and leaves him to his fate. Here, then, we have a young fellow deliberately leading an old man astray. And why? Because he has "nothing better to do."[13] It is not remarkably edifying. True, he afterwards makes a kind of apology for "causing my brother to sin by over-indulgence...."

But if we close our eyes to the fact that Ramage, when he gave way to these excesses, was a young man and ought to have known better, what an agreeable companion we find him!

He never rails at anything. Had I been subjected to half the annoyances he endured, my curses would have been loud and long. Under such provocation, Ramage contents himself with reproving his tormentors in rounded phrases of oratio obliqua which savour strongly of those Latin classics he knew so well. What he says of the countryfolk is not only polite but true, that their virtues are their own, while their vices have been fostered by the abuses of tyranny. "Whatever fault one may find with this people for their superstition and ignorance, there is a loveableness in their character which I am not utilitarian enough in my philosophy to resist." This comes of travelling off the beaten track and with an open mind; it comes of direct contact. When one remembers that he wrote in 1828 and was derived from a bigoted stock, his religious tolerance is refreshing—astonishing. He studies the observances of the poorer classes with sympathetic eye and finds that they are "pious to a degree to which I am afraid we must grant that we have no pretensions." That custom of suspending votive offerings in churches he does not think "worthy of being altogether condemned or ridiculed. The feeling is the same that induces us, on recovery from severe illness, to give thanks to Almighty God, either publicly in church or privately in our closets." How many Calvinists of to-day would write like this?

We could do with more of these sensible and humane reflections, but unfortunately he is generally too "pressed for time" to indulge in them. That mania of hustling through the country....

One morning he finds himself at Foggia, with the intention of visiting Mons Garganus. First of all he must "satisfy his curiosity" about Arpi; it is ten miles there and back. Leaving Foggia for the second time he proceeds twenty miles to Manfredonia, and inspects not only this town, but the site of old Sipontum. Then he sails to the village of Mattinata, and later to Vieste, the furthermost point of the promontory. About six miles to the north are the presumable ruins of Merinum; he insists upon going there, but the boatmen strike work; regretfully he returns to Manfredonia, arriving at 11 p.m., and having covered on this day some sixty or seventy miles. What does he do at Manfredonia? He sleeps for three hours—and then a new hustle begins, in pitch darkness.

Another day he wakes up at Sorrento and thinks he will visit the Siren Islets. He crosses the ridge and descends to the sea on the other side, to the so-called Scaricatojo—quite a respectable walk, as any one can find out for himself. Hence he sails to the larger of the islets, climbs to the summit and makes some excavations, in the course of which he observes what I thought I was the first to discover—the substructures of a noble Roman villa; he also scrambles into King Robert's tower. Then to the next islet, and up it; then to the third, and up it. After that, he is tempted to visit the headland of Minerva; he goes there, and satisfies his curiosity. He must now hence to Capri. He sails across, and after a little refreshment, walks to the so-called Villa of Jupiter at the easterly apex of the island. He then rows round the southern shore and is taken with the idea of a trip to Misenum, twenty miles or so distant. Arrived there, he climbs to the summit of the cape and lingers a while—it is pleasant to find him lingering—to examine something or other. Then he "rushes" down to the boat and bids them row to Pozzuoli, where he arrives (and no wonder) long after sunset. A good day's hustle….

The ladies made a great impression on his sensitive mind; yet not even they were allowed to interfere with his plans. At Strongoli the "sparkling eyes of the younger sister" proved the most attractive object in the place. He was strongly urged to remain a while and rest from his fatigues. But no; there were many reasons why he should press forward. He therefore presses forward. At another place, too, he was waited upon by his entertainer's three daughters, the youngest of whom was one of the most entrancing girls he had ever met with—in fact, it was well that his time was limited, else "I verily believe I should have committed all kinds of follies." That is Ramage. He parts from his host with "unfeigned regret"—but—parts. His time is always limited. Bit for that craze of pressing forward, what fun he could have had!

Stroll to that grove of oaks crowning a hill-top above the Serpentaro stream. It has often been described, often painted. It is a corner of Latium in perfect preservation; a glamorous place; in the warm dusk of southern twilight—when all those tiresome children are at last asleep—it calls up suggestions of A Midsummer Night's Dream. Here is a specimen of the landscape as it used to be. You may encounter during your wanderings similar fragments of woodland, saved by their inaccessibility from the invading axe. "Hands off the Oak!" cries an old Greek poet.

The Germans, realizing its picturesque value, bought this parcel of land and saved the trees from destruction. It was well done. Within, they have cut certain letterings upon the rock which violate the sylvan sanctity of the place—Germans will do these things; there is no stopping them; it is part of their crudely expansive temperament—certain letterings, among other and major horrors, anent the "Law of the Ever-beautiful" (how truly Teutonic!)—lines, that is, signed by the poet Victor von Scheffel, and dated 2 May, 1897. Scheffel was a kindly and erudite old toper, who toped himself into Elysium via countless quarts of Affenthaler. I used to read his things; the far-famed Ekkehardt furnishing an occasion for a visit to the Hohentwiel mountain in search of that golden-tinted natrolite mineral, which was duly found (I specialized in zeolites during that period).

Now what was Scheffel doing at this Serpentaro in 1897? For I attended his funeral, which took place in the 'eighties. Can it be that his son, a scraggy youth in those days, inherited not only the father's name but his poetic mantle? Was it he who perpetrated those sententious lines? I like to think so. That "law of the ever-beautiful" does not smack of the old man, unless he was more disguised than usual, and having a little fun with his pedantic countrymen....

Climb hence—it is not far—to the village of Civitella, now called Bellegra, a prehistoric fastness with some traces of "cyclopean" defences. Those ancients must have had cisterns; inconceivable that springs should ever have issued from this limestone crag. You can see the women of to-day fetching water from below, from a spot which I was too lazy to investigate, where perhaps the soft tertiary rock leans upon this impervious stuff and allows the liquid to escape into the open. An unclean place is Bellegra, and loud, like all these Sabine villages, with the confused crying of little children. That multiple wail of misery will ring in your ear for days afterwards. They are more neglected by their mothers than ever, since women now have all the men's work in the fields to do. They are hungrier than ever, on account of the war which has imposed real hardships on these agricultural folk; hardships that seize them by the throat and make them sit down, with folded hands, in dumb despair: so I have seen them. How many of these unhappy babies will grow to maturity?

Death-rate must anyhow be high hereabouts, for nothing is done in the way of hygiene. In the company of one who knows, I perambulated the cemetery of Olevano and was astonished at the frequency of tombstones erected to the young. "Consumption," my friend told me. They scorn prophylactics. I should not care to send growing children into these villages, despite their "fine air." Here, at Bellegra, the air must be fine indeed in winter; too fine for my taste. It lies high, exposed to every blast of Heaven, and with noble views in all directions.

Rest awhile, on your homeward march, at the small bridge near Olevano where the road takes a turn. A few hundred yards up the glen on your left is a fountain whose waters are renowned for their purity; the bridge itself is not a favourite spot after sunset; it is haunted by a most malignant spectre. That adds considerably, in my eyes, to the charm of the place. Besides, here stands an elder tree now in full flower. What recollections does that scent evoke! What hints of summer, after rain!

A venerable tree, old as the hills; that last syllable tells its tale—you may read it in the Sanscrit. A man-loving tree; seldom one sees an elder by itself, away from human habitations, in the jungle. I have done so; but in that particular jungle, buried beneath the soil, were the ruins of old houses. When did it begin to attach itself to the works of man, to walls and buildings? And why? Does it derive peculiar sustenance from the lime of the masonry? I think not, for it grows in lands where lime is rare, and in the shadow of log-huts. It seeks shelter from the wind for its frail stalks and leaves, that shrivel wondrously when the plant is set in exposed situations.

The Sabine mountains are full of elders. They use the berries to colour the wine. A German writer, R. Voss, wove their fragrance into a kind of Leit-motif for one of his local novels. I met him once by accident, and am not anxious to meet him again. A sacerdotal and flabbily pompous old man—straightway my opinion of his books, never very high, fell to zero, and has there remained. He knew these regions well, and doubtless sojourned at one time or another at yonder caravanserai-hotel, abandoned of late, but then filled with a crowd of noisy enthusiasts who have since been sacrificed to the war-god. Doubtless he drank wine with them on that terrace overlooking the brown houses of Olevano, though I question whether he then paid as much as they are now charging me; doubtless he rejoiced to see that stately array of white lilies fronting the landscape, though I question whether he derived more pleasure from them than I do....

While at Bellegra, this afternoon, I gazed landwards to where, in the Abruzzi region, the peaks are still shrouded in snow.

How are they doing our there, at Scanno? Is that driving-road at last finished? Can the "River Danube" still be heard flowing underground in the little cave of Saint Martin? Are the thistles of violet and red and blue and gold and silver as gorgeous as ever?[14] And those legions of butterflies—do they still hover among the sunny patches in the narrow vale leading to Mount Terrata? And Frattura, that strange place—what has happened to Frattura? Built on a fracture, on the rubble of that shattered mountain which produced the lake lower down, it has probably crumbled away in the last earthquake. Well I remember Frattura! It was where the wolf ate the donkey, and where we, in our turn, often refreshed ourselves in the dim hovel of Ferdinando—never with greater zest than on the hot downward march from Mount Genzana. Whether those small purple gentians are still to be found on its summit? And the emerald lizard on the lower slopes? Whether the eagles still breed on the neighbouring Montagna di Preccia? They may well be tired of having their nest plundered year after year.

What foreigner has older and pleasanter memories of Scanno? I would like to meet that man, and compare notes.

And so, glancing over the hills from Bellegra, I sent my thoughts into those Abruzzi mountains, and registered a vow to revisit Scanno—if only in order to traverse once more by moonlight, for the sake of auld lang syne, the devious paths to Roccaraso, or linger in that moist nook by the lake-side where stood the Scanno of olden days (the Betifuli, if such it was, of the Pelignians), where the apples grow, where the sly dabchick plays among the reeds, and where, one evening, I listened to something that might have been said much sooner. Acque Vive....

I kept my vow. Our bill at Scanno for wine alone was 189 francs, and for beer 92 francs; figures which look more formidable than they are and which I cite only to prove that we—for of course I was not alone—enjoyed ourselves fairly well during those eighteen days. By the way, what does Baedeker mean by speaking of the "excellent wines" of Scanno, where not a drop is grown? He might have said the same of Aberdeen.

The season was too late for the thistles, too late for the little coppers and fritillaries and queens of Spain and commas and all the rest of that fluttering tribe in the narrow vale leading to Terrata, though wood-pigeons were still cooing there. Scanno has been spared by the earthquake which laid low so many other places; it has prospered; prospered too much for my taste, since those rich smoky tints, especially of the vaulted interiors, are now disappearing under an invasion of iron beams and white plaster. The golden duskiness of Scanno, heightened as it was by the gleaming copper vessels borne on every young girl's head, will soon be a thing of the past. Young trees along the road-side—well-chosen trees: limes, maples, willows, elms, chestnuts, ashes—are likewise doing well and promise pretty effects of variegated foliage in a few years' time; so are the plantations of pines in the higher regions of the Genzana. In this matter of afforestation, Scanno continues its system of draconic severity. It is worth while, in a country which used to suffer so much from reckless grazing of goats on the hill-sides, and the furious floods of water. The Sagittario stream is hemmed in by a cunning device of stones contained within bags of strong wire; it was introduced many years ago by an engineer from Modena. And if you care to ascend the torrents, you will find they have been scientifically dammed by the administration, whereas the peasant, when they overflow and ruin his crops, contents himself with damning them in quite an amateurish fashion. Which reminds me that I picked up during this visit, and have added to my collection, a new term of abuse to be addressed to your father-in-law: Porcaccio d'un cagnaccio! Novel effects, you perceive, obtained by a mere intensification of colour.

As to Frattura—yes, it is shattered. Vainly we tried to identify Ferdinando's abode among all that debris. The old man himself escaped the cataclysm, and now sells his wares in one of the miserable wooden shanties erected lower down. The mellow hermit at St. Egidio, of whom more on p. 171, has died; his place is taken by a worthless vagabond. Saint Domenico and his serpents, the lonely mead of Jovana (? Jovis fanum), that bell in the church-tower of Villalago which bears the problematical date of 600 A.D.—they are all in their former places. Mount Velino still glitters over the landscape, for those who climb high enough to see it. The cliff-swallows are there, and dippers skim the water as of old. Women, in their unhygienic costume, still carry those immense loads of wood on their heads, though payment is considerably higher than the three half-pence a day which it used to be.

Enough of Scanno!

Whoever wishes to leave the place on foot and by an unconventional route, may go to Sora via Pescasseroli. Adventurous souls will scramble over the Terrata massif, leaving the summit well on their right, and descend on its further side; others may wander up the Valle dei Prati and then, bending to the right along the so-called Via del Campo, mount upwards past a thronged alp of sheep, over the watershed, and down through charming valleys of beechen timber. A noble walk, and one that compares favourably with many Abruzzi excursions. What deserts they often are, these stretches of arid limestone, voiceless and waterless, with the raven's croak for your only company!

I am glad to have seen Pescasseroli, where we arrived at about 9 a.m. For the rest, it is only one of many such places that have been brought to a state of degradation by the earthquake, the present war, and governmental neglect. Not an ounce of bread was procurable for money, or even as a gift. The ordinary needs of life—cigars, matches, maccheroni and so forth: there were none of them. An epidemic of the gapes, infecting the entire race of local hens, had caused the disappearance of every egg from the market. And all those other countless things which a family requires for its maintenance—soap and cloth and earthenware and kitchen utensils and oils—they have become rarities; the natives are learning to subsist without them; relapsing into a kind of barbarism. So they sit among the cracked tenements; resentful, or dumbly apathetic.

"We have been forgotten," said one of them.

The priests inculcate submission to the will of God. What else should they teach? But men will outgrow these doctrines of patience when suffering is too acute or too prolonged. "Anything is better than this," they say. Thus it comes about that these ruined regions are a goodly soil for the sowing of subversive opinions; the land reeks of ill-digested socialism.

We found a "restaurant" where we lunched off a tin of antediluvian Spanish sardines, some mouldy sweet biscuits, and black wine. (A distinction is made in these parts between black and red wine; the former is the Apulian variety, the other from Sulmona.) During this repast, we were treated to several bear-stories. For there are bears at Pescasseroli, and nowhere else in Italy; even as there are chamois nearby, between Opi and Villetta Barrea, among the crags of the Camosciara, which perpetuates their name. One of those present assured us that the bear is a good beast; he will eat a man, of course, but if he meets a little boy, he contents himself with throwing stones at him—just to teach him good manners. Certain old bears are as big as a donkey. They have been seen driving into their cave a flock of twenty-five sheep, like any shepherd. It is no rare thing to encounter in the woods a bear with a goat slung over his shoulder; he must breakfast, like anybody else. One of these gentlemen told us that the bears, not long ago, were a source of considerable profit to the peasantry round about. It was in this wise. Their numbers had been reduced, it seems, to a single pair and the species was threatened with extinction, when, somehow or other, this state of affairs became known to the King who, alarmed at the disappearance from his realm of a venerable and autochtonous quadruped, the largest European beast of prey, conceived the happy idea of converting the whole region into a Royal Preserve. On pain of death, no bear was to be molested or even laughed at; any damage they might do would be compensated out of the Royal Purse.

For a week or so after this enactment, nothing was heard of the bears. Then, one morning, the conscientious Minister of the Royal Household presented himself at the palace, with a large sheaf of documents under his arm.

"What have we here?" inquired the King.

"Attestations relating to the bears of Pescasseroli, Your Majesty. They seem to be thriving."

"Ah! That is nice of them. They are multiplying once more, thanks to Our Royal protection. We thought they would."

"Multiplying indeed, Sire. Here are testimonials, sworn before the local syndic, showing that they have devoured 18 head of cattle and 43 sheep."

"In that short time? Is it possible? Well, well! The damage must be paid. And yet We never knew the bears could propagate so fast. Maybe our Italian variety is peculiarly vigorous in such matters."

"Seems so, Your Majesty. Very prolific."

A week or so passed and, once more, His Excellency was announced. The King observed:

"You are not looking quite yourself this morning, my good Minister. Would it be indiscreet to inquire the cause? No family or parliamentary worries, We trust?"

"Your Majesty is very kind! No. It is the bears of Pescasseroli. They have eaten 75 head of cattle, 93 sheep, and 114 goats. Ah—and 18 horses. Here are the claims for damages, notarially attested."

"We must pay. But if only somebody could teach the dear creatures to breed a little more reasonably!"

"I cannot but think, Sire, that the peasants are abusing Your Majesty's——"

"May We never live to hear anything against Our faithful and well-beloved Abruzzi folk!"

Nearly a month elapsed before the Minister again presented himself. This time he looked really haggard and careworn, and was bowed down under an enormous bundle of papers. The King glanced up from that writing-desk where, like all other sovereigns, he had been working steadily since 4.30 a.m., and at once remarked, with that sympathetic intuition for which he is famous among crowned heads:

"We think We know. The bears."

Your Majesty is never wrong. They have devoured 126 cows and calves and bullocks, 418 sheep and goats, 62 mules, 37 horses, and 96 donkeys. Also 55 shepherd dogs and 827 chickens. Here are the claims."

"Dear, dear, dear. This will never do. If it is a question of going to ruin, We prefer that it should be the bears rather than Ourselves. We must withdraw Our Royal protection, after settling up these last items. What say you, my good Minister?"

"Your Majesty is always right. A private individual may indulge in the pastime of breeding bears to the verge of personal bankruptcy. Ruling sovereigns will be guided by juster and more complex considerations."

And from that moment, added our gentlemanly informant, there began a wonderful shrinkage in the numbers of the bears. Within a day or two, they were again reduced to a single couple.

Gladly would I have listened to more of these tales but, having by far the worst of the day's walk still before us, we left the stricken regions about midday and soon began an interminable ascent, all through woods, to the shrine of Madonna di Tranquillo. Hereabouts is the watershed, whence you may see, far below, the tower of Campoli Apennino. That village was passed in due course, and Sora lay before us, after a thirteen hours' march….

That same night in Sora—it may have been 2 a.m.—some demon drew nigh to my bedside and whispered in my ear: "What are you doing here, at Sora? Why not revisit Alatri? (I had been there already in June.) Just another little promenade! Up, sluggard, while the night-air is cool!"

I obeyed the summons and turned to rouse my slumbering companion, to whom I announced my inspiration. His remarks, on that occasion, were well worth listening to.

Next evening found us at Alatri.

Now whoever, after walking from Scanno over Pescasseroli to Sora in one day, and on the next, in the blazing heat of early autumn, from Sora over Isola Liri and Veroli to Alatri—touching in two days the soil of three Italian provinces: Aquila, Caserta, and Rome—whoever, after doing this, and inspecting the convent of Casamari en route, feels inclined for a similar promenade on the third day: let him rest assured of my profound respect.

Calm, sunny days at Olevano. And tranquil nights, for some time past.

The nightingale has been inspired to move a little up country, into another bush. Its rivals have likewise retired further off, and their melodramatic trills sound quite pleasant at this distance.

So tin cans have their uses, even when empty. Certain building operations may have been interrupted. I apologise, though I will not promise not to repeat the offence. They can move their nests; I cannot move this house. Bless their souls! I would not hurt a hair on their dear little heads, but one must really have a few hours' sleep, somehow or other. A single night's repose is more precious to me than a myriad birds or quadrupeds or bipeds; my ideas on the sacred nature of sleep being perfectly Oriental. That Black Hole of Calcutta was an infamous business. And yet, while nowise approving the tyrant's action, I can thoroughly understand his instructions on the subject of slumber.

Not every one at Olevano is so callous. Waiting the other day at the bifurcation of the roads for the arrival of the station motor-car—the social event of the place—I noticed two children bringing up to a bigger one the nest of a chaffinch, artfully frosted over with silver lichen from some olive, and containing a naked brood which sprawled pathetically within. Wasn't it pretty, they asked?

"Very pretty," he replied. "Now you will take it straight back where you found it. Go ahead. I am coming with you." And he marched them off.

I am glad to put this incident on record. It is the second of its kind which I have observed in this country, the first being when a fisherman climbed up a bad piece of rock to replace a nest—idle undertaking—which some boys had dislodged with stones. At a short distance from the scene sat the mother-bird in pensive mood, her head cocked on one side. What did she think of the benevolent enthusiast?...

Olevano is said to have been discovered by the Germans. I am sceptical on this point, having never yet found a place that was discovered by them. An English eccentric or two is sure to have lived and died here all by himself; though doubtless, once on the spot, they did their best to popularise and vulgarise it. In this matter, as in art or science or every department of life, a German requires forerunners. He must follow footsteps. He gleans; picks the brains of other people, profits by their mistakes and improves on their ideas.

I know nothing of the social history of Olevano—of its origin, so far as foreigners are concerned. It is the easiest and the flimsiest thing in the world to invent; there are so many analogies!

The first foreign resident of Olevano was a retired Anglo-Indian army officer with unblemished record, Major Frederick Potter. He came across the place on a trip from Rome, and took a fancy to it. Decent climate. Passable food. You could pick up a woodcock or two. He was accustomed to solitude anyhow, all his old friends being dead or buried, or scattered about the world. He had tried England for a couple of years and discovered that people there did not like being ordered about as they should be; they seemed to mind it less, at Olevano. He had always been something of a pioneer, and the mere fact of being the first "white man" in the place gave him a kind of fondness for it.

It was he, then, who discovered Olevano—Freddy Potter. We can see him living alone, wiry and whiskered and cantankerous, glorying in his solitude up to the fateful day when, to his infinite annoyance, a fellow-countryman turns up— Mr. Augustus Browne of London. Mr. Browne is a blameless personality who, enjoying indifferent health, brings an equally blameless old housekeeper with him. He is not a sportsman like Potter, but indulges in a pretty taste for landscape painting, with elaborate flowers and butterflies worked into the foreground. So they live, each in jealous seclusion, drinking tea at fixed hours, importing groceries from England, dressing for dinner, avoiding contact with the "natives" and, of course, pretending to be unaware of one another's existence.

As time goes on, their mutual distrust grows stronger. The Major has never forgiven that cockney for invading Olevano, his private domain, while Browne finds no words to express his disgust at Potter, who presumably calls himself a Briton and yet smokes those filthy cheroots in public (this was years and years ago). Why is the fellow skulking here, all by himself? Some hanky-panky with regimental money; every one knows how India plays the devil with a man's sense of right and wrong. And Potter is not long in making up his mind that this civilian has bolted to Olevano for reasons which will not bear investigation and is living in retirement, ten to one, under an assumed name. Browne! He really might have picked out a better one, while he was about it. That water-colour business—a blind, a red herring; the so-called lady companion——

The natives, meanwhile, observe with amazement the mutual conduct of two compatriots. They are known, far and wide, as "the madmen" till some bright spirit makes the discovery that they are not madmen at all, but only homicides hiding from justice; whereupon contempt is changed to grudging admiration.

Browne dies, after many years. His lady packs up and departs. The old Major's delight at being once more alone is of short duration; he falls ill and is entombed, his last days being embittered by the arrival of a party of German tourists who declare they have "discovered" this wonderful new spot, and threaten to bring more Teutons in their rear to participate in its joys.

They come, singly and in batches, and soon make Olevano uninhabitable to men of the Potter and Browne type. They keep the taverns open all night, sing boisterous choruses, kiss each other in the street "as if they were in their bedrooms," organise picnics in the woods, sketch old women sitting in old doorways, start a Verschoenerungsverein and indulge in a number of other antics which, from the local point of view, are held to be either coarse or childish. The natives, after watching their doings with critical interest, presently pronounce a verdict—a verdict to which the brightest spirits of the place give their assent—a verdict which, by the way, I have myself heard uttered.

"Those Englishmen"—thus it runs—"were at least assassins. These people are merely fools."

POSTSCRIPT—One thing has occurred of late which would hardly have happened were the Germans still in occupation of Olevano. At the central piazza is a fountain where the cattle drink and where, formerly, you could rest and glance down upon the country lying below—upon a piece of green landscape peering in upon the street. This little view was like a window, it gave an aerial charm to the place. They have now blocked it up with an ugly house. The beauty of the site is gone. It is surprising that local municipalities; however stupid, however corrupt, should not be aware of the damage done to their own interests when they permit such outrages. The Germans—were any of them still here—would doubtless have interfered en masse and stopped the building.

Something should be done about these reviewers.

There has followed me hither a bundle of press notices of a recent book of mine. They are favourable. I ought to be delighted. I happen to be annoyed.

What takes place in this absurd book? The three unities are preserved. A respectable but rather drab individual, a bishop, whose tastes and moods are fashioned to reflect those of the average drab reader, arrives at a new place and is described as being, among other things, peculiarly sensitive on the subject of women. He cannot bear flippant allusions to the sex. He has preserved a childlike faith in their purity, their sacred mission on earth, their refining influence upon the race. His friends call him old-fashioned and quixotic on this point. A true woman, he declares, can do no wrong. And this same man, towards the end of the book, watches how the truest woman in the place, the one whom he admires more than all the rest, his own cousin and a mother, calmly throws her legitimate husband over a cliff. He realises that he is "face to face with an atrocious and carefully planned murder." Such, however, has been the transformation of his mind during a twelve days' sojourn that he understands the crime, he pardons it, he approves it.

Can this wholesale change of attitude be brought about without a plot? Yet many of these reviewers discover no such thing in the book. "It possesses not the faintest shadow of a plot," says one of the most reputable of them. This annoys me.

I see no reason why a book should have a plot. In regard to this one, it would be nearer the truth to say that it is nothing but plot from beginning to end. How to make murder palatable to a bishop: that is the plot. How? You must unconventionalise him, and instil into his mind the seeds of doubt and revolt. You must shatter his old notions of what is right. It is the only way to achieve this result, and I would defy the critic to point to a single incident or character or conversation in the book which does not further the object in view. The good bishop soon finds himself among new influences; his sensations, his intellect, are assailed from within and without. Figures such as those in chapters 11, 19 and 35; the endless dialogue in the boat; the even more tedious happenings in the local law-court; the very externals—relaxing wind and fantastic landscape and volcanic phenomena—the jovial immoderation of everything and everybody: they foster a sense of violence and insecurity; they all tend to make the soil receptive to new ideas.

If that was your plot, the reviewer might say, you have hidden it rather successfully. I have certainly done my best to hide it. For although the personalities of the villain and his legal spouse crop up periodically, with ominous insistence, from the first chapter onwards, they are always swallowed up again. The reason is given in the penultimate chapter, where the critic might have found a résumé of my intentions and the key to this plot—to wit, that a murder under those particular circumstances is not only justifiable and commendable but—insignificant. Quite insignificant! Not worth troubling about. Hundreds of decent and honest folk are being destroyed every day; nobody cares tuppence; "one dirty blackmailer more or less—what does it matter to anybody"? There are so many more interesting things on earth. That is why the bishop—i.e. the reader—here discovers the crime to be a "contemptible little episode," and decides to "relegate it into the category of unimportant events." He was glad that the whole affair had remained in the background, so to speak, of his local experiences. It seemed appropriate. In the background: it seemed appropriate. That is the heart, the core, of the plot. And that is why all those other happenings find themselves pushed into the foreground.

I know full well that this is not the way to write an orthodox English novel. For if you hide your plot, how shall the critic be expected to see it? You must serve it on a tray; you must (to vary the simile) hit the nail on the head and ask him to be so good as to superintend the operation. That is the way to rejoice the cockles of his heart. He can then compare you to someone else who has also hit the nail on the head and with whose writings he happens to be familiar. You have a flavour of Dostoievsky minus the Dickens taint; you remind him of Flaubert or Walter Scott or somebody equally obscure; in short, you are in a condition to be labelled—a word, and a thing, which comes perilously near to libelling. If, to this description, he adds a short summary of your effort, he has done his duty. What more can he do? He must not praise overmuch, for that might displease some of his own literary friends. He must not blame overmuch, else how shall his paper survive? It lives on the advertisements of publishers and—say those persons, perhaps wisely—"if you ill-treat our authors, there's an end to our custom." Commercialism....

Which applies far less to literary criticism than to other kinds. Of most of the critics of music and art the best one can say is that there are hearty fellows among them who, with the requisite training, might one day become fit for their work. England is the home of the amateur in matters intellectual, the specialist in things material. No bootmaker would allow an unpractised beginner to hack his leather about in a jejune attempt to construct a pair of shoes. The other commodity, being less valuable than cowhide, may be entrusted to the hands of any 'prentice who cares to enliven our periodicals with his playful hieroglyphics. Criticism in England—snakes in Iceland.[15]

All alone, for a wonder, I climbed up to the sanctuary of St. Michael above Serrone, that solitary white speck visible from afar on the upper slopes of Mount Scalambra. It is a respectable walk, and would have been inconveniently warm but for the fact that I rose with the nightingales, reaching my destination at the very moment when the sun peered over the ridge of the mountain at its back. A delicious ramble in the dewy shade of morning, with ten minutes' rest on a wall at Serrone, talking to an old woman who wore those ponderous red ornaments designed, I suppose, to imitate coral.

I had hoped to meet at this hermitage some amiable and garrulous anchorite who would share my breakfast. It is the ideal place for such a life, and many are the mountain solitaries of this species I have known in Italy (mostly retired shepherds). There was he of Scanno—dead, I doubt not, by this time—that simple-hearted venerable with whom I whiled away the long evenings at the shrine of Sant' Egidio, gazing over the placid lake below, or up stream, at the dusky houses of Scanno theatrically ranged against their hill-side. I became his friend, once and for ever, after finding a wooden snuff-box he had lost—his only snuff-box; it lay at the edge of the path among thick shrubs, and he could hardly believe his eyes when he saw it again. One of my many strokes of luck! Once I found a purse—

The little structure here was barred and deserted. I had no company save a couple of ravens who, after assuring themselves, with that infernal cunning of theirs, that I carried no gun, became as friendly as could be expected of such solemn fowls. They are always in pairs—incurably monogamous; whereas the carrion crow, for reasons of its own, has a fondness for living in trios. This ménage à trois may have subtle advantages and seems to be a step in the direction of the truly social habits of the rook; it enables them to fight with more success against their enemies, the hawks, and fosters, likewise, a certain lightheartedness which the sententious raven lacks. No one who has watched the aerial antics of a triplet of carrion crows can deny them a sense of fun.

After an hour's contemplation of the beauties of nature I descended once more through that ilex grove to Serrone. And now it began to grow decidedly warm. The wide depression between this village and Olevano used to be timbered and is still known as la selva or la foresta. Vines now occupy the whole ground. If they had only left a few trees by the wayside! Walking along, I encountered a sportsman who said he was on the look-out for a hare. Always that hare! They might as well lie in wait for the Great Auk. Not long ago, an old visionary informed me that he had killed a hare beside the Ponte Milvio at Rome. Hares at Ponte Milvio! They reminded me of those partridges in Belgrave Square. In my younger days there was not a general in the British army who had not (1) shot partridges in Belgrave Square and (2) been the chosen lover of Queen Isabella of Spain....

Up to the castle, in the afternoon, for a final chat. We sit under the vine near the entrance of that decayed stronghold, while babies and hens scramble about the exposed rock; he talks, as usual, about the war. He can talk of nothing else. No wonder. One son is maimed for life; the other has been killed outright, and it looks as if no amount of ironmongery (medals, etc.) would ever atone for the loss. This happy land is full of affliction. Mourning everywhere, and hardships and bitterness and ruined homes. Vineyards are untilled, olives unpruned, for lack of labourers. It will take years to bring the soil back into its old state of productivity. One is pained to see decent folk suffering for a cause they fail to understand, for something that happens beyond their ken, something dim and distant—unintelligible to them as that Libyan expedition. None the less, he tells me, there is not a single deserter in Olevano. An old warrior-brood, these men of Latium....

Thence onward and upward, towards evening by that familiar path, for a second farewell visit to Giulio's farm. It is a happy homestead, an abode of peace, with ample rooms and a vine-wreathed terrace that overlooks the smiling valley to the south. A mighty bush of rosemary stands at the door. The mother is within, cooking the evening meal for her man and the elder boys who work in the fields so long as a shred of daylight flits about the sky. The little ones are already half asleep, tired with a long day's playing in the sunshine.

Here is my favourite, Alberto, an adorable cherub and the pickle of the family. I can see at a glance that he has been up to mischief. Alberto is incorrigible. No amount of paternal treatment will do him any good. He hammers nails into tables and into himself, he tumbles down from trees, he throws stones at the girls and cuts himself with knives and saws; he breaks things and loses things, and chases the hens about—disobeys all the time. Every day there is some fresh disaster and fresh chastisement. Two weeks ago he was all but run over by the big station motor—pulled out from the wheels in the nick of time; that scar across his forehead will remain for life, a memento of childish naughtiness. Alberto understands me thoroughly. He is glad to see me.

But a certain formality must be gone through; every time we meet there is a moment of shy distrust, while the ice has to be broken afresh—he must assure himself that I have not changed since our last encounter. Everything, apparently, is in order to-night, for he curls up comfortably on my knee and is soon fast asleep, all his little tragedies forgotten.

"It appears you like children," says the mother.

"I like this one, because he is never out of trouble. He reminds me of myself. I shall steal him one of these days, and carry him off to Rome. From there we will walk on foot to Brindisi, along an old track called the Via Appia. It will require two of three years, for I mean to stop a day, or perhaps a week, at every single tavern along the road. Then I will write a book about it; a book to make myself laugh with, when I am grown too old for walking."

"Giulio is big enough."

"I'll wait."

No chance of undertaking such a trip in these times of war, when a foreigner is liable to be arrested at every moment. Besides, how far would one get, with Giulio? Nevermore to Brindisi! As far as Terracina; possibly even to Formia. There, at Formia, we would remain for the rest of our natural lives, if the wine at the Albergo della Quercia is anything like what it used to be; there, at Formia, we would pitch our tent, enacting every day, or perhaps twice a day, our celebrated Faun-and-Silenus entertainment for the diversion of the populace. I have not forgotten Giulio's besetting sin. How nearly he made me exceed the measure of sobriety at Rojate!…

Night descends. I wander homewards. Under the trees of the driving-road fireflies are dancing; countrymen return in picturesque groups, with mules and children, from their work far afield; that little owl, the aluco, sits in the foliage overhead, repeating forever its plaintive note. The lights of Artena begin to twinkle.

This Artena, they say, had such a sorry reputation for crime and brigandage that the authorities at one time earnestly considered the proposition of razing it to the ground. Then they changed their minds. It seemed more convenient to have evil-doers all collected into one place than scattered about the country. To judge by the brightness of the lamps at this distance of twelve miles, the brigands have evidently spared no expense in the matter of street-illumination.

And now the lights of Segni station are visible, down in the malarious valley, where the train passes from Rome to Naples. Every night I have beheld them from my window; every night they tinged my thoughts with a soft sadness, driving them backwards, northwards—creating a link between present and past. Now, for the last time, I see them and recall those four journeys along that road; four, out of at least a hundred; only four, but in what rare company!

Valmontone

Back to Valmontone.

At Zagarolo, where you touch the Rome-Naples line, I found there was no train to this place for several hours. A merchant of straw hats from Tuscany, a pert little fellow, was in the same predicament; he also had some business to transact at Valmontone. How get there? No conveyance being procurable on account of some local fair or festival, we decided to walk. A tiresome march, in the glow of morning. The hatter, after complaining more or less articulately for an hour, was reduced to groans and almost tears; his waxed moustache began to droop; he vowed he was not accustomed to this kind of exercise. Would I object to carrying his bundle of hats for him? I objected so vigorously that he forthwith gave up all hope. But I allowed him to rest now and then by the wayside. I also offered him, gratis, the use of a handful of my choicest Tuscan blasphemies,[16] for which he was much obliged. Most of them were unfamiliar to him. He had been brought up by his mother, he explained. They seemed to make his burden lighter.

Despite wondrous stretches of golden broom, this is rather a cheerless country, poorly cultivated, and still bearing the traces of mediaeval savagery and insecurity. It looks unsettled. One would like to sit down here and let the centuries roll by, watching the tramp of Roman legions and Papal mercenaries and all that succession of proud banners which have floated down this ancient Via Labiena.

That rock-like structure, visible in the morning hours from Olevano, is a monstrous palace containing, among other things, a training school for carbineers. Attached thereto is a church whose interior has an unusual shape, the usual smell, and a tablet commemorating a visit from Pius IX.

There is a beautiful open space up here, with wide views over the surrounding country. It gives food for thought. What an ideal spot, one says, for the populace to frequent on the evenings of these sultry days! It is empty at that hour, utterly deserted. Now why do they prefer to jostle each other in the narrow, squalid and stuffy lane lower down? One would like to know the reason for this preference. I enquired, and was told that the upper place was not sufficiently well-lighted. The explanation is not wholly convincing, for they have the lighting arrangements in their own hands, and could easily afford the outlay. It may be that they like to remain close to the shops and to each other's doors for conversational purposes, since it is a fact that, socially speaking, the more restricted the area, the more expansive one grows. We broaden out, in proportion as the environment contracts. A psychological reason....

I leaned in the bright sunshine over the parapet of this terrace, looking at Artena near-by. It resembled, now, a cluster of brown grapes clinging to the hillside. An elderly man, clean-shaven, with scarred and sallow face, drew nigh and, perceiving the direction of my glance, remarked gravely:

"Artena."

"Artena," I repeated.

He extracted half a toscano cigar from his waistcoat pocket, and began to smoke with great gusto. A man of means, I concluded, to be able to smoke at this hour of an ordinary week-day. He was warmly dressed, with flowing brown tie and opulent vest and corduroy trousers. His feet were encased in rough riding-boots. Some peasant proprietor, very likely, who rode his own horses. Was he going to tell me anything of interest about Artena? Presumably not. He said never another word, but continued to smile at me rather wearily. I tried to enliven the conversation by pointing to a different spot on the hills and observing:

"Segni."

"Segni," he agreed.

His cigar had gone out, as toscanos are apt to do. He applied a match, and suddenly remarked:

"Velletri."

"Velletri."

We were not making much progress. A good many sites were visible from here, and at this rate of enumeration the sun might well set on our labours.

"How about all those deserters?" I inquired.

There was a fair number of them, he said. Young fellows from other provinces who find their way hither across country, God knows how. It was a good soil for deserters—brushwood, deep gullies, lonely stretches of land, and, above all, la tradizione. The tradition, he explained, of that ill-famed forest of Velletri, now extirpated. The deserters were nearly all children—the latest conscripts; a grown man seldom deserts, not because he would not like to do so, but because he has more "judgment" and can weigh the risks. The roads were patrolled by police. A few murders had taken place; yes, just a few murders; one or two stupid people who resented their demands for money or food—

He broke off with another weary smile.

"You have had malaria," I suggested.

"Often."

The fact was patent, not only from his sallow face, but from the peculiar manner....

They brought in a deserter that very afternoon. He lay groaning at the bottom of a cab, having broken his leg in jumping down from somewhere. The rest of the conveyance was filled to overflowing with carbineers. A Sicilian, they said. The whole populace followed the vehicle uphill, reverently, as though attending a funeral. "He is little," said a woman, referring either to his size or his age.

An hour later there was a discussion anent the episode in the fashionable café of Valmontone. A citizen, a well-dressed man, possibly a notary, put the case for United Italy, for intervention against Germany, for military discipline and the shooting of cowardly deserters, into a few phrases so clear, so convincing, that there was a general burst of approval. Then another man said:

"I hate those Sicilians; I have good personal reasons for hating them. But no Sicilian fears death. If they are not brilliant soldiers, they certainly make first-class assassins, which is only another branch of the same business. This boy deserts not because he is afraid of death, but because he still owes a debt. He feels he ought to do something to repay his parents who nursed him when he was a child, and not be sacrificed to that kidnapping camorra of blackguards out yonder"—and he pointed with his thumb, spitting contemptuously the while, in the direction of Rome.

Nobody had any comment to make on this speech. Not a word of protest was raised. The man was entitled to an opinion like everybody else, and might even have obtained his share of approval had the victim been a native. He was only a Sicilian—an outsider. What is one to say of this patriarchal, or parochial, attitude? The enlargement of Italy's boundaries—Albania, Cyrenaica, Asia Minor and so forth—is an ideal that few Italians bother their heads about. They are not sufficiently dense—not yet.[17] To found a world-empire like the British or Roman calls for a certain bullet-headed crassness. One has only to look at the Germans, who have been trying to do so for some time past. That collecting mania.... One single boy who collects postage stamps can infect his whole school with the complaint, and make them all jealous of his fine specimens. England has been collecting, for many centuries, islands and suchlike; she is paying the penalty of her acquisitive mania. She has infected others with the craze and cannot help incurring their envy, seeing that they are now equally acquisitive, but less fortunate. All the good specimens are gone!

That Pergola tavern deserves its name, the courtyard being overhung with green vines and swelling clusters of grapes. The host is a canny old boy, up to any joke and any devilry, I should say. He had already taken a fancy to me on my first visit, for I cured his daughter Vanda of a raging toothache by the application of glycerine and carbolic acid. We went into his cellar, a dim tunnel excavated out of the soft tufa, from whose darkest and chilliest recesses he drew forth a bottle of excellent wine—it might have lain on a glacier, so cold it was. How thoughtful of Providence to deposit this volcanic stuff within a stone's-throw of your dining-table! Nobody need ice his wine at the Pergola.

After a capital repast I sallied forth late at night and walked, striving to resemble a rich English tourist who has lost his way, along the lonely road to Artena, in order to be assassinated by the deserters or, failing that, to hear at least what these fellows have got to say for themselves. My usual luck! Not a deserter was in sight.

Of my sleeping accommodation with certain old ladies, of what happened to their little dog and of other matters trivial to the verge of inanity, I may discourse upon the occasion of some later visit to Valmontone. For this, the second, was by no means the last. Meanwhile, we proceed southwards.

Sant' Agata, Sorrento

Siren-Land revisited….

A delightful stroll, yesterday, with a wild youngster from the village of Torco—what joy to listen to analphabetics for a change: they are indubitably the salt of the earth—down that well-worn track to Crapolla, only to learn that my friend Garibaldi, the ancient fisherman, the genius loci, has died in the interval; thence by boat to the lonely beach of Recomone (sadly noting, as we passed, that the rock-doves at the Grotto delle Palumbe are now all extirpated), where, for the sake of old memories, I indulged in a bathe and then came across an object rare in these regions, a fragment of grey Egyptian granite, relic of some pagan temple and doubtless washed up here in a wintry gale; thence, for a little light refreshment, to Nerano; thence to that ill-famed "House of the Spirits" where my Siren-Land was begun in the company of one who feared no spirits—victim, already, of this cursed war, but then a laughter-loving child—and down to the bay and promontory of Ierate, there to make the unwelcome discovery that certain hideous quarrying operations on the neighbouring hill have utterly ruined the charm of this once secluded site; thence laboriously upwards, past that line of venerable goat-caves, to the summit of Mount San Costanzo.

Nothing has changed. The bay of Naples lay at my feet as of old, flooded in sunshine.

There is a small outdoor cistern here. Peering into its darkness through an aperture in the roof, I noticed that there was water at the bottom; out of the water projected a stone; on the stone, a prisoner for life, sat the most disconsolate lizard imaginable. It must have tumbled through the chink, during some scuffle with a companion, into this humid cell, swum for refuge to that islet and there remained, feeding on the gnats which live in such places. I observed that its tail had grown to an inordinate length—from disuse, very likely; from lack of the usual abrasion against shrubs and stones. An unenviable fate for one of these restless and light-loving creatures, never again to see the sun; to live and die down here, all alone in the dank gloom, chained, as it were, to a few inches of land amid a desolation of black water.

It took my thoughts back to what I saw two days ago while climbing in the torrid hour of noon up that shadeless path where the vanilla-scented orchids grow—the path which runs from Sant' Elia past the shattered Natural Arch to Fontanella. Here, at the hottest turning of the road, sat a woman in great distress. Beside her was a pink pig she had been commissioned to escort down to the farm of Sant' Elia. This beast was suffering hellish torments from the heat and vainly endeavouring, with frenzied grunts of despair, to excavate for itself a hollow in the earth under a thinly clothed myrtle bush. I told the woman of shade lower down. She said she knew about it, but the pig—the pig refused to move! It had been engaged upon this hopeless occupation, without a moment's respite, for an hour or more; nothing would induce it to proceed a step further;

it had plainly made up its mind to find shelter here from the burning rays, or die. And of shelter there was none.

What would not this pig (I now thought) have given to be transported into the lizard's cool aquatic paradise; and the lizard, into that scorching sunlight!...

It was not to muse upon the miseries of the animal creation that I have revisited these shores. I came to puzzle once more over the site of that far-famed Athene temple which gave its name to the whole promontory. Now, after again traversing the ground with infinite pleasure, I fail to find any reason for changing what I wrote years ago in a certain pamphlet which some scholar, glancing through these pages and anxious to explore for himself a spot of such celebrity in ancient days, is so little likely to see that he may not be sorry if I here recapitulate its arguments. Others will be well advised to pass over what follows.

Let me begin by saying that the temple, in every probability, stood at the Punta Campanella facing Capri, the actual headland of the Sorrentine peninsula, where—apart from every other kind of evidence—you may pick up to this day small terra-cotta figures of Athene, made presumably to be carried away as keepsakes by visitors to the shrine.

Now for alternative suggestions.

Strabo tells us that the temple was placed on the akron of the promontory; that is, the summit of Mount San Costanzo where we are now standing. (He elsewhere describes it as being "on the straits.") This summit is nearly 500 metres above the sea-level, and here no antique building seems ever to have been erected. No traces of old life are visible save some fragments of Roman pottery which may have found their way up in early Byzantine days, even as modern worshippers carry up the ephemeral vessels popularly called "caccavelle"[18] and scatter them about. With the exception of one fragment of white Pentelic marble, no materials of an early period have been incorporated into the masonry of the little chapel or the walls of the fields below. It is incredible that no vestige of a structure like the Athene temple should remain on a spot of this kind, so favourably situated as regards immunity from depredations, owing to its isolated and exalted position. The rock-surface around the summit has not undergone that artificial levelling which an edifice of this importance would necessitate; the terrace is of mediaeval construction, as can be seen by its supporting walls. No doubt the venerable Christian sanctuary there has been frequently repaired and modified; on the terrace-level to the south can be seen the foundations of an earlier chapel, and the slopes are littered with broken bricks, Sorrentine tufa, and old battuto floors. But there is no trace of antique workmanship or material, nor has the rocky path leading up to the shrine been demarcated with chisel-cuts in the ancient fashion. The sister-summit of La Croce is equally unproductive of classical relics.

We must therefore conclude that Strabo was mistaken. And why not? His accounts of many parts of the Roman world are surprisingly accurate, but, according to Professor Pais, "of Italy Strabo seems to have known merely the road which leads from Brindisi to Rome, the road between Rome and Naples and Pozzuoli, and the coast of Etruria between Rome and Populonia." If so, he probably saw no more of the district than can be seen from Naples. He attributes the foundation of this Athene temple to Odysseus: statements of such a kind make one wonder whether the earlier portions of his lost history were more critical than other old treatises which have survived.

So much for Strabo.

Seduced by a modern name, which means nothing more or less than "a temple"—strong evidence, surely—I was inclined to locate the Athene shrine at a spot called Ierate (marked also as Ieranto on some maps, and popularly pronounced Ghiérate the Greek aspirate still surviving) which lies a mile or more eastwards of the Punta Campanella and faces south. "Hieron," I thought: that settles it. You may guess I was not a little proud of this discovery, particularly when it turned out that an ancient building actually did stand there— on the southern slope, namely, of the miniature peninsula which juts into Ierate bay. Here I found fragments of antique bricks, tegulae bipedales, amphoras, pottery of the lustrous Sorrentine ware—Surrentina bibis?—pavements of opus signinum, as well as one large Roman paving flag of the type that is found on the road between Termini and Punta Campanella. (How came this stone here? Did the old road from Stabiae Athene temple go round the promontory and continue as far as Ierate along the southern slope of San Costanzo hill? No road could pass there now; deforestation has denuded the mountain-side of its soil, laying bare the grey rock—a condition at which its mediaeval name of Mons Canutarius already hints.) Well, a more careful examination of the site has convinced me that I was wrong. No temple of this magnificence can have stood here, but only a Roman villa—one of the many pleasure-houses which dotted these shores under the Empire.

So much for myself.

PEUTINGER'S CHART

Showing ancient road rounding the headland and terminating at "Templum Minervae."

None the less—and this is a really curious point—an inspection of Peutinger's Tables seems to bear out my original theory of a temple at Ierate. For the structure is therein marked not at the Punta Campanella but, approximately, at Ierate itself, facing south, with the road from Stabiae over Surrentum rounding the promontory and terminating at the temple's threshold. Capri and the Punta Campanella are plainly drawn, though not designated by name. Much as I should like my first speculation to be proved correct on the evidence of this old chart of A.D. 226, I fear both of us are mistaken.

So much for Peutinger's Tables.

Beloch makes a further confusion in regard to the local topography. He says that the "three-peaked rock" which Eratosthenes describes as separating the gulfs of Cumae and Paestum (that is, of Naples and Salerno) is Mount San Costanzo. I do not understand Beloch falling into this error, for the old geographer uses the term skopelos, which is never applied to a mountain of this size, but to cliffs projecting upon the sea. Moreover, the landmark is there to this day. I have not the slightest doubt that Eratosthenes meant the pinnacle of Ierate, which is three-peaked in a remarkably, and even absurdly, conspicuous manner, both when viewed from the sea and from the land (from the chapel of S. M. della Neve, for instance).

Now this projecting cliff of three peaks—they are called, respectively, Montalto, Ierate, and Mortella; Ierate for short—is not the actual boundary between the two gulfs; not by a mile or more. No; but from certain points it might well be mistaken for it. The ancients had no charts like ours, and the world in consequence presented itself differently to their senses; even Strabo, says Bunbury, "was so ignorant of the general form and configuration of the North African coast as to have no clear conception of the great projection formed by the Carthaginian territory and the deep bay to the east of it"; and, coasting along the shore line, this triple-headed skopelos, behind which lies the inlet of Ierate, might possibly be mistaken for the turning-point into the gulf of Naples. So it looks when viewed from the S.E. of Capri; so also from the Siren islets—a veritable headland.

So much for Beloch and Eratosthenes.

To sum up: Strabo is wrong in saying that the temple of Athene stood on the summit of Mount San Costanzo; I was wrong in thinking that this temple lay at Ierate; Peutinger's Chart is wrong in figuring the structure on the south side of the Sorrentine peninsula; Beloch is wrong in identifying the skopelos trikoruphos of Eratosthenes with Mount San Costanzo; Eratosthenes is wrong in locating his rock at the boundary between the two gulfs.

The shrine of Athene lay doubtless at Campanella, whose crag is of sufficient altitude to justify Roman poets like Statius in their descriptions of its lofty site. So great a number of old writers concur in this opinion—Donnorso, Persico, Giannettasio, Mazzella, Anastasio, Capaccio—that their testimony would alone be overwhelming, had these men been a little more careful as to what they called a "temple." Capasso, the acutest modern scholar of these regions, places it "in the neighbourhood of the Punta Campanella." Professor Pais, in 1900, wrote a paper on this "Atene Siciliana" which I have not seen. The whole question is discussed in Filangieri's recent history of Massa (1908-1910). It also occurs to me that Strabo's term akron may mean an extremity or point projecting into the sea (a sense in which Homer used it), and be applicable, therefore, to the Punta Campanella.

Rome

Here we are.

That mysterious nocturnal incident peculiar to Rome has already occurred—sure sign that the nights are growing sultry. It happens about six times in the course of every year, during the hot season. You may read about it in the next morning's paper which records how some young man, often of good family and apparently in good health, was seen behaving in the most inexplicable fashion at the hour of about 2 a.m.; jumping, that is, in a state of Adamitic nudity, into some public fountain. It goes on to say that the culprit was pursued by the police, run to earth, and carried to such-and-such a hospital, where his state of mind is to be investigated. Will our rising generation, it gravely adds, never learn the most elementary rules of decency?

If I have not had the curiosity to inquire at one of these establishments what has been the result of the medical examination, it is because I will wager my last shirt that the invalid's health leaves nothing to be desired. The genesis of the affair, I take it, is this. He is in bed, suffering from the heat. Sleep refuses to come. He has already passed half the night in agony, tossing on his couch during those leaden hours when not a breath of air is astir. In any other town he would submit to the torture, knowing it to be irremediable. But Rome is the city of fountains. It is they who are responsible for this sad lapse. Their sound is clear by day; after midnight, when the traffic has died down, it waxes thunderous. He hears it through the window—hears it perforce, since the streets are ringing with that music, and you cannot close your ears. He listens, growing hotter and more restless every moment. He thinks…. That splash of waters! Those frigid wavelets and cascades! How delicious to bathe his limbs, if only for a moment, in their bubbling wetness; he is parched with heat, and at this hour of the night, he reflects, there will not be a soul abroad in the square. So he hearkens to the seductive melody, conjuring up the picture of that familiar fountain; he remembers its moistened rim and basin all alive with jolly turmoil; he sees the miniature cataracts tumbling down in streaks of glad confusion, till the longing grows too strong to be controlled.

The thing must be done.

Next day he finds a handful of old donkeys solemnly inquiring into his state of mind….

I can sympathise with that state of mind, having often undergone the same purgatory. My room at present happens to be fairly cool; it looks north, and the fountain down below, audible at this moment, has not yet tempted me to any breach of decorum. Night is quiet here, save for the squeakings of some strange animals in the upper regions of the neighbouring Pantheon; they squeak night and day, and one would take them to be bats, were it not that bats are supposed to be on the wing after sunset. There are no mosquitoes in Rome—none worth talking about. It is well. For mosquitoes have a deplorable habit of indulging in a second meal, an early breakfast, at about four a.m.—a habit more destructive to slumber than that regular and legitimate banquet of theirs. No mosquitoes, and few flies. It is well.

It is more than merely well. For the mosquito, after all, when properly fed, goes to bed like a gentleman and leaves you alone, whereas that insatiable and petty curiousness of the fly condemns you to a never-ending succession of anguished reflex movements. What a malediction are those flies; how repulsive in life and in death: not to be touched by human hands! Their every gesture is an obscenity, a calamity. Fascinated by the ultra-horrible, I have watched them for hours on end, and one of the most cherished projects of my life is to assemble, in a kind of anthology, all the invectives that have been hurled since the beginning of literature against this loathly dirt-born insect, this living carrion, this blot on the Creator's reputation—and thereto add a few of my own. Lucian, the pleasant joker, takes the fly under his protection. He says, among other things, that "like an honest man, it is not ashamed to do in public what others only do in private." I must say, if we all followed the fly's example in this aspect, life would at last be worth living....

Morning sleep is out of the question, owing to the tram-cars whose clangour, both here and in Florence, must be heard to be believed. They are fast rendering these towns uninhabitable. Can folks who cherish a nuisance of this magnitude compare themselves, in point of refinement, with those old Hellenic colonists who banished all noises from their city? Nevermore! Why this din, this blocking of the roadways and general unseemliness? In order that a few bourgeois may be saved the trouble of using their legs. And yet we actually pride ourselves on these detestable things, as if they were inventions to our credit. "We made them," we say. Did we? It is not we who make them. It is they who make us, who give us our habits of mind and body, our very thoughts; it is these mechanical monsters who control our fates and drive us along whither they mean us to go. We are caught in their cog-wheels—in a process as inevitable as the revolution of the planets. No use lamenting a cosmic phenomenon! Were it otherwise, I should certainly mope myself into a green melancholy over the fact, the most dismal fact on earth, that brachycephalism is a Mendelian dominant.[19] No use lamenting. True.

But the sage will reserve to himself the right of cursing. Those morning hours, therefore, when I would gladly sleep but for the tram-car shrieking below, are devoted to the malediction of all modern progress, wherein I include, with fine impartiality, every single advancement in culture which happens to lie between my present state and that comfortable cavern in whose shelter I soon see myself ensconced as of yore, peacefully sucking somebody's marrow while my women, round the corner, are collecting a handful of acorns for my dessert.... The telephone, that diabolic invention! It might vex a man if his neighbour possessed a telephone and he none; how would it be, if neither of them had it? We can hardly realise, now, the blissful quietude of the pre-telephone epoch. And the telegraph and the press! They have huddled mankind together into undignified and unhygienic proximity; we seem to be breathing each other's air. We know what everybody is doing, in every corner of the earth; we are told what to think, and to say, and to do. Your paterfamilias, in pre-telegraph days, used to hammer out a few solid opinions of his own on matters political and otherwise. He no longer employs his brain for that purpose. He need only open his morning paper and in it pours—the oracle of the press, that manufactory of synthetic fustian, whose main object consists in accustoming humanity to attach importance to the wrong things. It furnishes him with opinions ready made, overnight, by some Fleet Street hack at so much a column, after a little talk with his fellows over a pint of bad beer at the Press Club. He has been told what to say—yesterday, for instance, it was some lurid balderdash about a steam-roller and how the Kaiser is to be fed on dog biscuits at Saint Helena—he has been "doped" by the editor, who gets the tip—and out he goes! unless he take it—from the owner, who is waiting for a certain emolument from this or that caucus, and trims his convictions to their taste. That is what the Press can do. It vitiates our mundane values. It enables a gang to fool the country. It cretinises the public mind. The time may come when no respectable person will be seen touching a daily, save on the sly. Newspaper reading will become a secret vice. As such, I fear, its popularity is not likely to wane. Having generated, by means of sundry trite reflections of this nature, an enviable appetite for breakfast, I dress and step out of doors to where, at a pleasant table, I can imbibe some coffee and make my plans for loafing through the day.

Hot, these morning hours. Shadeless the streets. The Greeks, the Romans, the Orientals knew better than to build wide roadways in a land of sunshine.

There exists an old book or pamphlet entitled "Napoli senza sole"—Naples without sun. It gives instructions, they say (for I have never seen it) how foot passengers may keep for ever in the shade at all hours of the day; how they may reach any point of the town from another without being forced to cross the squares, those dazzling patches of sunlight. The feat could have been accomplished formerly even in Rome, which was always less umbrageous than Naples. It is out of the question nowadays. You must do as the Romans do—walk slowly and use the tram whenever possible.

That is what I purpose to do. There is a line which will take me direct to the Milvian bridge, where I mean to have a bathe, and then a lunch at the restaurant across the water. Its proprietor is something of a brigand; so am I, at a pinch. It is "honour among thieves," or "diamond cut diamond."

Already a few enthusiasts are gathered here, on the glowing sands. But the water is still cold; indeed, the Tiber is never too warm for me. If you like it yet more chill, you must walk up to where the Aniene discharges its waves whose temperature, at this season, is of a kind to tickle up a walrus.

Whether it be due to the medley of races or to some other cause, there is a singular variety of flesh-tints among the bathers here. I wish my old friend Dr. Bowles could have seen it; we used to be deeply immersed, both of us, in the question of the chromatophores, I observing their freakish behaviour in the epidermis of certain frogs, while he studied their action on the human skin and wrote an excellent little paper on sunburn—a darker problem than it seems to be. [20]

These men and boys do not grow uniformly sunburnt. They display so many different colour-shades on their bodies that an artist would be delighted with the effect. From that peculiar milky hue which, by reason of some pigment, contrives to resist the rays, the tints diverge; the reds, the scarcer group, traversing every gradation from pale rose to the ruddiest of copper—not excluding that strange marbled complexion concerning which I cannot make up my mind whether it be a beauty or a defect; while the xanthous tones, the yellows, pass through silvery gold and apricot and café au lait to a duskiness approaching that of the negro. At this season the skins are still white. Your artist must come later—not later, however, than the end of August, for on the first of September the bathing, be the weather never so warm, is officially, and quite suddenly, at an end. Tiber water is declared to be "unhealthy" after that date, and liable to give you fever; a relic of the days when the true origin of malaria was unknown.

A glance at the papers is sufficient to prove that bathing has not yet begun in earnest. No drowning accidents, up to the present. Later on they come thick and fast. For this river, with its rapid current and vindictive swirling eddies, is dangerous to young swimmers; it grips them in its tawny coils and holds them fast, often within a few yards of friend or parent who listens, powerless to help, to the victim's cries of anguish and sees his arm raised imploringly out of that serpent-like embrace. So it hurries him to destruction, only to be fished up later in a state, as the newspapers will be careful to inform us, of "incipient putrefaction."

A murderous flood....

That hoary, trickling structure—that fountain which has forgotten to be a fountain, so dreamily does the water ooze through obstructive mosses and emerald growths that dangle in drowsy pendants, like wet beards, from its venerable lips—that fountain un-trimmed, harmonious, overhung by ancient ilexes: where shall a more reposeful spot be found? Doubly delicious, after the turmoil and glistening sheen by the river-bank. For the foliage of the oaks and sycamores is such that it creates a kind of twilight, and all around lies the tranquillity of noon. Here, on the encircling stone bench, you may idle through the sultry hours conversing with some favourite disciple while the cows trample up to drink amid moist gurglings and tail-swishings. They gaze at you with gentle eyes, they blow their sweet breath upon your cheek, and move sedately onward. The Villa Borghese can be hushed, at such times, in a kind of enchantment.

"You never told me why you come to Italy."

"In order," I reply, "to enjoy places like this."

"But listen. Surely you have fountains in your own country?"

"None quite so golden-green."

"Ah, it wants cleaning, doesn't it?"

"Lord, no!" I say; but only to myself. One should never pass for an imbecile, if one can help it.

Aloud I remark:—

"Let me try to set forth, however droll it may sound, the point of view of a certain class of people, supposing they exist, who might think that this particular fountain ought never to be cleaned"—and there ensued a discussion, lasting about half an hour, in the course of which I elaborated, artfully and progressively, my own thesis, and forged, in the teeth of some lively opposition, what struck me as a convincing argument in favour of leaving the fountain alone.

"Then that is why you come to Italy. On account of a certain fountain, which ought never to be cleaned."

"I said on account of places like this. And I ought to have added, on account of moments such as these."

"Are those your two reasons?"

"Those are my two reasons."

"Then you have thought about it before?"

"Often."

One should never pass for an imbecile, if one can help it.

"But listen. Surely it is sometimes two o'clock in the afternoon, in your country?"

"I used that word moment in a pregnant sense," I reply. "Pregnant: when something is concealed or enclosed within. What is enclosed within this moment? Our friendly conversation."

"But listen. Surely folks can converse in your country?"

"They can talk."

"I begin to understand why you come here. It is that difference, which is new to me, between conversing and talking. Is the difference worth the long journey?"

"Not to everybody, I daresay."

"Why to you?"

"Why to me? I must think about it."

One should never pass for an imbecile, if one can help it.

"What is there to think about? You said you had thought about it already.... Perhaps there are other reasons?"

"There may be."

"There may be?"

"There must be. Are you satisfied?"

"Ought I to be satisfied before I have learnt them?"

"I find you rather fatiguing this afternoon. Did you hear about that murder in Trastevere last night and how the police——"

"But listen. Surely you can answer a simple question. Why do you come to Italy...?"

Why does one come here?

A periodical visit to this country seems an ordinary and almost automatic proceeding—a part of one's regular routine, as natural as going to the barber or to church. Why seek for reasons? They are so hard to find. One tracks them to their lair and lo! there is another one lurking in the background, a reason for a reason.

The craving to be in contact with beauty and antiquity, the desire for self-expression, for physical well-being under that drenching sunshine, which while it lasts, one curses lustily; above all, the pleasure of memory and reconstruction at a distance. Yes; herein lies, methinks, the secret; the reason for the reason. Reconstruction at a distance.... For a haze of oblivion is formed by lapse of time and space; a kindly haze which obliterates the thousand fretting annoyances wherewith the traveller's path in every country is bestrewn. He forgets them; forgets that weltering ocean of unpleasantness and remembers only its sporadic islets—those moments of calm delight or fiercer joy which he would fain hold fast for ever. He does not come here on account of a certain fountain which ought never to be cleaned.[21] He comes for the sake of its mirage, that sunny phantom which will rise up later, out of some November fog in another land. Italy is a delightful place to remember, to think and talk about. And is it not the same with England? Let us go there as a tourist—only as a tourist. How attractive one finds its conveniences, and even its conventionalities, provided one knows, for an absolute certainty, that one will never be constrained to dwell among them.

What lovely things one could say about England, in Timbuktu!

Rome is not only the most engaging capital in Europe, it is unusually heterogeneous in regard to population. The average Parisian will assure you that his family has lived in that town from time immemorial. It is different here. There are few Romans discoverable in Rome, save across the Tiber. Talk to whom you please, you will soon find that either he or his parents are immigrants. The place is filled with hordes of employees—many thousands of them, high and low, from every corner of the provinces; the commoner sort, too, the waiters, carpenters, plasterers, masons, painters, coachmen, all the railway folk—they are hardly ever natives. Your Roman of the lower classes does not relish labour. He can do a little amateurish shop-keeping, he is fairly good as a cook, but his true strength, as he frankly admits, consists in eating and drinking. That is as it should be. It befits the tone of a metropolis that outsiders shall do its work. That undercurrent of asperity is less noticeable here than in many towns of the peninsula. There is something of the grande dame in Rome, a flavour of old-world courtesy. The inhabitants are better-mannered than the Parisians; a workday crowd in Rome is as well-dressed as a Sunday crowd in Paris. And over all hovers a gentle weariness.

The city has undergone orgies of bloodshed and terror. Think only, without going further back, of that pillage by the Spanish and German soldiery under Bourbon; half a year's pandemonium. And all those other mediaeval scourges, epidemics and floods and famines. That sirocco, the worst of many Italian varieties: who shall calculate its debilitating effect upon the stamina of the race? Up to quite a short time ago, moreover, the population was malarious; older records reek of malaria; that, assuredly, will leave its mark upon the inhabitants for years to come. And the scorching Campagna beyond the walls, that forbidden land in whose embrace the city lies gasping, flame-encircled, like the scorpion in the tale....

A well-known scholar, surveying Rome with the mind's eye, is so impressed with its "eternal" character that he cannot imagine this site having ever been occupied otherwise than by a city. To him it seems inevitable that these walls must always have stood where now they stand—must have risen, he suggests, out of the earth, unaided by human hands. Yet somebody laid the foundation-stones, once upon a time; somebody who lived under conditions quite different from those that supervened. For who—not five thousand, but, say, five hundred years ago—who would have thought of building a town on a spot like this? None but a crazy despot, some moonstruck Oriental such as the world has known, striving to impress his dreams upon a recalcitrant nature. No facilities for trade or commerce, no scenic beauty of landscape, no harbour, no defence against enemies, no drinking water, no mineral wealth, no food-supplying hinterland, no navigable river—a dangerous river, indeed, a perpetual menace to the place—every drawback, or nearly so, which a town may conceivably possess, and all of them huddled into a fatally unhealthy environment, compressed in a girdle of fire and poison. Human ingenuity has obviated them so effectually, so triumphantly that, were green pastures not needful to me as light and air, I, for one, would nevermore stray beyond those ancient portals....

The country visits you here. It comes in the wake of that evening breeze which creeps about with stealthy feet, winding its way into the most secluded courtyards and sending a sudden shiver through the frail bamboos that stand beside your dinner-table in some heated square. Then the zephyr departs mysteriously as it came, and leaves behind a great void—a torrid vacuum which is soon filled up by the honey-sweet fragrance of hay and aromatic plants. Every night this balsamic breath invades the town, filling its streets with ambrosial suggestions. It is one of the charms of Rome at this particular season; quite a local speciality, for the phenomenon could never occur if the surrounding regions were covered with suburbs or tilth or woodland—were aught save what they are: a desert whose vegetation of coarse herbage is in the act of withering. The Campagna once definitely dried, this immaterial feast is at an end.

I am glad never to have discovered anyone, native or foreign, who has been aware of the existence of this nocturnal emanation; glad because it corroborates a theory of mine, to wit, that mankind is forgetting the use of its nose; and not only of nose, but of eyes and ears and all other natural appliances which help to capture and intensify the simple joys of life. We all know the civilised, the industrial eye—how atrophied, how small and formless and expressionless it has become. The civilised nose, it would seem, degenerates in the other direction. Like the cultured potato or pumpkin, it swells in size. The French are civilised and, if we may judge by old engravings (what else are we to take as guide, seeing that the skull affords some criterion as to shape but not size of nose?) they certainly seem to accentuate this organ in proportion as they neglect its use. Parisians, it strikes me, are running to nose; they wax more rat-like every day. Here is a little problem for anthropologists. There may be something, after all, in the condition of Paris life which fosters the development of this peeky, rodential countenance. Perfumery, and what it implies? There are scent-shops galore in the fashionable boulevards, whereas I defy you to show me a single stationer. Maupassant knew them fairly well, and one thinks of that story of his:—

"Le parfum de Monsieur?"
"La verveine...." [22]

Speaking of the French, I climbed those ninety odd stairs the other day to announce my arrival in Italy to my friend Mrs. N., who, being vastly busy at that moment and on no account to be disturbed, least of all by a male, sent word to say that I might wait on the terrace or in that microscopic but well-equipped library of hers. I chose the latter, and there browsed upon "Emaux et Camées" and the "Fleurs du Mal" which happened, as was meet and proper, to lie beside each other.

Strange reading, at this distance of time. These, I thought—these are the things which used to give us something of a thrill.

If they no longer provide that sensation, it may well be that we have absorbed their spirit so thoroughly into our system that we forget whence we drew it. They have become part of ourselves. Even now, one cannot help admiring Gautier's precision of imagery, his gift of being quaint and yet lucid as a diamond; one pictures those crocodiles fainting in the heat, and notes, too, whence the author of the "Sphinx" drew his hard, glittering, mineralogical flavour. The verse is not so much easy as facile. And not all the grace of internals can atone for external monotony. That trick—that full stop at the end of nearly every fourth line—it impairs the charm of the music and renders its flow jerky; coming, as it does, like an ever-repeated blow, it grows wearisome to the ear, and finally abhorrent.

Baudelaire, in form, is more cunning and variegated. He can also delve down to deeps which the other never essayed to fathom. "Fuyez l'infini que vous portez en vous"—a line which, in my friend's copy of the book, had been marked on the margin with a derisive exclamation-point. (It gave me food for thought, that exclamation-point.) But, as to substance, he contains too many nebulosities and abstractions for my taste; a veritable mist of them, out of which emerges—what? The figure of one woman. Reading these "Fleurs du Mal" we realise, not for the first time, that there is something to be said in favour of libertinage for a poet. We do not need Petrarca, much less the Love-Letters of a Violinist—no, we do not need those Love-Letters at all—to prove that a master can draw sweet strains from communion with one mistress, from a lute with one string; a formidable array of songsters, on the other hand, will demonstrate how much fuller and richer the melody grows when the instrument is provided with the requisite five, the desirable fifty. Monogamous habits have been many a bard's undoing.

Twenty years' devotion to that stupid and spiteful old cat of a semi-negress! They make one conscious of the gulf between the logic of the emotions and that other one—that logic of the intellect which ought to shape our actions. Here was Baudelaire, a man of ruthless self-analysis. Did he never see himself as others saw him? Did he never say: "You are making a fool of yourself"?

Be sure he did.

You are making a fool of yourself: are not those the words I ought to have uttered when, standing in the centre of the Piazza del Popolo—the sunny centre: so it had been inexorably arranged—I used to wait and wait, with eyes glued to the clock hard by, in the slender shadow of that obelisque which crawled reluctantly, like the finger of fate, over the burning stones?

And I crawled with it, more than content.

Days of infatuation!

I never pass that way now without thanking God for a misspent youth. Why not make a fool of yourself? It is good fun while it lasts; it yields mellow mirth for later years, and are not our fellow-creatures, those solemn buffoons, ten times more ridiculous? Where is the use of experience, if it does not make you laugh? The Logic of the Intellect—what next! If any one had treated me to such tomfoolery while standing there, petrified into a pillar of fidelity in that creeping shadow, I should have replied gravely:

"The Logic of the Intellect, my dear Sir, is incompatible with situations like mine. It was not invented for so stupendous a crisis. I am waiting for my negress—can't you understand?—and she is already seven minutes late...."

A flaming morning, forestaste of things to come.

I find myself, after an early visit to the hospital where things are doing well, glancing down, towards midday, into Trajan's Forum, as one looks into some torrid bear-pit.

Broken columns glitter in the sunshine; the grass is already withered to hay. Drenched in light and heat, this Sahara-like enclosure is altogether devoid of life save for the cats. The majority are dozing in a kind of torpor, or moribund, or dead. My experiences in the hospital half an hour ago dispose me, perhaps, to regard this menagerie in a more morbid fashion than usual. To-day, in particular, it seems as if all the mangy and decrepit cats of Rome had given themselves a rendezvous on this classic soil; cats of every colour and every age—quite young ones among them; all, one would say, at the last gasp of life. This pit, this crater of flame, is their "Home for the Dying." Once down here, nothing matters any more. They are safe at last from their old enemies, from dogs and carriages and boys. Waiting for death, they move about in a stupid and dazed manner. Sunlight streams down upon their bodies. One would think they preferred to expire in the shade of some pillar or slab. Apparently not. Apparently it is all the same. It matters nothing where one dies.

There is one immediately below me, a moth-eaten desiccated tortoiseshell; its eyes are closed and a red tongue hangs out of the mouth. I drop a small pebble. It wakes up and regards me stoically for a moment. Nothing more.

These cats have lost their all—their self-respect. Grace and ardour, sleekness of coat and buoyancy of limbs are gone out of them. Tails are knotted with hunger and neglect; bones protrude through the skin. So they strew the ground in discomposed, un-catlike attitudes, while the sun burns through their parched anatomy. Do they remember their kittenish pranks, those moonlight ecstasies on housetops, that morsel snatched from a fishmonger's barrow and borne through the crowded traffic in a series of delirious leaps? Who can tell! They are not even bored with themselves. Their fur is in patches. They are alive when they ought to be dead. Nobody knows it better than they do. They are too ill, too far gone, to feel any sense of shame at their present degradation. Nothing matters! What would Baudelaire, that friend of cats, have said to this macabre exhibition?

Yonder is an old one, giving milk to the phantom of a kitten. The parent takes no interest in the proceedings; she lies prone, her head on the ground. Her eyes have a stony look. Is she dead? Possibly. Her own kitten? Who cares! Her neighbour, once white but now earth-coloured, rises stiffly as though dubious whether the joints are still in working order. What does she think of doing? It would seem she has formed no plan. She walks up to the mother, peers intently into her face, then sits apart on her haunches and begins gazing at the sun. Presently she rises anew and proceeds five or six paces for no imaginable reason—collapses; falls, quite abruptly, on her side. There she lies, flat, like a playing-card.

A sinister aimlessness pervades the actions of those that move at all. The shadow of death is upon these creatures in the scorching sunshine. They stare at columns of polished granite, at a piece of weed, at one another, as though they had never seen such things before. They totter about on tip-toe; they yawn and forget to shut their mouths. Here is one, stretching out a hind leg in a sustained cramp; another is convulsed with nervous twitchings; another scratches the earth in a kind of mechanical trance. One would say she was preparing a grave for herself. The saddest of all is an old warrior with mighty jowl and a face that bears the scars of a hundred fights. One eye has been lost in some long-forgotten encounter. Now they walk over him, kittens and all, and tread about his head, as if he were a hillock of earth, while his claws twitch resentfully with rage or pain. Too ill to rise!

Most of them are thus stretched out blankly, in a faint. Are they suffering? Hungry or thirsty?[23] I believe they are past troubling about such things. It is time to die. They know it....

"L'albergo dei gatti," says a cheery voice at my side—some countryman, who has also discovered Trajan's Forum to be one of the sights of Rome. "The cats' hotel. But," he adds, "I see no restaurant attached to it."

That reminds me: luncheon-time.

Via Flaminia—what a place for luncheon! True; but this is one of the few restaurants in Rome where, nowadays, a man is not in danger of being simultaneously robbed, starved, and poisoned. Things have come to a pretty pass. This starvation-fare may suit a saint and turn his thoughts heavenwards. Mine it turns in the other direction. Here, at all events, the food is straightforward. Our hostess, a slow elderly woman, is omnipresent; one realises that every dish has been submitted to her personal inspection. A primeval creature; heaviness personified. She moves in fateful fashion, like the hand of a clock. The crack of doom will not avail to accelerate that relentless deliberation. She reminds me of a cousin of mine famous for his imperturbable calm who, when his long curls once caught fire from being too near a candle, sleepily remarked to a terrified wife: "I think you might try to blow it out."

But where shall a man still find those edible maccheroni—those that were made in the Golden Age out of pre-war-time flour?

Such things are called trifles.... Give me the trifles of life, and keep the rest. A man's health depends on trifles; and happiness on health. Moreover, I have been yearning for them for the last five months. Hope deferred maketh the heart sick.... There are none in Rome. Can they be found anywhere else?

Mrs. Nichol: she might know. She has the gift of knowing about things one would never expect her to know. If only one could meet her by accident in the street! For at such times she is gay and altogether at your disposal. She is up to any sport, out of doors. To break upon her seclusion at home is an undertaking reserved for great occasions. The fact is, we are rather afraid of Mrs. Nichol. The incidents of what she describes as a tiresome life have taught her the value of masculine frankness—ultra-masculine, I call it. She is too frank for subterfuge of any kind. When at home, for instance, she is never "not at home." She will always see you. She will not detain you long, if you happen to be de trop.

This, I persuade myself, is a great occasion—my health and happiness.... Besides, I am her oldest friend in this part of the world; was I not on the spot when she elected, for reasons which nobody has yet fathomed, to make Rome her domicile? Have I not more than once been useful to her, nay, indispensable? I therefore climb, not without trepidation, those ninety-three stairs to the very summit of the old palace, and presently find myself ushered into the familiar twilight.

Nothing has changed since I was here some little time ago to announce my arrival in Italy (solemn occasion), when I had to amuse myself for an hour or so with Baudelaire in the library, Mrs. Nichol being engaged upon "house-accounts." This time, as I enter the studio, she is playing cards with a pretty handmaiden, amid peals of laughter. She often plays cards. She is puffing at a cigarette in a long mouthpiece which keeps the smoke out of her olive-complexioned face and which she holds firm-fixed between her teeth, in a corner of the mouth, after the perky fashion of a schoolboy. I have interrupted a game, and at once begin to feel de trop under a glance from those smouldering grey eyes.

"It is not a trifle. It is a matter of life and death. Will you please listen for half a minute? Then I will evaporate, and you can go on with your ridiculous cards. The fact is, I am being assassinated by inches. Do you know of a place where a man can get eatable macaroni nowadays? The old kind, I mean, made out of pre-war-time flour...."

She lays her hand on the cards as though to suspend the game, and asks the girl in Italian:

"What was the name of that place?"

"That place——"

"Oh, stupid! Where I stayed with Miranda last September. Where I tore my skirt on the rock. Where I said something nice about the white macaroni?"

"Soriano in Cimino."

"Soriano," echoes the mistress in a cloud of smoke. "There is a tram from here every morning. They can put you up."

A pause follows. I would like to linger and talk to this sultry and self-centred being; I would like to wander with her through these rooms, imbibing their strange Oriental spirit—not your vulgar Orient, but something classic and remote; something that savours, for aught I know, of Indo-China, where Mrs. Nichol, in one of her immature efforts at self-realisation, spent a few years as the wife of a high French official, ere marrying, that is, the late lamented Nichol—another unsuccessful venture.

Now why did she marry all these people (for I fancy there was yet an earlier alliance of some kind)? A whim, a freak? Or did they plague her into it? If so, I suspect they lived and died to repent their manly persistence. She could grind any ordinary male to powder. And why has she now flitted here, building herself this aerial bower above the old roofs of Rome? Is she in search of happiness? I doubt whether she will find it. She possesses that fatal craving—the craving for disinterested affection, a source of heartache to the perfect egoist for whom affection of this particular kind is not a necessity but a luxury, and therefore desirable above all else—desirable, and how seldom attained!

The pause continues. I make a little movement, to attract notice. She looks up, but only her eyes reply.

"Now, my good fellow," they seem to say, "are you blind?"

That is the drawback of Mrs. Nichol. Phenomenally absent-minded, she always knows at a given moment exactly what she wants to do. And she never wants to do more than one thing at a time. It is most unwomanly of her. Any other person of her sex would have left a game of cards for the sake of an attractive visitor like myself. Or, for that matter, an ordinary lady would have played cards, given complicated orders to dressmakers and servants, and entertained half a dozen men at the same time. Mrs. Nichol cannot do these things. That hand, that rather sunburnt little hand without a single ring on it, has not moved from the table. No, I am not blind. It is quite evident that she wants to play cards; only that, and nothing more.

I withdraw, stealthily.

Not downstairs. I go to linger awhile on the broad terrace where jessamine grows in Gargantuan tubs; there I pace up and down, admiring the cupolas and towers of Rome that gleam orange-tawny against the blue background of distant hills. How much of its peculiar flavour a town will draw—not from artistic monuments but from the mere character of building materials! How many variations on one theme! This mellow Roman travertine, for instance…. I call to mind those disconsolate places in Cornwall with their chill slate and primary rock, the robust and dignified bunter-sandstone of the Vosges, the satanic cheerfulness of lava, those marble-towns that blind you with their glare, Eastern cities of brightly tinted stucco or mere clay, the brick-towns, granite-towns, wood-towns—how they differ in mood from one another!…Here I pace up and down, rejoicing in the spacious sunlit prospect, and endeavouring to disentangle from one another the multitudinous street-cries that climb to this hanging garden in confused waves of sound. Harsh at close quarters, they weave themselves into a mirthful symphony up here.

From that studio, too, comes a lively din—the laughter has begun again. Mrs. Nichol is having a good time. It will be followed, I daresay, by a period of acute depression. I shall probably be consulted with masonic frankness about some little tragedy of the emotions which is no concern of mine. She can be wondrously engaging at such times—like a child that has got into trouble and takes you into its confidence.

One of these days I must write a character-sketch of Mrs. Nichol. She foreshadows a type—represents it, very possibly—a type which will grow commoner from day to day. She dreams of a Republic of women, vestals or otherwise, wherefrom all men are to be excluded unless they possess qualifications of a rather unusual nature. I think she would like to draft a set of rules and regulations for that community. She could be trusted, I fancy, to make them sufficiently stringent.

I think I understand, now, why a certain line in her copy of Baudelaire was marked with that derisive exclamation-point on the margin: "Fuyez l'infini que vous portez en vous."

"Fuyez?" it seemed to say. "Why 'fuyez'?"

Fulfil it!

Soriano

Amid clouds of dust you are whirled to Soriano, through the desert Campagna and past Mount Soracte, in a business-like tramway—different from that miserable Olevano affair which, being narrow gauge, can go but slowly and even then has a frolicsome habit of jumping off the rails every few days. From afar you look back upon the city; it lies so low as to be invisible; over its site hovers the dome of Saint Peter, like an iridescent bubble suspended in the sky.

This region is unfamiliar to me. Soriano lies on the slope of an immense old volcano and conveys at first glance a somewhat ragged and sombre impression. It was an unpleasantly warm day, but those macaroni—they atoned for everything. So exquisite were they that I forthwith vowed to return to Soriano, for their sake alone, ere the year should end. (I kept my vow.) The right kind at last, of lily-like candour and unmistakably authentic, having been purchased in large quantities at the outbreak of hostilities by the provident hostess, who must have anticipated a rise in price, a deterioration in quality, or both, as the result of war.

How came Mrs. Nichol to discover their whereabouts? That is her affair. I know not how she has managed, in so brief a space of time, to collect such a variety of useful local information. I can only testify that on her arrival in Rome she knew no more about the language and place than the proverbial babe unborn, and that nowadays, when anybody is faced with a conundrum like mine, one always hears the words: "Try Mrs. Nichol." And how many women, by the way, would have made a note of the particular quality of those macaroni? One in a hundred? These are temperamental matters....

We also—for of course I took a friend with me, a well-preserved old gentleman of thirty-two, whose downward career from a brilliant youth into hopeless mediocrity has been watched, by both of us, with philosophic unconcern—we also consumed a tender chicken, a salad containing olive oil and not the usual motor-car lubricant, an omelette made with genuine butter, and various other items which we enjoyed prodigiously, eating, one would think, not only for the seven lean years just past but for seven—yea, seventy times seven—lean years to come. So great a success was this open-air meal that my companion, a case-hardened Roman, was obliged to confess:

"It seems one fares better in the province than at home. You could not get such bread in Rome, not if you offered fifty francs a pound."

As for myself, I had lost all interest in the bread by this time, but grown fairly intimate with the wine, a rosy muscatel, faintly sparkling—very young, but not altogether innocent.

There were flies, however, and dogs, and children. We ought to have remained indoors. Thither we retired for coffee and cigars and a liqueur, of the last of which my friend refused to partake. He fears and distrusts all liqueurs; it is one of his many senile traits. The stuff proved, to my surprise, to be orthodox Strega, likewise a rarity nowadays.

It is a real shame—what is happening to Strega at this moment. It has grown so popular that the country is flooded with imitations. There must be fifty firms manufacturing shams of various degrees of goodness and badness; I have met their travellers in the most unexpected places. They reproduce the colour of Strega, its minty flavour—everything, in short, except the essential: its peculiar strength of aroma and of alcohol. They can afford to sell this poison at half the price of the original, and your artful restaurateur keeps an old bottle or two of the real product which he fills up, when empty, out of some hidden but never-failing barrel of the fraudulent mixture round the corner, charging you, of course, the full price of true Strega. If you complain, he proudly points to the bottle, the cork, the label: all authentic! No wonder foreigners, on tasting these concoctions, vow they will never touch Strega again....

We had a prolonged argument, over the coffee, about this Strega adulteration, during which I tried to make my friend comprehend how I thought the grievance ought to be remedied. How? By an injunction. That was the way to redress these wrongs. You obtain an injunction, I said, such as the French Chartreuse people obtained against the manufacturers of the Italian "Certosa," which was thereafter obliged to change its name to "Val D'Emma." More than once I endeavoured to set forth, in language intelligible to his understanding, what an injunction signified; more than once I explained how well-advised the Strega Company would be to take this course.

In vain!

He always missed my point. He always brought in some personal element, whereas I, as usual, confined myself to general lines, to the principle of the thing. Italians are sometimes unfathomably obtuse.

"But what is an injunction?" he repeated.

"If you were a little younger, there might be some hope for you. I would then try to explain it again, for the fiftieth time. Instead of that, what do you say to taking a nap?"

"Ah! You have eaten too much."

"Not at all. But please to note that I am tired of explaining things to people who refuse to understand."

"No doubt, no doubt. Yes. A little sleep might freshen you up."

"And perhaps inspire you with another subject of conversation."

In the little hotel there were no rooms available just then wherein we might have slumbered, and another apartment higher up the street promising lively sport for which we were disinclined at that hour, we moved laboriously into the chestnut woods overhead. Fine old timber, part of that mysterious Ciminian forest which still covers a large tract, from within whose ample shade one looks downhill towards the distant Orte across a broiling stretch of country. There were golden orioles here, calling to each other from the tree-tops. My friend, having excavated himself a couch among the troublesome prickly seeds of this plant, was soon snoring—another senile trait—snoring in a rhythmical bass accompaniment to their song. I envied him. How some people can sleep! It is a thing worth watching. They shut their eyes, and forget to be awake. With a view to imitating his example, I wearied myself trying to count up the number of orioles I had shot in my bird-slaying days, and where it happened. Not more than half a dozen, all told. They are hard to stalk, and hard to see. But of other birds—how many! Forthwith an endless procession of massacred fowls began to pass before my mind. One would fain live those ornithological days over again, and taste the rapturous joy with which one killed that first nutcracker in the mountain gulley; the first wall-creeper which fluttered down from the precipice hung with icicles; the Temminck's stint—victim of a lucky shot, late in the evening, on the banks of the reservoir; the ruff, the grey-headed green woodpecker, the yellow-billed Alpine jackdaw, that lanius meridionalis——

And all those slaughtered beasts—those chamois, first and foremost, sedulously circumvented amid snowy crags. Where are now their horns, the trophies? The passion for such sport died out slowly and for no clearly ascertainable reason, as did, in its turn, the taste for art and theatres and other things. Sheer satiety, a grain of pity, new environments—they may all help to explain what was, in its essence, a molecular change in the brain, driving one to explore new departments of life.

And now latterly, for some reason equally obscure, the natural history fancy has revived after lying dormant so long. It may be those three months spent on the pavements of Florence which incline one's thoughts to the country and wild things. Social reasons too—a certain weariness of humanity, and more than weariness; a desire to avoid contact with creatures Who kill each other so gracelessly and in so doing—for the killing alone would pass—invoke specially manufactured systems of ethics and a benevolent God overhead. What has one in common with such folk?

That may be why I feel disposed to forget mankind and take rambles as of yore; minded to shoulder a gun and climb trees and collect birds, and begin, of course, a new series of "field notes." Those old jottings were conscientiously done and registered sundry things of import to the naturalist; were they accessible, I should be tempted to extract therefrom a volume of solid zoological memories in preference to these travel-pages that register nothing but the crosscurrents of a mind which tries to see things as they are. For the pursuit brought one into relations not only with interesting birds and beasts, but with men.

There was Mr. H. of the Linnean Society, whose waxed moustache curled round upon itself like an ammonite. A great writer of books was Mr. H., and a great collector of them. He collected, among other things, a rare monograph belonging to me and dealing with the former distribution of the beaver in Bavaria (we were both absorbed in beavers). Nothing I could do or say would induce him to disgorge it again; he had always lent it to a friend, who was just on the point of returning it, etc. etc. Bitterly grieved, I not only forgave him, but put him into communication with my friend Dr. Girtanner of St. Gallen, another beaver—and marmot—specialist. It stimulated his love of Swiss zoology to such an extent that he straightway borrowed a still rarer pamphlet of mine, J. J.

Tschudi's "Schweizer Echsen," which I likewise never saw again. What an innocent one was! Where is now the man who will induce me to lend him such books?

In those days I held a student's ticket at the South Kensington Museum, an institution I enriched with specimens of rana graeca from near Lake Stymphalus, and lizards from the Filfla rock, and toads from a volcanic islet (toads, says Darwin, are not found on volcanic islets), and slugs from places as far apart as Santorin and the Shetlands and Orkneys, whither I went in search of Asterolepis and the Great Skua. The last gift was a seal from the fresh-water lake of Saima in Finland. Who ever heard of seals living in sweet land-locked waters? This was one of my happiest discoveries, though the delight of my friend the Curator was tempered by the fact that this particular specimen happened to be an immature one, and did not display any pronounced race-characters. I have early recollections of the rugged face and lovely Scotch accent of Tam Edwards, the Banffshire naturalist; and much later ones of J. Young,[24] who gave me a circumstantial account of how he found the first snow bunting's nest in Sutherlandshire; I recall the Rev. Mathew (? Mathews) of Gumley, an ardent Leicestershire ornithologist, whose friendship I gained at a tender age on discovering the nest of a red-legged partridge, from which I took every one of the thirteen eggs. "Surely six would have been enough," he said—a remark which struck me as rather unreasonable, seeing that French partridges were not exactly as common as linnets. He afterwards showed me his collection of birdskins, dwelling lovingly, for reasons which I cannot remember, upon that of a pin-tail duck.

He it was who told me that no collector was worth his salt until he had learnt to skin his own birds. Fired with enthusiasm, I took lessons in taxidermy at the earliest possible opportunity—from a grimy old naturalist in one of the grimiest streets of Manchester, a man who relieved birds of their jackets in dainty fashion with one hand, the other having been amputated and replaced by an iron hook. During that period of initiation into the gentle art, the billiard-room at "The Weaste," Manchester, was converted every morning, for purposes of study, into a dissecting-room, a chamber of horrors, a shambles, where headless trunks and brains and gouged-out eyes of lapwings and other "easy" birds (I had not yet reached the arduous owl-or-titmouse stage of the profession) lay about in sanguinary morsels, while the floor was ankle-deep in feathers, and tables strewn with tweezers, lancets, arsenical paste, corrosive sublimate and other paraphernalia of the trade. The butler had to be furiously tipped.

There were large grounds belonging to this estate, fields and woodlands once green, then blackened with soot, and now cut up into allotments and built over. Here, ever since men could remember—certainly since the place had come into the possession of the never-to-be-forgotten Mr. Edward T.—a kingfisher had dwelt by a little streamlet of artificial origin which supported a few withered minnows and sticklebacks and dace. This kingfisher was one of the sights of the domain. Visitors were taken to see it. The bird, though sometimes coy, was generally on view. Nevertheless it was an extremely prudent old kingfisher; to my infinite annoyance, I never succeeded in destroying it. Nor did I even find its nest, an additional source of grief. Lancashire naturalists may be interested to know that this bird was still on the spot in the 'eighties (I have the exact date somewhere[25])—surely a noteworthy state of affairs, so near the heart of a smoky town like Manchester.

Later on I learnt to slay kingfishers—the first victim falling to my gun on a day of rain, as it darted across a field to avoid the windings of a brook. I also became a specialist at finding their nests. Birds are so conservative! They are at your mercy, if you care to study their habits. The golden-crested wren builds a nest which is almost invisible; once you have mastered the trick, no gold-crest is safe. I am sorry, now, for all those plundered gold-crests' eggs. And the rarer ones—the grey shrike, that buzzard of the cliff (the most perilous scramble of all my life), the crested titmouse, the serin finch on the apple tree, that first icterine warbler whose five eggs, blotched with purple and quite unfamiliar at the time, gave me such a thrill of joy that I nearly lost my foothold on the swerving alder branch——

At this point, my meditations were suddenly interrupted by a vigorous grunt or snort; a snort that would have done credit to an enraged tapir. My friend awoke, refreshed. He rubbed his eyes, and looked round.

"I remember!" he began, sitting up. "I remember everything. Are you feeling better? I hope so. Yes. Exactly. Where were we? An injunction—what did you say?"

At it again!

"I said it was the drawback of old people that they never know when they have had enough of an argument."

"But what is an injunction?"

"How many more times do you wish me to make that clear? Shall I begin all over again? Have it your way! When you go into Court and ask the judge to do something to prevent a man from doing something he wants to do when you do not want him to do it. Like that, more or less."

"So I gather. But I confess I do not see why a man should not do something he wants to do just because you want him not to do it. You might as well go into Court and ask the judge to do something to make a man do something he does not want to do just because you want him to do it."

"Ah, but he must not, in this case. Good Lord, have I not explained that a thousand times already? You always miss my point. It is illegal, don't you understand? Illegal, illegal."

"Anybody can say that. It would be a very natural thing to say, under the circumstances. I should say it myself! Now just take my advice. You go and tell your brother——"

"My brother? It is not my brother. You are quite beside the point. Why introduce this personal element? It is the Strega Company. Strega, a liqueur. I am talking about a commercial concern obtaining an injunction. Burroughs and Wellcome—they got injunctions on the same grounds. I know a great deal of such things, though I don't talk about them all day long as other people would, if they possessed half my knowledge. A company, don't you see? An injunction. A liqueur. Please to note that I am talking about a company, a company. Have I now made myself clear, or how many more times——"

"One would think he was at least your brother, from the way you take his part. Let us say he is a friend, then; some never-to-be-mentioned friend who is interested in a shady liqueur business and now wants to make a judge do something to make a man do something——"

"Wrong again! To prevent a man doing something——"

"—Wants to do something to make a judge do something to prevent a man doing something he wants to do because he does not want him to do it. Is that right? Very well. You tell your friend that no Italian judge is going to do dirty work of that kind for nothing."

"Dirty work. God Almighty! I don't want any judge to do dirty work——"

"No doubt, no doubt. I am quite convinced you don't. But your priceless friend does. Come now! Why not be open about it?"

"Open about what?"

"It is positively humiliating for me to be treated like this, after all the years we have known each other. I wish you would try to cultivate the virtue of frankness. You are far too secretive. Something will really have to be done about it."

"A company, a company."

"A company consists of a certain number of human beings. Why make mysteries about one of them? It may happen to the best of mankind to be mixed up——"

"Mixed up——"

"You are going to be disagreeable about my choice of words. Have it your way! We all know you think you can talk better Italian than the Pope. My own father, I was going to say, has been involved in some pretty dirty work in the course of his professional career——"

"No doubt, no doubt."

"And please to note that he is as good a man as any brother of yours."

"You always miss my point."

"Now try to be truthful, for once in your life. Out with it!"

"A liqueur."

"Is that all? Sleep does not seem to have sharpened your wits to any great extent."

"I was not asleep. I was thinking about eggs. A company."

"A company? You are waking up. Anything else?"

"An injunction…."

A distinguished writer some years ago started a crusade in favour of pure English. He wished to counteract those influences which are forever at work debasing the standard of language; whether, as he seemed to think, that standard should be inalterably fixed, is yet another question. For in literature as in conversation there is a "pure English" for every moment of history; that of our childhood is different from to-day's; and to adopt the tongue of the Bible or Shakespeare, because it happens to be pure, looks like setting back the hands of the clock. Men would surely be dull dogs if their phraseology, whether written or spoken, were to remain stagnant and unchangeable. We think well of Johnson's prose. Yet the respectable English of our own time will bear comparison with his; it is more agile and less infected with Latinisms; why go back to Johnson? Let us admire him as a landmark, and pass on! Some literary periods may deserve to be called good, others bad; so be it. Were there no bad ones, there would be no good ones, and I see no reason why men should desire to live in a Golden Age of literature, save in so far as that millennium might coincide with a Golden Age of living. I doubt, in the first place, whether they would be even aware of their privilege; secondly, every Golden Age grows fairer when viewed from a distance. Besides, and as a general consideration, it strikes me that a vast deal of mischief is involved in these arbitrary divisions of literature into golden or other epochs; they incite men to admire some mediocre writers and to disparage others, they pervert our natural taste, and their origin is academic laziness.

Certain it is that every language worthy of the name should be in a state of perennial flux, ready and avid to assimilate new elements and be battered about as we ourselves are—is there anything more charming than a thoroughly defective verb?—fresh particles creeping into its vocabulary from all quarters, while others are silently discarded. There is a bar-sinister on the escutcheon of many a noble term, and if, in an access of formalism, we refuse hospitality to some item of questionable repute, our descendants may be deprived of a linguistic jewel. Is the calamity worth risking when time, and time alone, can decide its worth? Why not capture novelties while we may, since others are dying all the year round; why not throw them into the crucible to take their chance with the rest of us? An English word is no fossil to be locked up in a cabinet, but a living thing, liable to the fate of all such things. Glance back into Chaucer and note how they have thriven on their own merits and not on professorial recommendations; thriven, or perished, or put on new faces!

I would make an exception to this rule. Foreign importations which do not belong to us by right, idioms we have enticed from over the sea for one reason or another, ought to remain, as it were, stereotyped. They are respected guests and cannot decently be jostled in our crowd; let them be jostled in their own; here, on British soil, they should be allowed to retain that primal signification which, in default of a corresponding English term, they were originally taken over to express.

What prompts me to this exordium is the discovery that a few pages back, with a blameworthy hankering after the picturesque, I have grossly misused a foreign word. Those cats in Trajan's Forum at Rome are nowise a "macabre exhibition"; they are not macabre in the least; they are sad, or saddening. The charnel-house flavour is absent.

My apologies to the French language, to the cats, and to the reader....

Now whoever wishes to see a truly macabre exhibition at Rome may visit the Peruvian mummies in the Kircher Museum. It is characteristic of the spirit in which guide-books are written that, while devoting long paragraphs to some worthless picture of a hallucinated venerable, they hardly utter a word about these most remarkable and gruesome objects.

Those old Peruvians, like the Egyptians, had necrophilous leanings. They cultivated an unwholesome passion for corpses, and called it religion. Many museums contain such relics from the New World in various attitudes of discomfort; frequently seated, as though trying to be at rest after life's long journey. No two are alike; and all are horrible of aspect. Some have been treated with balsam to preserve the softer parts; others are shrivelled. Some are filled with chopped straw, like any stuffed crocodile in a show; others contain precious coca-leaves and powdered fragments of shell, which were doubtless placed there so that the defunct might receive nourishment up to the time when his soul should once more have rejoined the body. Every one knows, furthermore, that these American ancients were fond of playing tricks with the shape of the skull—a custom which was forbidden by the Synod of Lima in 1585 and which Hippocrates describes as being practised among the inhabitants of the Crimea.[26] It adds considerably to their ghastly appearance.

One looks at them and asks oneself: what are they now, these gentle Incas who loved the arts and music, these children of the Sun, whose civic acquirements amazed their conquerors? They have contrived to transform themselves into something quite unusual. Staring orbits and mouths agape, colour-patches here and there, morsels of muscle and hair attached to contorted limbs—they suggest a half-way house, a loathsome link, between a living man and his skeleton; and not only a link between them, but a grim caricature of both. Some have been coated with varnish. They glisten infamously. Picture a decrepit and rather gaunt relative of your own, writhing in a fit, stark naked, and varnished all over——

Different are these mummies from those of the tenaciously unimaginative and routine-bound Egyptians. Theirs are dead as a door-nail; torpid lumps, undistinguishable one from the other. Here we have a rare phenomenon—life, and individuality, after death. They are more noteworthy than the cowled and desiccated monks of Italy or Sicily, or at least differently so; undraped, for the most part, though some of them may be seen, mere skin-covered heads, peering with dismal coyness out of a brown sack. And the jabbering teeth.... We dream as children of night-terrors, of goblins and phantoms that start out of the gloom and flit about with hideous grimaces. They are gone, while yet we shudder at that momentary flash of grizzliness; intangibilities, whose image is not easily detained. To see spectral visions embodied, and ghosts made flesh, one should come here. Had the excruciating operation of embalming been performed upon live men and women, their poses could hardly have been more multifariously agonised; and an aesthete may speculate as to how far such objects offend, in expression of blank misery and horror, against the canons of what is held to be artistically desirable. The nearest approach to them in human craftsmanship, and as regards Auffassung, are perhaps some little Japanese wood-carvings whose creators, labouring consciously, likewise overstepped the boundaries of the grotesque and indulged in nightmarish effects of line similar to those which the old Peruvians, all unconsciously, have achieved upon the bodies of their dear friends and relatives....

Drive swiftly thence, if you are in the mood, as you should be, for something at the other pole of feeling, to view that wonder, the kneeling boy at the Museo delle Terme. Headless and armless though he be, he displays as much vitality as the Peruvians; every inch of the body is alive, and one may well marvel at the skill of the artist who, during his interminable task of sculpture, held fast the model's fleeting outline—so fleeting, at that particular age of life, that every month, and every week, brings about new conditions of surface and texture. A child of Niobe? Very likely. There is suffering also here, a suffering different from theirs; struck by the Sun-God's arrow, he is in the act of sinking to earth. Over this tension broods a divine calm. Here is the antidote to mummified Incas.

Alatri

What brought me to Alatri?

Memories of a conversation, by Tiber banks, with Fausto, who was born here and vaunted it to be the fairest city on earth. Rome was quite a passable place, but as to Alatri——

"You never saw such walls in all your life. They are not walls. They are precipices. And our water is colder than the Acqua Marcia."

"Walls and water say little to me. But if the town produces other citizens like yourself——"

"It does indeed! I am the least of the sons of Alatri."

"Then it must be worthy of a visit...."

In the hottest hour of the afternoon they deposited me outside the city gate at some new hotel—I forget its name—to which I promptly took an unreasoning dislike. There was a fine view upon the mountains from the window of the room assigned to me, but nothing could atone for that lack of individuality which seemed to exhale from the establishment and its proprietors. It looked as though I were to be a cypher here. Half an hour was as much as I could endure. Issuing forth despite the heat, I captured a young fellow and bade him carry my bags whithersoever he pleased. He took me to the Albergo della——

The Albergo della——is a shy and retiring hostelry, invisible as such to the naked eye, since it bears no sign of being a place of public entertainment at all. Here was individuality, and to spare. Mine host is an improvement even upon him of the Pergola at Valmontone; a man after my own heart, with merry eyes, drooping white moustache and a lordly nose—a nose of the right kind, a flame-tinted structure which must have cost years of patient labour to bring to its present state of blossoming. That nose! I felt as though I could dwell for ever beneath its shadow. The fare, however, is not up to the standard of the "Garibaldi" inn at Frosinone which I have just left.

Now Frosinone is no tourist resort. It is rather a dull little place; I am never likely to go there again, and have therefore no reason for keeping to myself its "Garibaldi" hotel which leaves little to be desired, even under these distressful war-conditions. It set me thinking—thinking that there are not many townlets of this size in rural England which can boast of inns comparable to the "Garibaldi" in point of cleanliness, polite attention, varied and good food, reasonable prices. Not many; perhaps very few. One remembers a fair number of the other kind, however; that kind where the fare is monotonous and badly cooked, the attendance supercilious or inefficient, and where you have to walk across a cold room at night—refinement of torture—in order to turn out the electric light ere going to bed. That infamy is alone enough to condemn these establishments, one and all.

Yes! And the beds; those frowsy, creaky, prehistoric wooden concerns, always six or eight inches too short, whose mattresses have not been turned round since they were made. What happens? You clamber into such a receptacle and straightway roll downhill, down into its centre, into a kind of river-bed where you remain fixed fast, while that monstrous feather-abomination called a pillow, yielding to pressure, rises up on either side of your head and engulfs eyes and nose and everything else into its folds. No escape! You are strangled, smothered; you might as well have gone to bed with an octopus. In this horrid contrivance you lie for eight long hours, clapped down like a corpse in its coffin. Every single bed in rural England ought to be burnt. Not one of them is fit for a Christian to sleep in....

The days are growing hot.

A little tract of woodland surrounded by white walls and attached to the convent on the neighbouring hill is a pleasant spot to while away the afternoon hours. You can have it to yourself. I have all Alatri to myself; a state of affairs which is not without its disadvantages, for, being the only foreigner here, one is naturally watched and regarded with suspicion. And it would be even worse in less civilised places, where one could count for certain on trouble with some conscientious official. So one remains on the beaten track, although my reputation here as non-Austrian (nobody bothers about the Germans) is fairly well established since that memorable debate, in the local cafe, with a bootmaker who, having spent three years in America, testified publicly that I spoke English almost as well as he did. The little newsboy of the place, who is a universal favourite, seeing that his father, a lithographer, is serving a stiff sentence for forgery—he brings me every day with the morning's paper the latest gossip concerning myself.

"Mr. So-and-so still says you are a spy. It is sheer malice."

"I know. Did you tell him he might——?"

"I did. He was very angry. I also told him the remark you made about his mother."

"Tell him again, to-morrow."

It seldom pays to be rude. It never pays to be only half rude.

In October—and we are now at midsummer—there occurred a little adventure which shows the risks one may run at a time like this.

I was in Rome, walking homewards at about eleven at night along the still crowded Corso and thinking, as I went along, of my impending journey northwards for which the passport was already viséd, when there met me a florid individual accompanied by two military officers. We stared at one another. His face was familiar to me, though I knew not where I had seen it. Then he introduced himself. He was a director of the Banca d'Italia. And was I not the gentleman who had recently been to Orvinio? I remembered.

"The last time I was there," I said, "was about a month ago. I fancy we had some conversation in the motor up from Mandela."

"That is so. And now, however disagreeable it may be, I feel myself obliged to perform a patriotic duty. This is war-time. I would ask you to be so good as to accompany us to the nearest police-station."

"Which is not far off," I replied. "There is one up the next street on our right."

We walked there, all four of us, without saying another word. "What have I been doing?" I wondered. Then we climbed upstairs.

Here, at a well-lighted table in a rather stuffy room, sat a delegato or commissario—I forget which—surrounded, despite the lateness of the hour, by one or two subordinates. He was of middle age, and not prepossessing. He looked as if he could make himself unpleasant, though his face was not of that actively vicious—or actively stupid: the terms are interconvertible—kind. While scanning his countenance, during those few moments, sundry thoughts flitted through my mind.

These then, I said to myself—these are the functionaries, whether executive or administrative, whether Italian or English or Chinese, whom a man is supposed to respect. Who are they? God knows. Nine-tenths of them are in a place where they have no business to be: so much is certain. And what are they doing, these swarms of parasites? Justifying their salaries by inventing fresh regulations and meddlesome bye-laws, and making themselves objectionable all round. Distrust of authority should be the first civic duty, even as the first military duty is said to be the reverse of it. We catch ourselves talking of the "lesson of history." Why not take that lesson to heart? Reverence of the mandarin destroyed the fair life of old China, which was overturned by the Tartars not because Chinamen were too weak or depraved, but because they were the opposite: too moral, too law-abiding, too strong in their sense of right. They paid for their virtue with the extinction of their wonderful culture. They ought to have known better; they ought to have rated morality at its true worth, since it was the profoundest Chinaman himself who said that virtue is merely etiquette—or something to that effect.

I found myself studying the delegato's physiognomy. What could one do with such a composite face? It is a question which often confronts me when I see such types. It confronted me then, in a flash. How make it more presentable, more imposing? By what alterations? Shaving that moustache? No; his countenance could not carry the loss; it would forfeit what little air of dignity it possessed. A small pointed beard, an eye-glass? Possibly. Another trimming of the hair might have improved him, but, on the whole, it was a face difficult to manipulate, on account of its inherent insipidity and self-contradictory features; one of those faces which give so much trouble to the barbers and valets of European royalties.

He took down the names and addresses of all four of us, and it was then that I missed my chance. I ought to have spoken first instead of allowing this luscious director to begin as follows:—

"The foreign gentleman here was at Orvinio about a month ago. He admits it himself and I can corroborate the fact, as I was there at the same time. Orvinio is a small country place in the corner of Umbria. There is a mountain in the neighbourhood, remote and very high—altissima! It is called Mount Muretta and occupies a commanding situation. For reasons which I will leave you, Signer

Commissario, to investigate, this gentleman climbed up that mountain and was observed, on the very summit, making calculations and taking measurements with instruments."

Now why did I climb up that wretched Muretta? For an all sufficient reason: it was a mountain. There is no eminence in the land, from Etna and the Gran Sasso downwards, whose appeal I can resist. A bare wall-like patch on the summit (whence presumably the name) visible from below and promising a lively scramble up the rock, was an additional inducement. Precipices are not so frequent at Orvinio that one can afford to pass them by, although this one, as a matter of fact, proved to be a mighty tame affair. There was yet another object to my trip. I desired to verify a legend connected with this mountain, the tradition of a vanished castle or hamlet in its upper regions to whose former existence the name of a certain old family, still surviving at Orvinio, bears witness. "We are not really from Orvinio," these people will tell you. "We are from the lost castle of the Muretta." (There is not a vestige of a castle left. But I found one brick in the jungle which covers, on the further side of the summit, a vast rock-slide dating, I should say, from early mediaeval days, under whose ruins the fastness may lie buried.) Reasons enough for visiting Muretta.

As to taking measurements—well, a man is naturally accused of a good many things in the course of half a century. Nobody has yet gone so far as to call me a mathematician. These "calculations and instruments" were a local mirage; as pretty an instance of the mythopoeic faculty as one could hope to find in our degenerate days, when gods no longer walk the earth. [27]

The official seemed to be impressed with the fact that my accuser was director of a bank. He inquired what I had to say.

This was a puzzle. They had sprung the thing on me rather suddenly. One likes to have notice of such questions. Tell the truth? I am often tempted to do so; it saves so much trouble! But truth-telling is a matter of longitude, and the further east one goes, the more one learns to hold in check that unnatural propensity. (Mankind has a natural love of the lie itself. Bacon.) Which means nothing more than that one will do well to take account of national psychology. An English functionary, athlete or mountaineer, might have glimpsed the state of affairs. But to climb in war-time, without any object save that of exercising one's limbs and verifying a questionable legend, a high and remote mountain— Muretta happens to be neither the one nor the other—would have seemed to an Italian an incredible proceeding. I thought it better to assume the role of accuser in my turn: an Oriental trick.

"This director," I said, "calls himself a patriot. What has he told us? That while at Orvinio he knew a foreigner who climbed a high mountain to make calculations with instruments. What does this admirable citizen do with regard to such a suspicious character? He does nothing. Is there not a barrack-full of carbineers at the entrance of the place ready to arrest such people? But our patriotic gentleman allows the spy to walk away, to climb fifty other mountains and take five thousand other measurements, all of which have by this time safely reached Berlin and Vienna. That, Signor Commissario, is not our English notion of patriotism. I shall certainly make it my business to write and congratulate the Banca d'Italia on possessing such a good Italian as director. I shall also suggest that his talents would be more worthily employed at the Banca—"(naming a notoriously pro-German establishment).

A poor speech; but it gave me the satisfaction of seeing the fellow grow purple with fury and so picturesquely indignant that he soon reached the spluttering stage. In fact, there was nothing to be done with him. The delegato suggested that inasmuch as he had said his say and deposited his address, he was at liberty to depart, whenever so disposed.

They went—he and his friends.

The other was looking serious—as serious as such a face could be made to look. He must not be allowed to think, I decided, for once an official begins to think he is liable to grow conscientious and then—why, any disaster might happen, the least of them being that I should remain in custody pending investigations. In how many more countries was I going to be arrested for one crime or another? This joke had lost its novelty a good many years ago.

"A pernicious person," I began, "—you have but to look at him. And now he has invited me here in order to make a patriotic impression on his friends, those poor little devils in uniform (a safe remark, since no love is lost hereabouts between police and military). Such silly talk about measurements! It should be nipped in the bud. Here you have an intelligent young subordinate, if I mistake not. Let him drive home with me at my expense; we will go through all papers and search for instruments and bring everything that savours of suspicion back to this office, together with my passport which I never carry on my person. This, meanwhile, is my carta di soggiorno."

The document was in order. Still he hesitated. I thought of those miserable three days' grace which were all that the French consulate had accorded me. If the man grew conscientious, I might remain stranded in Rome, and all that passport trouble must begin again. And to tell him of this dilemma would make him more distrustful than ever.

I went on hastily to admit that my request might not be regular, but how natural! Were we not allies? Was it not my duty to clear myself of such an imputation at the earliest moment and to spare no efforts to that end? I felt sure he could sympathise with the state of my mind, etc. etc.

Thus I spoke while perfect innocence, mother of invention, lent wings to my words, and while thinking all the time: You little vermin, what are you doing here, in that chair, when you should be delving the earth or breaking stones, as befits your kind? I tried to picture myself climbing up Muretta with a theodolite bulging out of my pocket. A flagon of port would have been more in my line. Calculations! It is all I can do to control my weekly washing bill, and even for that simple operation I like to have a quiet half hour in a room by myself. Instruments! If this young fellow, I thought, discovers so much as an astrolabe among my belongings, let them hang me from the ramparts at daybreak! And the delegato, listening, was finally moved by my rhetoric, as they often are, if you can throw not only your whole soul, but a good part of your body, into the performance. He found the idea sufficiently reasonable. The subordinate, as might have been expected, had nothing whatever to do; like all of his kind, he was only in that office to evade military service.

We drove away and, on reaching our destination, I insisted, despite his polite remonstrances, on turning everything upside down. We made hay of the apartment, but discovered nothing more treasonable than some rather dry biscuits and a bottle of indifferent Marsala.

"And now I must really be going," he said. "Half-past one! He will be surprised at my long absence."

"I am coming with you. I promised him the passport."

"Don't dream of it. To-morrow, to-morrow. You will have no trouble with him. You can bring the passport, but he will not look at it. Yes; ten o'clock, or eleven, or midday."

So it happened. The passport was waived aside by the official, a little detail which, I must say, struck me as more remarkable than anything else. He did not even unfold it.

"E stato un' equivoco," was all he condescended to say, still without a smile. There had been a misunderstanding.

The incident was closed.

Things might have gone differently in the country. I would either have been marched to the capital under the escort of a regiment of carbineers, or kept confined in some rural barracks for half a century while the authorities were making the necessary researches into the civil status of my grandmother's favourite poet—an inquiry without which no Latin dossier is complete.

POSTSCRIPT.—Why are there so many carbineers at Orvinio? And how many of these myriad public guardians scattered all over the country ever come into contact with a criminal, or even have the luck to witness a street accident? And would the taxpayer not profit by a reduction in their numbers? And whether legal proceedings of every kind would not tend to diminish?

There is a village of about three hundred inhabitants not far from Rome; fifteen carbineers are quartered there. Before they came, those inevitable little troubles were settled by the local mayor, things remained in the family, so to speak. Now the place has been set by the ears, and a tone of exacerbation prevails. The natives spend their days in rushing to Rome and back on business connected with law-suits, not a quarter of which would have arisen but for the existence of the carbineers. Let me not be misunderstood. Individually, these men are nowise at fault. They desire nothing better than to be left in peace. Seldom do they meddle with local concerns—far from it! They live in sacerdotal isolation, austerely aloof from the populace, like a colony of monks. The institution is to blame. It is their duty, among other things, to take down any charge which anybody may care to prefer against his neighbour. That done, the machinery of the law is automatically set in motion. Five minutes' talk among the village elders would have settled many affairs which now degenerate into legal squabbles of twice as many years; chronic family feuds are fostered; a man who, on reflection, would find it more profitable to come to terms with his opponent over a glass of wine, or even to square the old syndic with a couple of hundred francs, sees himself obliged to try the same tactics on a judge of the high court—which calls for a different technique.

Altogether, the country is flagrantly over-policed.[28] It gives one a queer sense of public security to see, at Rome for instance, every third man you meet—an official, of course, of some kind—with a revolver strapped to his belt, as if we were still trembling on the verge of savagery in some cowboy settlement out West. Greek towns of about ten thousand inhabitants, like Argos or Megara, have about ten municipal guardians each, and peace reigns within their walls. How can ten men perform duties which, in Italy, would require ten times as many? Is it a question of climate, or national character? A question, perhaps, of common sense—of realising that local institutions often work with less friction and less outlay than that system of governmental centralisation of which the carbineers are an example.

Meanwhile we are still at Alatri which, I am glad to discover, possesses five gateways—five or even more. It is something of a relief to be away from that Roman tradition of four. Military reasons originally, fixing themselves at last into a kind of sacred tradition.... So it is, with unimaginative races. Their pious sentimentalism crystallises into inanimate objects. The English dump down Gothic piles on India's coral strand, and the chimes of Big Ben, floating above that crowd of many-hued Orientals, give to the white man a sense of homeliness and racial solidarity. The French, more fluid and sensitive to the incongruous, have introduced local colour into some of their Colonial buildings, not without success. As to this particular Roman tradition, it pursues one with meaningless iteration from the burning sands of Africa to Ultima Thule. Always those four gateways!

For a short after-breakfast ramble nothing is comparable to that green space on the summit of the citadel. Hither I wend my way every morning, to take my fill of the panorama and meditate upon the vanity of human wishes. The less you have seen of localities like Tiryns the more you will be amazed at this impressive and mysterious fastness. That portal, those blocks—what Titans fitted them into their places? Well, we have now learnt a little something about those Titans and their methods. From this point you can see the old Roman road that led into Alatri; it climbs up the hill in straightforward fashion, intersecting the broad modern "Via Romana"—a goat-track, nowadays....

These Alatri remains are wonderful—more so than many of the sites which old Ramage so diligently explored. Why did he fail to "satisfy his curiosity" in regard to them? He utters not a word about Alatri. Yet he stayed at the neighbouring Frosinone and makes some good observations about the place; he stayed at the neighbouring Ferentino and does the same. Was he more "pressed for time" than usual? We certainly find him "hurrying down" past Anagni near-by, of whose imposing citadel he again says nothing whatever....

I am now, at the end of several months, beginning to know Ramage fairly well. I hope to know him still better ere we part company, if ever we do. It takes time, this interpretation, this process of grafting one mind upon another. For he does not supply mere information. A fig for information. That would be easy to digest. He supplies character, which is tougher fare. His book, unassuming as it is, comes up to my test of what such literature should be. It reveals a personality. It contains a philosophy of life.

And what is the dominating trait of this old Scotsman? The historical sense. Ancient inscriptions interested him more than anything else. He copied many of them during his trip; fifty, I should think; and it is no small labour, as any one who has tried it can testify, to decipher these half-obliterated records often placed in the most inconvenient situations (he seems to have taken no squeezes). To have busied himself thus was to his credit in an age whose chief concern, as regards antiquity, consisted in plundering works of art for ornamental purposes. Ramage did not collect bric-a-brac like other travellers; he collected knowledge of humanity and its institutions, such knowledge as inscriptions reveal. It is good to hear him discoursing upon these documents in stone, these genealogies of the past, with a pleasingly sentimental erudition. He likes them not in any dry-as-dust fashion, but for the light they throw upon the living world of his day. Speaking of one of them he says: "It is when we come across names connected with men who have acted an illustrious part in the world's history, that the fatigues of such a journey as I have undertaken are felt to be completely repaid." That is the humanist's spirit.

His equipment in the interpretation of these stones and of all else he picked up in the way of lore and legend was of the proper kind. Boundless curiosity, first of all. And then, an adequate apparatus of learning. He knew his classics—knew them so well that he could always put his finger on those particular passages of theirs which bore upon a point of interest. We may doubtless be able to supply some apt quotation from Virgil or Martial. It is quite a different thing remembering, and collating, references in. Aelian or Pliny or Aristotle or Ptolemy. And wide awake, withal; not easily imposed upon. He is not of the kind to swallow the tales of the then fashionable cicerone's. He has critical dissertations on sites like Cannae and the Bandusian Fountain and Caudine Forks; and when, at Nola, they opened in his presence a sepulchre containing some of those painted Greek vases for which the place is famous, he promptly suspects it to be a "sepulchre prepared for strangers," and instead of buying the vases allows them to remain where they are "for more simple or less suspicious travellers." On the way to Cape Leuca he passes certain mounds whose origin he believes to be artificial and the work of a prehistoric race. I fancy his conjecture has proved correct. On page 258, speaking of an Oscan inscription, he mentions Mommsen, which shows that he kept himself up to date in such researches....

Of course it would be impossible to feel any real fondness for Ramage before one has discovered his failings and his limitations. Well, he seems to have taken Pratilli seriously. I like this. A young fellow who, in 1828, could have guessed Pratilli to have been the arch-forger he was—such a young fellow would be a freak of learning. He says little of the great writers of his age; that, too, is a weakness of youth whose imagination lingers willingly in the past or future, but not in the present. The Hohenstauffen period does not attract him. He rides close to the magnificent Castel del Monte but fails to visit the site; he inspects the castle of Lucera and says never a word about Frederick II or his Saracens. At Lecce, renowned for its baroque buildings, he finds "nothing to interest a stranger, except, perhaps, the church of Santa Croce, which is not a bad specimen of architectural design." True, the beauty of baroque had not been discovered in his day.

What pleases me less is that there occurs hardly any mention of wild animals in these pages, and that he seems to enjoy natural scenery in proportion as it reminds him of some passage in one of those poets whom he is so fond of quoting. This love of poetic extracts and citations is a mark of his period. It must have got the upper hand of him in course of time, for we find, from the title-page of these "Nooks and Byways," that he was the author of "Beautiful Thoughts from Greek authors; Beautiful Thoughts from French and Italian authors, etc.";[29] indeed, the publication of this particular book, as late as 1868, seems to have been an afterthought. How greatly one would prefer a few more "Nooks and By-ways" to all these Beautiful Thoughts! He must have been at home again, in some bleak Caledonian retreat, when the poetic flowers were gathered. If only he had lingered longer among the classic remains of the south, instead of rushing through them like an express train. That mania of "pressing forward"; that fatal gift of hustle....

His body flits hither and thither, but his mind remains observant, assimilative. It is only on reading this book carefully that one realises how full of information it is. Ay, he notices things, does Ramage—non-antiquarian things as well. He always has time to look around him. It is his charm. An intelligent interest in the facts of daily life should be one of the equipments of the touring scholar, seeing that the present affords a key to the past. Ramage has that gift, and his zest never degenerates into the fussiness of many modern travellers. He can talk of sausages and silkworms, and forestry and agriculture and sheep-grazing, and how they catch porcupines and cure warts and manufacture manna; he knows about the evil eye and witches and the fata morgana and the tarantula spider, about figs in ancient and modern times and the fig-pecker bird—that bird you eat bones and all, the focetola or beccafico (garden warbler). In fact, he has multifarious interests and seems to have known several languages besides the classics. He can hit off a thing neatly, as, when contrasting our sepulchral epitaphs with those of olden days, he says that the key-note of ours is Hope, and of theirs, Peace; or "wherever we find a river in this country (Calabria) we are sure to discover that it is a source of danger and not of profit." He knew these southern torrents and river-beds! He garners information about the Jewish and Albanian colonies of South Italy; he studies Romaic "under one of the few Greeks who survived the fatal siege of Missolonghi" and collects words of Greek speech still surviving at Bova and Maratea (Maratea, by the way, has a

Phoenician smack; the Greeks must have arrived later on the scene, as they did at Marathon itself).

A shrewd book, indeed. Like many of his countrymen, he was specially bent on economic and social questions; he is driven to the prophetic conclusion, in 1828, that "the government rests on a very insecure basis, and the great mass of the intelligence of the country would gladly welcome a change." Religion and schooling are subjects near his heart and, in order to obtain a first-hand knowledge of these things in Italy, he enters upon a friendship, a kind of intellectual flirtation, with the Jesuits. That is as it should be. Extremes can always respect one another. The Jesuits, I doubt not, learnt as much from Ramage as he from them....

I wish I had encountered this book earlier. It would have been useful to me when writing my own pages on the country it describes. I am always finding myself in accord with the author's opinions, even in trivial matters such as the hopeless inadequacy of an Italian breakfast. He was personally acquainted with several men whose names I have mentioned—Capialbi, Zicari, Masci; he saw the Purple Codex at Rossano; in fact, there are numberless points on which I could have quoted him with profit. And even at an earlier time; for I once claimed to have discovered the ruins of a Roman palace on the larger of the Siren islets (the Galli, opposite Positano)—now I find him forestalling me by nearly a century. It is often thus, with archaeological discoveries.

He saw, near Cotrone, that island of the enchantress Calypso which has disappeared since his day, and would have sailed there but for the fact that no boat was procurable. I forget whether Swinburne, who landed here, found any prehistoric remains on the spot; I should doubt it. On another Mediterranean island, that of Ponza, I myself detected the relics of what would formerly have been described as the residence of that second Homeric witch, Circe.[30]

The mention of discoveries reminds me that I have already, of course, discovered my ideal family at Alatri. Two ideal families....

One of them dwells in what ought to be called the "Conca d'Oro," that luxuriant tract of land beyond the monastery where the waters flow—that verdant dale which supplies Alatri, perched on its stony hill, with fruit and vegetables of every kind. The man is a market-gardener with wife and children, a humble serf, Eumaeus-like, steeped in the rich philosophy of earth and cloud and sunshine. I bring him a cigar in the cool of the evening and we smoke on the threshold of his two-roomed abode, or wander about those tiny patches of culture, geometrically disposed, where he guides the water with cunning hand athwart the roots of cabbages and salads. He is not prone to talk of his misfortunes; intuitive civility has taught him to avoid troubling a stranger with personal concerns.

The mother is more communicative; she suffers more acutely. They are hopelessly poor, she tells me, and in debt; unlucky, moreover, in their offspring. Two boys had already died. There are only two left.

"And this one here is in a bad way. He has grown too ill to work. He can only mope about the place. Nothing stays in his stomach—nothing; not milk, not an egg. Everything is rejected. The Alatri doctor treated him for stomach trouble; so did he of Frosinone. It has done no good. Now there is no more money for doctors. It is hard to see your children dying before your eyes. Look at him! Just like those two others."

I looked at him.

"You sent him into the plains last summer?" I ventured.

"To Cisterna. One must make a little money, or starve."

"And you expect to keep your children alive if you send them to Cisterna?"

I was astonished that the local medicine man had not diagnosed malaria. I undertook that if she would put him into the train when next I went to Rome, I would have him overhauled by a competent physician and packed home again with written instructions. (I kept my word, and the good doctor Salatino of the Via Torino—a Calabrian who knows something about malaria—wrote out a treatment for this neglected case, no part of which, I fear, has been observed. Such is the fatalism of the country-folk that if drugs and injections do not work like magic they are quietly discarded. This youth may well have gone the way of "those other two"—who, by the by, were also sent into the Pontine Marshes— since you cannot reject your food for ever, and grow more anaemic every day, without producing some such result.)

Meanwhile my friendly offer caused so great a joy in the mother's heart that I became quite embarrassed. She likened me, among other things, to her favourite Saint.

All comparisons being odious, I turned the conversation by asking:

"And that last one?"

"Here," she said, pushing open the door of the inner room.

He lay on the couch fast asleep, in a glorious tangle of limbs, the picture of radiant boyhood.

"This one, I think, has never been to Cisterna."

"No. He goes into the mountains with the woodcutters every morning an hour before sunrise. It is up beyond Collepardo—seven hours' labour, and seven hours' march there and back. The rest of the time he sleeps like a log...."

Children from these hill-places often accompany their parents into the plains to work; more commonly they go in droves of any number under the charge of some local man. They are part of that immense army of hirelings which descends annually, from the uplands of Tuscany to the very toe of Italy, into these low-lying regions, hardly an inch of which is fever-free. I do not know even approximately the numbers of these migratory swarms of all ages and both sexes; let us say, to be on the safe side, a quarter of a million. They herd down there, in the broiling heat of summer and autumn, under conditions which are not all that could be desired.[31] Were they housed in marble palaces and served on platters of gold, the risk would not be diminished by a hair. How many return infected? I have no idea. It cannot be less than sixty per cent. How many of these perish? Perhaps five per cent. A few thousand annual deaths are not worth talking about. What concerns the country—and what the country, indeed, has taken seriously in hand—is this impoverishment of its best blood; this devitalising action of malaria upon unnumbered multitudes of healthy men, women, and children who do not altogether succumb to its attacks.

I sometimes recognise them on the platform of Rome station—family parties whom I have met in their country villages, now bound for Maccarese or one of those infernal holes in the Campagna, there to earn a little extra money with hay, or maize, or wheat, or tomatoes, or whatever the particular crop may be. You chat with the parents; the youngsters run up to you, all gleeful with the change of scene and the joy of travelling by railway. I know what they will look like, when they return to their mountains later on....

And so, discoursing of this and that, one rambles oneself into a book....

Into half a book; for here—at Alatri, and now—midsummer, I mean to terminate these non-serious memories and leave unrecorded the no less insignificant events which followed up to the mornings in October, those mornings when jackdaws came cawing past my window from the thickly couched mists of the Borghese Gardens, and the matutinal tub began to feel more chilly than was altogether pleasant.

Half a book: I perceive it clearly. These pages might be rounded by another hundred or two. The design is too large for one volume; it reminds me of those tweed suits we used to buy long ago whose pattern was so "loud" that it "took two men to show it off." Which proves how a few months' self-beguilement by the wayside of a beaten track can become the subject of disquisitions without end. Maybe the very aimlessness of such loiterings conduces to a like method of narrative. Maybe the tone of the time fosters a reminiscential and intimately personal mood, by driving a man for refuge into the only place where peace can still be found—into himself. What is the use of appealing in objective fashion to the intelligence of a world gone crazy? Say your say. Go your way. Let them rave! We shall all be pro-German again to-morrow.[32]

Half a book: it strikes me, on reflection, as curiously appropriate. To produce something incomplete and imperfect, a torso of a kind—is it not symbolical of the moment? Is not this an age of torso's? We are manufacturing them every hour by the score. How many good fellows are now crawling about mutilated, converted into torso's? There is room for a book on the same lines....

I glance through what has been written and detect therein an occasional note of exacerbation and disharmony which amuses me, knowing, as I do, its transitory nature. Dirty work, touching dirt. One cannot read for three consecutive years of nothing but poison-gas and blood and explosives without engendering a corresponding mood—a mood which expresses itself in every one according to whether he thinks individually or nationally; whether he cultivates an impartial conscience or surrenders to that of the crowd. For the man and his race are everlastingly tugging in different directions, and unreasoning subservience to race-ideals has clouded many a bright intellect. How many things a race can do which its component members, taken separately, would blush to imitate! Our masses are now fighting for commercial supremacy. The ideal may well be creditable to a nation. It is hardly good enough for a gentleman. He reacts; he meditates a Gospel of Revolt against these vulgarities; he catches himself saying, as he reads the morning paper full of national-flag fetishism and sanguinary nonsense: "One Beethoven symphony is a greater victory than the greatest of these, and reasonable folks may live under any rule save that of a wind-fed herd."

It avails nothing. The day has dawned, the day of those who pull downwards—stranglers of individualism. Can a man subscribe to the aspirations of a mob and yet think well of himself? Can he be black and white? He can be what he is, what most of us are: neutral tint. Look around you: a haze of cant and catchwords. Such things are employed on political platforms and by the Press as a kind of pepsine, to aid our race-stomach in digesting certain heavy doses of irrationalism. The individual stomach soon discovers their weakening effect....

Looking back upon these months of uneventful wanderings, I became aware of a singular phenomenon. I find myself, for some obscure reason, always returning to the same spot. I was nine times in Rome, twice in Florence and Viareggio and Olevano and Anticoli and Alatri and Licenza and Soriano, five times at Valmontone, thrice at Orvinio; and if I did not go a second time to Scanno and other places, there may be a reason for it. Why this perpetual revisiting? How many new and interesting sites might have been explored during that period! Adventures and discoveries might have fallen to my lot, and been duly noted down. As it is, nothing happened, and nothing was noted down. I have only a diary of dates to go upon, out of which, with the help of memory and imagination, have been extracted these pages. For generally, delving down into memory, a man can bring up at least one clear-cut fragment, something still fervid and flashing, a remembered voice or glimpse of landscape which helps to unveil the main features of a scenario already relegated to the lumber-room. And this detail will unravel the next; the scattered elements jostle each other into place, as in the final disentangling of some complicated fugue.

Such things will do for a skeleton. Imagination will kindly provide flesh and blood, life, movement. Imagination—why not? One suppresses much; why not add a little? Truth blends well with untruth, and phantasy has been so sternly banned of late from travellers' tales that I am growing tender-hearted towards the poor old dame; quite chivalrous, in fact—especially on those rather frequent occasions when I find myself unable to dispense with her services.

Yes; truth blends well with untruth. It is one of the maladies of our age, a sign of sheer nervousness, to profess a frenzied allegiance to truth in unimportant matters, to refuse consistently to face her where graver issues are at stake. We cannot lay claim to a truthful state of mind. In this respect the eighteenth century, for all its foppery, was ahead of ours. What is the basic note of Horace Walpole's iridescent worldliness—what about veracity? How one yearns, nowadays, for that spacious and playful outlook of his; or, better still, for some altogether Golden Age where everybody is corrupt and delightful and has nothing whatever to do, and does it well....

My second ideal family at Alatri lives along a side path which diverges off the main road to Ferentino. They are peasant proprietors, more wealthy and civilised than those others, but lacking their terrestrial pathos. They live among their own vines and fruit-trees on the hillside. The female parent, a massive matron, would certainly never send those winsome children into the Pontine Marshes, not for a single day, not for their weight in gold. The father is quite an uncommon creature. I look at him and ask myself; where have I seen that face before, so classic and sinewy and versatile? I have seen it on Greek vases, and among the sailors of the Cyclades and on the Bosphorus. It is a non-Latin face, with sparkling eyes, brown hair, rounded forehead and crisply curling beard; a legendary face. How came Odysseus to Alatri?

Not far from this homestead where I have spent sundry pleasant hours there is a fountain gushing out of a hollow. In olden days it would have been hung with votive offerings to the nymphs, and rightly. One appreciates this nature-cult in a dry land. I have worshipped at many such shrines where the water bounds forth, a living joy, out of the rocky cleft—unlike those sluggish springs of the North that ooze regretfully upwards, as though ready to slink home again unless they were kicked from behind, and then trickle along, with barely perceptible movement, amid weeds and slime.

Now this particular fountain (I think it is called acqua santa), while nowise remarkable as regards natural beauty, is renowned for curing every disease. It is not an ordinary rill; it has medicinal properties. Hither those two little demons, the younger children, conducted me all unsuspecting two days ago, desirous that I should taste the far-famed spring.

"Try it," they said.

I refused at first, since water of every kind has a knack of disagreeing with my weak digestion. As for them, they gulped down tumblers of it, being manifestly inured to what I afterwards discovered to be its catastrophic effects.

"Look at us drinking it," they went on. "Ah, how good! Delicious! It is like Fiuggi, only better."

"Am I an invalid, to drink Fiuggi water?"

"It is not quite the same as Fiuggi. (True. I was soon wishing it had been.) How many men would pay dearly for your privilege! Never let it be said that you went away thirsting from this blessed spot."

"I am not thirsty just now. Not at all thirsty, thank you."

"We have seen you drink without being thirsty. Just one glass," they pleaded. "It will make you live a hundred years."

"No. Let us talk about something else."

"No? Then what shall we tell our mother? That we brought you here, and that you were afraid of a little mouthful of acqua santa? We thought you had more courage. We thought you could strangle a lion."

"Something will happen," I said, as I drained that glass.

Nothing happened for a few hours.

Two days' rest is working wonders....

I profit by the occasion of this slight indisposition to glance backwards—and forwards.

I am here, at Alatri, on the 22 June: so much is beyond contestation.

A later page of that old diary of dates. August 31: Palombara. Well I remember the hot walk to Palombara!

August 3: Mons Lucretilis, that classical mountain from whose summit I gazed at the distant Velino which overtops like a crystal of amethyst all the other peaks. This was during one of my two visits to Licenza. Pleasant days at Licenza, duly noting in the house of Horace what I have noted with Shelley and other bards, namely, that these fellows who sing so blithely of the simple life yet contrive to possess extremely commodious residences; pleasant days among those wooded glens, walking almost every morning in the footsteps of old Ramage up the valley in whose streamlet the willow-roots sway like branches of coral—aloft under the wild walnuts to that bubbling fountain where I used to meet my two friends, Arcadian goat-herds, aboriginal fauns of the thickets, who told me, amid ribald laughter, a few personal experiences which nothing would induce me to set down here.

July 26: La Rocca. What happened at La Rocca?

October 2: Florence. What happened at Florence? A good deal, during those noteworthy twelve hours!

Some memories have grown strangely nebulous; impossible to reconstruct, for example, what went on during the days of drowsy discomfort at Montecelio. A lethargy seems to have fallen on me; I lived in a dream out of which there emerges nothing save the figure of the local tobacconist, a ruddy type with the face of a Roman farmer, who took me to booze with him, in broad patriarchal style, every night at a different friend's house. Those nights at Montecelio! The mosquitoes! The heat! Could this be the place which was famous in Pliny's day for its grove of beeches? How I used to envy the old Montecelians their climate!

July 23: Saracinesca. What happened? I recollect the view over the sweltering Campagna from the dizzy castle-ruin, in whose garden I see myself nibbling a black cherry, the very last of the season, plucked from a tree which grows beside the wall whereon I sat. That suffices: it gives a key to the situation. I can now conjure up the gaunt and sombre houses of this thick-clustering stronghold; the Rembrandtesque shadows, the streets devoid of men, the picture of some martial hero in a cavern-like recess where I sought shelter from the heat, a black crucifix planted in the soil below the entrance of the village—my picture of Saracinesca is complete, in outline.

July 31: Subiaco. Precisely! A week later, then, I walk thirty-two chilometres along the shadeless high road, an insane thing to do, to Subiaco and back. There, in the restaurant Aniene, when all the luncheon-guests have departed for their noonday nap, the cook of the establishment, one of those glorious old Roman he-cooks, comes up to my table. Did I like the boiled trout?

Rather flabby, I reply. A little tasteless. Let him try, next time, some white vinegar in the water and a bay-leaf or two.

He pricks up his ears: we are gens du metier. I invite him to sit down and inquire: how about a bottle of Cesanese, now that we are alone? An excellent idea! And he, in his turn, will permit himself to offer me certain strawberries from his own private store.

"Strawberries?" I ask. "Who ever heard of strawberries in Central Italy on the 31 July? Why, I devoured the last cherry a week ago, and it was only alive because it grew above the clouds."

These, he explains mysteriously, are special strawberries, brought down from near the snow-line by a special goat-boy. They are not for the guests, but "only for myself." Strawberries are always worth paying for; they are mildly purging, they go well with the wine. And what a wonderful scent they have! "You remind me of a certain Lucullo," I said, "who was also nice about strawberries. In fact, he made a fine art of eating and drinking."

"Your Lucullo, we may take it, was a Roman?"

"Romano di Roma."

Thus conversing with this rare old ruffian, I forget my intention of leaving a card on Saint Scolastica. She has waited for me so long. She can wait a little longer....

August 9: Villa Lante.

August 12: Ferento. What happened at Ferento?

Now what happened at Ferento? Let me try to reconstruct that morning's visit.

I have clear memories of the walk from Viterbo—it would be eighteen chilometres there and back, they told me. I had slept well in my quaint little room with the water rushing under the window, and breakfasted in receptive and responsive mood. I recall that trudge along the highway and how I stepped across patches of sunlight from the shade of one regularly planted tree into that of another. The twelfth of August.... It set me thinking of heathery moorlands and grouse, and of those legions of flies that settle on one's nose just as one pulls the trigger. It all seemed dim and distant here, on this parching road, among southern fields. I was beginning to be lost in a muse as to what these boreal flies might do with themselves during the long winter months while all the old women of the place are knitting Shetland underwear when, suddenly, a little tune came into my ears—a wistful intermezzo of Brahms. It seemed to spring out of the hot earth. Such a natural song, elvishly coaxing! Would I ever play it again? Neither that, nor any other.

It turned my thoughts, as I went along, to Brahms and led me to understand why no man, who cares only for his fellow-creatures, will ever relish that music. It is an alien tongue, full of deeps and rippling shallows uncomprehended of those who know nothing of lonely places; full of thrills and silences such as are not encountered among the habitations of men. It echoes the multitudinous voice of nature, and distils the smiles and tears of things non-human. This man listened, all alone; he overheard things to which other ears are deaf—things terrible and sweet; the sigh of some wet Naiad by a reedy lake, the pleadings and furies of the genii—of those that whisper in woodlands and caverns by the sea, and ride wailing on thunder-laden clouds, and rock with ripe laughter in sunny wildernesses. Brahms is the test. Whoso dreads solitude will likewise dread his elemental humour.

It kept me company, this melodious and endearing fairy, till where a path, diverging to the right, led up to the ruins already visible. There the ethereal comrade took flight, scared, maybe, because my senses took on a grossly mundane complexion—it is a way they have, thank God—became absorbed, that is, in the contemplation of certain blackberries wherewith the hedge was loaded. I thought: the tons of blackberries that fall to earth in Italy, unheeded! And not even a Scotsman knows what blackberries are, until he has tasted these. I am no gourmet of such wild things; I rather agree with Goethe when he says: "How berries taste, you must ask children." But I can sympathise with the predilections of others, having certain predilections of my own.

Once, at a miserable place in North Ireland, region of bad whisky and porter, they brought me at dinner some wine of which they knew nothing—they had got it from a shipwreck or some local sale. I am rather fond of hock. And this particular bottle bore on its label the magic imprint of a falcon sitting on a hilltop. Connoisseurs will know that falcon. They will understand how it came about that I remained in the inn till the last bottle of nectar was cracked. What a shame to leave a drop for anybody else! Once again, on a bicycle trip from Paris to the Mediterranean, I came upon a broad, smiling meadow somewhere in the Auvergne, thickly besprinkled with mushrooms. There was a village hard by. In that village I remained till the meadow was close cropped. Half a ton of mushrooms—gone. Some people are rather fond of mushrooms. And that is the right spirit: to leave nothing but a tabula rasa for those that come after. It hurt me to think that anybody else should have a single one of those particular mushrooms. Let them find new ones, in another field; not in mine.

Now what would your amateur of blackberries do in Italy? From the fate which nearly overtook me he might save himself by specialising; by dividing the many local varieties into two main classes and devoting his whole attention to one or the other; to the kind such as I found on Elba—small and round and fragrant, of ruddy hue, and palpitating with warm sunbeams; or to that other kind, those that grow in clearings of the Apennines where the boughs droop to earth with the weight of their portentous clusters—swarthy as night, huge in size, oval, and fraught with chilly mountain dews.

No true enthusiast, I feel sure, would ever be satisfied with such an unfair division of labour—so one-sided an arrangement. He would curse his folly for having specialised. While engaged upon one variety, he would always be hankering after that other kind and thinking how much better they were. What shall he do, then? Well, he might devote one year to one species, the next to another, and so on. Or else—seeing that every zone of altitude bears brambles at its season and that the interval between the maturing of the extreme varieties is at least four months—he might pilgrimage athwart the country in a vertical sense, devouring blackberries of different flavour as he went along; he might work his way upwards, boring a tunnel through the landscape as a beetle drills an oak, and leaving a track of devastation in his rear—browsing aloft from the sea-board, where brambles are black in June, through tangled macchia and vine-clad slopes into the cooler acclivities of rock and jungle—grazing ever upward to where, at close of September and in the shadow of some lonely peak on which the white mantle of winter has already fallen, he finds a few more berries struggling for warmth and sunshine, and then, still higher up, just a few more—the last, the very last, of their race—dwarfs of the mountains, earthward-creeping, and frozen pink ere yet they have had time to ripen. Here, crammed to the brim, he may retire to hibernate, curled up like a full-gorged bear and ready to roll downhill with the melting snows and arrive at the sea-coast in time to begin again. What a jolly life! How much better than being Postmaster-General or Inspector of Nuisances! But such enthusiasts are nowhere to be found. I wish they were; the world would be a merrier place....

Here is the ruined town of Ferento, all alone on the arid brow of the hill. Nothing human in sight. A charming spot it must have been in olden times, when the country was more timbered; now all is bare—brown earth, brown stones. Dutifully I inspect the ruins and, applying the method of Zadig or something of that kind, conclude that Ferento, this particular Ferento, was relatively unimportant and relatively modern, although so fine a site may well have commended itself from early days as a settlement. I pick up, namely, a piece of verde antico, a green marble which came into vogue at a later period than many other coloured ones. Ergo, Ferento was relatively modern as antiquities go; else this marble would not occur there. I seek for coloured ones and find not the smallest fragment; nothing but white. Ergo, the place was relatively insignificant; else the reds and yellows would also be discoverable. I observe incidentally—quite incidentally!—that the architecture corroborates my theory; so do the guide-books, no doubt, if there are any. Now I know, furthermore, the origin of that small slab of verde antico which had puzzled me, mixed up, as it was, among the mosaics of quite modern marbles in that church whither I had been conducted by a local antiquarian to admire a certain fresco recently laid bare, and some rather crude daubs by Romanelli.

Out again, into the path that overlooks the steep ravine. Here I find, resting in the shadow of the wall, an aged shepherd and his flock and a shaggy, murderous-looking dog of the Campagna breed that shows his teeth and growls incessantly, glaring at me as if I were a wolf. "Barone" is the brute's name. I had intended to clamber down and see whether the rock-surface bears any traces of human workmanship; the rock-surface, I now decide, may take care of itself. It has waited for me so long. It can wait a little longer.

"Does that beast of yours eat Christians?"

"He? He is a perfect capo di c———. That is his trick, to prevent people from kicking him. They think he can bite."

I produce half a cigar which he crushes up into his black clay pipe.

"Yours is not a bad life."

"One lives. But I had better times in Zurich."

He had stayed there awhile, working in some factory. He praised its food, its beer, its conveniences.

Zurich: incongruous image! Straightway I was transported from this harmonious desolation of Ferento; I lost sight of yonder clump of withering thistles—thistles of recent growth; you could sit, you could stand, in their shade—and found myself glancing over a leaden lake and wandering about streets full of ill-dressed and ungracious folk; escaping thence further afield, into featureless hills encrusted with smug, tawdry villas and drinking-booths smothered under noisome horse-chestnuts and Virginia creepers. How came they to hit upon the ugliest tree, and the ugliest creeper, on earth? Infallible instinct! Zurich: who shall sum up thy merciless vulgarity?

So this old man had been there.

And I remembered an expression in a book recently written by a friend of mine who, oddly enough, had encountered some of these very Italians in Zurich. He talks of its "horrible dead ordinariness"—some such phrase.[33] It is apt. Zurich: fearsome town! Its ugliness is of the active kind; it grips you by the throat and sits on your chest like a nightmare.

I looked at the old fellow. He was sound; he had escaped the contagion. Those others, those many hundred thousand others in Switzerland and America—they can nevermore shake off the horrible dead ordinariness of that life among machines. Future generations will hardly recognise the Italian race from our descriptions. A new type is being formed, cold and loveless, with all the divinity drained out of them.

Having a long walk before me and being due home for luncheon, I rose to depart, and in so doing bestowed a vigorous kick upon Barone, in order to test the truth of his master's theory. It worked. The glowering and snarling ceased. He was a good dog—almost human. I think, with a few more kicks, he might have grown quite friendly.

Along that hot road the spectre of Zurich pursued me, in all its starkness. A land without atmosphere, and deficient in every element of the picturesque, whether of man or nature. Four harsh, dominant tones, which never overlap or intermingle: blue sky, white snow, black fir-woods, green fields, and, if you insist upon having a fifth, then take—yes, take and keep—that theatrical pink Alpenglühen which is turned on at fixed hours for the delectation of gaping tourists, like a tap of strontium light or the display of electric fluid at Schaffhausen Falls.

"Did you observe the illumination of the Falls, sir, last night?"

"How can one avoid seeing the beastly thing?"

"Ah! Then we must add two francs to the bill."

Many are the schools of art that have grown up in England and elsewhere and flourished side by side, vying with one another to express the protean graces of man, of architecture and domestic interior, of earth and sky and sea. Where is the Swiss school? Where, in any public gallery, will you find a masterpiece which triumphantly vindicates the charm of Swiss scenery? You will, find it vindicated only on condensed milk tins. These folks can write. My taste in lyrics may be peculiar, but I used to love my Leuthold—I wish I had him here at this moment; the bold strokes of Keller, the miniature work, the cameo-like touches, of C. F. Meyer—they can write! They would doubtless paint, were there anything to paint. Holbein: did the landscape of Switzerland seduce him? And Boecklin? He fled out of its welter of raw materialism. Even his Swiss landscapes are mediterraneanized. Boecklin——

And here, as the name formulated itself, that little sprite of Brahms, that intermezzo, once more leapt to my side out of the parched fields. I imagine it came less for my sake than for the companionship of Boecklin. They were comrades in the spirit; they understood. What one had heard, the other beheld—shapes of mystery, that peer out of forest gloom and the blue hush of midday and out of glassy waters—shapes that shudder and laugh. No doubt you may detect a difference between Boecklin's creations and those of classic days; it is as if the light of his dreamings had filtered through some medium, some stained-glass window in a Gothic church which distorted their outlines and rendered them somewhat more grotesque. It is the hand of time. The world has aged. Yet the shapes are young; they do but change their clothes and follow the fashion in externals. They laugh as of old. How they laugh! No mortal can laugh so heartily. No mortal has such good cause. Theirs is not the serene mirth of Olympian spheres; it sounds demoniac, from the midway region. What are they laughing at, these cheerful monsters? At the greatest jest in the universe. At us....

That lake of Conterano—the accent is on the ante-penultima—it looked appetising on the map, all alone out there. It attracted me strongly. I pictured a placid expanse, an eye of blue, sleepily embowered among wooded glens and throwing upward the gleam of its calm waters. Lakes are so rare in Italy. During the whole of this summer I saw only one other, fringed with the common English reed—two, rather, lying side by side, one turbid and the other clear, and filling up two of those curious circular depressions in the limestone. I rode past them on the watershed behind Cineto Romano. These were sweet water. Of sulphur lakelets I also saw two.

Sitting on a stone into which the coldness of midnight had entered (Alatri lies at a good elevation) I awaited my companion in the dusk of dawn. Soon enough, I knew, we should both be roasted. This half-hour's shivering before sunrise in the square of Alatri, and listening to the plash of the fountain, is one of those memories of the town which are graven most clearly in my mind. I could point out, to-day, the very spot whereon I sat.

We wandered along the Ferentino road to begin with, profiting by some short cuts through chestnut woods; turned to the right, ever ascending, behind that strange village of Fumone, aloft on its symmetrical hill; thence by a mule-track onward. Many were the halts by the way. A decayed roadside chapel with faded frescoes—a shepherd who played us some melodies on his pipe—those wondrous red lilies, now in their prime, glowing like lamps among the dark green undergrowth—the gateway of a farmhouse being repaired—a reservoir of water full of newts—a fascinating old woman who told us something about something—the distant view upon the singular peak of Mount Cacume, they all gave us occasion for lingering. Why not loaf and loiter in June? The days are so endless!

At last, through a gap in the landscape, we saw the lake at our feet, simmering in the noonday beams—an everyday sheet of water, brown in colour, with muddy banks and seemingly not a scrap of shade within miles; one of those lakes which, by their periodical rising and sinking, give so much trouble that there is talk, equally periodical, of draining them off altogether. This one, they say, shifts continually and sometimes reaches so low a level that rich crops are planted in its oozy bed.

Here are countless frogs, and fish—tench; also a boat that belongs to the man who rents the fishing. A sad accident happened lately with his boat. A party of youngsters came for an outing and two boys jumped into the tub, rowed out, and capsized it with their pranks. They were both drowned—a painful and piteous death—a death which I have tried, by accident, and can nowise recommend. They fished them out later from their slimy couch, and found that they had clasped one another so tightly in their mortal agony that it was deemed impious ever to unloosen that embrace. So they were laid to rest, locked in each other's arms.

While my companion told me these things we had plodded further and further along this flat and inhospitable shore, and grown more and more taciturn. We were hungry and thirsty and hot, for one feels the onslaught of these first heats more acutely than the parching drought of August. Things looked bad. The luncheon hour was long past, and our spirits began to droop. All my mellowness took flight; I grew snappy and monosyllabic. Was there no shade?

Yonder…that dusky patch against the mountain? Brushwood of some kind, without a doubt. The place seemed to be unattainable, and yet, after an inordinate outlay of energy, we had climbed across those torrid meadows. It proved to be a hazel copse mysteriously dark within, voiceless, and cool as a cavern.

Be sure that he who planted these hazels on the bleak hillside was no common son of earth, but some wise and inspired mortal. My blessings on his head! May his shadow never grow less! Or, if that wish be already past fulfilment, may he dwell in Elysium attended by a thousand ministering angels, every one of them selected by himself; may he rejoice in their caresses for evermore. Naught was amiss. All conspired to make the occasion memorable. I look back upon our sojourn among those verdant hazels and see that it was good—one of those moments which are never granted knowingly by jealous fate. So dense was the leafage in the greenest heart of the grove that not a shred of sunlight, not a particle as large as a sixpence, could penetrate to earth. We were drowned in shade; screened from the flaming world outside; secure—without a care. We envied neither God nor man.

I thought of certain of my fellow-creatures. I often think of them. What were they now doing? Taking themselves seriously and rushing about, as usual, haggard and careworn—like those sagacious ants that scurry hither and thither, and stare into each other's faces with a kind of desperate imbecility, when some sportive schoolboy has kicked their ridiculous nest into the air and upset all their solemn little calculations.

As for ourselves, we took our ease. We ate and drank, we slumbered awhile, then joked and frolicked for five hours on end, or possibly six.[34] I kept no count of what was said nor how the time flew by. I only know that when at last we emerged from our ambrosial shelter the muscles of my stomach had grown sore from the strain of laughter, and Arcturus was twinkling overhead.

THE END

---

[1] There exists a fine one, but you must go to San Remo to see it.

[2] Discovered, according to Corsi, in 1547, and not to be confounded with the yet more beautiful black and yellow Rhodian marble of the ancients.

[3] See North American Review, September, 1913. Ramage's Calabrian tour of 1828, by the way, was an extremely risky undertaking. The few travellers who then penetrated into this country kept to the main roads and never moved without a military escort. One of them actually hired a brigand as a protection.

[4] Sometimes at this season there is not the smallest trickle in the stream-bed—mere disconnected pools to show where the river was, and will be. Then you may walk across it, even in Florence. Grant Duff says he has seen the Arno "blue." So have I: a hepatic blue.

[5] It afterwards passed into the hands of the German Crown Prince.

[6] He was afterwards imprisoned for this, and has since died.

[7] I am told the Florentines at no period adopted the method of the Parisians, and that I am also wrong in saying that the older monuments are in better condition than the new ones. We live and learn.

[8] The late Henry Maudsley. He says, in one of his letters, "...I am writing without due consideration of the interesting point. But this possible explanation occurs to me: children are active motor machines, always restless and moving when not asleep. When asleep, the motor tendencies, being not quite passive, translate themselves into the dreaming consciousness of motion, pleasant or painful, according to bodily states pleasing or disturbing. As the muscles are almost passive in sleep, the outlet is into dreaming activity—into dreams of flying when bodily states are pleasant, into falling down precipices, etc., when they are out of sorts. This is quite a hasty reflection...."

[9] "The Prison. A Dialogue." By H. B. Brewster. (Williams and Norgate, 1891.)

[10] Parkstone, Dorset. July 19, 1894. "Many thanks for your reference to Schopenhauer's remarks on Recognition Marks, which I thought I was the first to fully point out. It is a most interesting anticipation. I do not read German, but from what I have heard of his works he was the last man I should have expected to make such an acute suggestion in Natural History."

[11] Written during the U-boat scare and food-restrictions.

[12] Fecit! He poisoned himself with hydrocyanic acid on the 4th November, 1920.

[13] This is the same gentleman who informs us, on page 166, "I have lived, however, very temperately, avoiding much wine." We learn from the Dictionary of National Biography that he was born in 1803; he must therefore have been twenty-five years old when he bemused the coastguard. Only twenty-five; and already at this stage. We are further told that he was tutor to somebody's son. Unhappy child!

[14] Not all of them are true thistles. Abbadé's Guide to the Abruzzi (1903) enumerates 1476 plants from this region.

[15] Manifestly unfair, all this. For the rest, the critic, in speaking of a plot, may have meant what young ladies call by that name—a love intrigue, in which case he is to be blamed solely for misuse of a good word. I am consoled by the New York Dial calling my plot "rightly filmy." Nobody could have expressed it better.

[16] Three spring months, at Florence, had been spent in making a scientific collection of local imprecations—abusive, vituperative or profane expletives; swear-words, in short—enriched with elaborate commentary. I would gladly print this little study in folk-lore as an appendix to the present volume, were it fit for publication.

[17] Since this was written, the gospel of imperialism has made considerable progress in the peninsula.

[18] This is a survival of the Greek kakkabos. Gargiuli and others have garnered Hellenic derivations among the place-names here, and to their list may be added that of the rock on which stood the villa of Pollius Felix; it is now known as Punta Calcarella, but used to be called Petrapoli; pure Greek: Pollio's rock. There is still a mine of such material to be exploited by all who care to study the vernacular. The giant euphorbia, for instance, common on these hills, is locally known as "totomaglie"; pure Greek again: tithymalos.

[19] Query: whether there be no connection between brachycephalism and this modern deification of machinery?

[20] Robert L. Bowles, M.D. "Sunburn on the Alps" (Alpine Journal, November, 1888) and "The Influence of Light on the Skin" (British Journal of Dermatology, No. 105, Vol. 9).

[21] It has now been cleaned—with inevitable results.

[22] Maupassant himself was partial to scents. See his valet's diary.

[23] Since this was written (1917) the condition of these beasts has improved. Somebody now feeds them—which could hardly have been expected during those stressful times of war, when bread barely sufficed for the human population. They are also fewer in numbers. Their owners, I fancy, can afford to keep them at home once more.

[24] This is my last (7 July, 1894) and somewhat mysterious letter from the old fellow. "The question you ask is one of great ornithological importance and I believe has never been worked out, but I am absolutely afraid to ask any questions in the British Museum, as they jump at an idea and cut the ground from under the original man's feet. This I regret to say is my experience. I have been asked what does it matter who makes the discovery? I reply, 'Render unto Caesar, etc.' If you are going to work it out, keep it dark. The British Museum have not the necessary specimens—in this country I believe it is not known how the change takes place. I tried some years ago to work it out with live specimens, but failed because I could not get young birds. Now in answer to your question, my belief is that the young bird moults into the winter plumages direct and that this is changed into the full plumage in spring either by a spring moult or by a shedding of the tips of the feathers. This is private because it is theoretical, and for your private use to verify...."

Of the Finland seal, by the way, Dr. Günther wrote: "The skin differs in nothing from that of Phoca foetida. In the skull I observe that the nasal bones are conspicuously narrower than in typical specimens from the northern coasts. There is also a remarkable thinness of bone, a want of osseous substance; but it is impossible to say whether this is due to altered physical conditions or should be accounted for by the youth of the specimen, or whether it is an individual peculiarity."

[25] Winter 1882-1883; possibly later.

[26] The centre of this usage, so far as Europe is concerned, seems to have been the Caucasus.

[27] I have been there since, and vainly endeavoured to track the legend to its lair. Its only possible foundation is that I possessed the ordinary tourists' map of the district.

[28] Add to all the other varieties, now, the countless legions of the guardie regie, which threaten to absorb the entire youth of Italy. At this moment there is a distressing dearth of housing accommodation all over the peninsula; in Rome alone, they say, apartments are needed for 10,000 practically homeless persons, and a mathematician may calculate

the number of houses required to contain them. How shall they ever be built, if all the potential builders are loafing about in uniforms at the public expense?

[29] Some of these Beautiful Thoughts went through more than one edition.

[30] From an old article: "I was pleased to observe on Ponza the relics of a great pre-Roman civilization. Above the town, where the cemetery now stands, is a likely site for a citadel, and on examining it from the sea I noticed, sure enough, a few blocks of prehistoric structure of the so-called Cyclopean type underneath a corner of the cemetery wall. There is a portion in better preservation between the 'Baths of Pilate' and the harbour, where a little path winds up from the sea. The blocks are joined without mortar, and some of them are over a metre in length. This megalithic wall may be taken to be contemporaneous with similar works of defence found in various parts of Italy, but I believe its existence on Ponza has not yet been recorded. Livy says that Volscians inhabited the island till they were supplanted by the Romans, and a tradition preserved by Strabo and Virgil locates here the palace of the enchantress Circe, who transformed the companions of Ulysses into bristly swine...." Some one may have anticipated me here again, as did Salis-Marschlins in the eighteenth century with those roses of Passtum whose disappearance Ramage, like every one else, laments—those roses which I thought I was the first to re-discover. They grow on the spot in considerable quantities, though one needs good eyes to see them. They are not flourishing as of yore, being dwarfs not more than a few inches in height. One which I carried away and kept three years in a pot and six more in the earth grew to a length of about sixteen feet, and is probably alive at this moment, I never saw a flower.

[31] For the abject condition of these slaves (such they are) see Chapter VII of The Roman Campagna by Arnaldo Cervesato.

[32] Written in 1917.

[33] D.H. Lawrence: Twilight in Italy.

[34] The title Alone strikes me, on reflection, as rather an inapt one for this volume. Let it stand!

CPSIA information can be obtained
at www.ICGtesting.com
Printed in the USA
BVHW042245031118
532107BV00001B/40/P

9 781406 825817